THE
BEAST
OF
BODMIN

The Beast of Bodmin

Published by The Conrad Press in the United Kingdom 2018

Tel: +44(0)1227 472 874
www.theconradpress.com
info@theconradpress.com

ISBN 978-1-911546-36-8

Typesetting and Cover Design by:
Charlotte Mouncey, www.bookstyle.co.uk

The Conrad Press logo was designed by Maria Priestley.

Printed and bound in Great Britain
by Clays Ltd, St Ives plc

For Dad
for your support at the beginning
sorry you missed the end

THE
BEAST
OF
BODMIN

MARK EDMONDSON

Chapter 1

While Steve drove the red Fiesta, Debbie looked around at the landscape in the summer dusk.

A June evening here on Bodmin Moor was about as different from one in Ealing as she could imagine. All around the solitary car was a vista of long, gently undulating green and brown-green moorland, dotted with occasional thin trees and narrow stone walls that rose higher in the far distance with rocky, hilly outcrops.

Debbie hoped they could find somewhere to stay before nightfall. She was enjoying the views now, but she knew that this beautiful place would become very creepy indeed once the sun had completely disappeared from the sky.

Steve had come into her life the previous July. They'd had a few weekends away: Oxford, Brighton, even Calais, but this was their first proper holiday. They'd decided on a tour of Devon and Cornwall. She told Steve she got easily sunburnt and right away he said, 'OK then, let's forget Majorca or the Canaries; let's go to the West Country.' That was just like him; he was just so considerate. She knew he really cared about her. That was one of the many reasons why she loved him.

They'd spent the first week in Devon, staying in Dartmouth before moving to Taunton for two nights, and then they began their journey through Cornwall. Debbie found it exciting travelling from place to place without booking anywhere first, but they left Devon later than they wanted to, and after spending a few hours in the town of Launceston, they reached their destination of Jamaica Inn at just before nine in the evening. At Jamaica Inn, they'd been told that there weren't any rooms available. Steve had been relaxed and OK about that, and they had dinner there before setting off again. Debbie had been worried that in June, the height of the holiday season, they might struggle to find a place to stay. They'd brought a tent with them but they hadn't used it yet, Debbie secretly hoped they wouldn't use it at all; she liked to sleep in a bed, not on a groundsheet. Besides, how could she get all cuddly and affectionate at night with the man she loved if they were sleeping on some bumpy ground in a tent? She loved Steve a lot and adored being with someone much bigger than she was. She enjoyed feeling protected by her gentle giant of a boyfriend who was six feet two inches tall. She herself was only five feet three inches.

'We should've booked somewhere this morning,' she said.

'I know; I'm sort of kicking myself for that. We'll keep going and stay in Truro. That's inland, so the hotels are less likely to be full, whereas in St Austell, I don't imagine we'd have much luck. Also Truro's the only city in Cornwall, so we should be able to get a room there, easily enough.'

Debbie looked at the map. Everything Steve said had made sense, but she was worried it was getting late. 'Steve, I don't think we should have eaten at Jamaica Inn. It's almost a quarter to ten and it'll be dark soon. We should've set off as soon as they told us there were no rooms.'

'I know, Debs, but I was starving hungry, and that steak really was worth waiting for.'

Debbie tied her long brown hair into a ponytail so she could read the map. 'How long before we get to Truro?'

'It'll most likely take us an hour to get to Truro on this road; it winds like a snake. We'll be driving in pitch darkness for the last part of the journey.'

'Yes, I know.'

'To be honest, I'm feeling a little light-headed after that beer.'

'You only had a pint, you won't be over the limit, will you, Steve?'

'Don't worry; I'm sure I'm not.'

He wiped his eyes one at a time as he tried to focus on the road. 'We could camp out instead,' he added, suddenly.

A twinge of unease pricked the back of Debbie's neck as he made this suggestion.

'Steve, do we have to?'

'What's the problem? It'll be exciting.'

'It'll be terrifying, you mean. Especially once it goes dark.'

'Come on, Debs, we'll be fine. It's a warm evening after all. We'll find somewhere secluded and near some greenery; you know, for if we need the loo. We've got the tent, and torches, and plenty of water for drinking and washing, and in the morning we'll find a cafe somewhere for breakfast. I'll set the tent up, which will only take ten minutes or so, and we've still got some bottles of lager left. We can watch the sun go down in the middle of nowhere, completely on our own.'

After Steve said that, Debbie found, rather to her surprise, that she was actually beginning to like the sound of his suggestion of camping on the moors. He made it sound quite romantic.

'And we can have sex as loudly as we want,' Steve said, with a smile. 'After all, we couldn't last night in Taunton, not with those two old women in the room next one along. Bloody hell, the look they gave us in the corridor in the morning! Anyone would have thought it was a crime.'

Steve carried on driving further along the road, which wound up and down and darted right and then left, then right again. Neither of them spoke for a few minutes. Debbie knew that, quite apart from anything else, they would save sixty or seventy pounds by staying in the tent and their holiday money was limited.

'I suppose it'll save us a few quid,' she said.

'That's the spirit,' he said. He then started looking more intently for somewhere they could camp. Finally, after about another ten minutes, the road went down a shallow hill, at the foot of which Debbie saw a rocky outcrop maybe a hundred yards from the road, with what looked like a small spinney close by.

'There,' she said, pointing to it. 'What d'you think?'

'Looks great,' he said. 'Well spotted.'

He drove down to where the road reached as close as it got to the place Debbie had seen, then he drove the car off the road for maybe fifty yards. They hadn't seen another car for ages; *it really is pretty creepy out here*, Debbie thought, but knowing she was with Steve made her feel safe.

They carried their supplies and equipment over to the rocky outcrop and found a secluded place to set up camp. They spent the next twenty minutes or so setting the tent up. This was a task Debbie had imagined she'd soon get bored with, but she was starting to share Steve's excitement as the daylight slowly disappeared and the sun stood alone in the late summer evening sky. Distracted by the intoxicating views and peaceful environment, she allowed Steve to do most of the work and passed him the tent pegs one at a time as he asked for them; he then hammered them into the ground with the rubber mallet.

She saw some sheep in the distance. There was a wooded area a couple of hundred yards away; but nothing else visible except for endless fields that seemed to her to go on for miles. The sun glowed in a dark red sky that had almost vanished from her view. She wanted to tell Steve to stop what he was doing and enjoy it with her, but on the other hand she wanted the job to be done before the darkness closed in around them; so she just soaked in the beautiful scenery and let him carry on.

Chapter 2

The camping chair sank into the soft grass as Debbie sat down with her bottle of lager.

'This is the life,' she said, with a smile.

'Coming around to the idea of wild camping now, are we?' Steve asked.

'I'm not looking forward to the morning when we can't have a shower, and I really don't fancy going in that spinney when I need the loo, though I know there isn't much choice. But yes, at this moment, I'm enjoying myself.'

Steve smiled. He leaned over to kiss her and clink her bottle with his. She felt as though there was something romantic about being out in the middle of nowhere, just her and Steve watching the sun go down, she wanted this moment to last forever. She held his hand as they enjoyed the silence together.

Minutes passed as the dark slowly surrounded them. She thought that she would be scared once the daylight disappeared, but she wasn't. She knew she would've been scared if she was there with anyone other than Steve, especially now that she couldn't see more than about twenty feet ahead of her; but now she was very relaxed as she held onto Steve's hand. As they sat there she couldn't hear a thing other than the occasional car in the distance, and the infrequent light breeze that whistled through her ears.

She thought of how at this time on a Sunday evening she would normally be getting ready for bed and setting her alarm for six thirty in the morning. Working in a sandwich bar was a job she found enjoyable, but not catching two trains to get there she didn't; but it was where she met Steve, so she felt as though it was worth the inconvenience. He'd been a regular customer of hers for several months before he nervously asked her out. He'd always come across to her as an extremely confident young guy who probably had oodles of girls chasing after him. If it wasn't for how nervous he was when he asked her to go out with him, she probably would've said no. She found it endearing that although he was a fit and healthy young man who obviously visited the gym and the barber on a regular basis, he wasn't so sure of himself as to ask a girl out without his hands shaking and his voice trembling. So she said yes, after letting him sweat for ten seconds or so first.

Debbie was used to the hustle and bustle of city life, so now she was enjoying the quiet of the moors. This peaceful serene location, being here with Steve; this was the happiest she'd ever been. This was her favourite part of the holiday so far.

An hour later, once it was dark - there was no moon that night - they took everything inside the tent and closed the front flap. They stripped down to their underwear before climbing inside the two sleeping bags that they had zipped together; this was something that made the idea of camping a little cosier, much better than being in separate sleeping bags, Debbie thought. Steve lay on his back as Debbie rested her head on his shoulder.

'Night night,' she said.

'Are we leaving noisy sex for another day then?' he asked.

'It's up to you,' she said. She waited for his answer. Although she was enjoying the romance of the evening, she was ready for sleep. She was still happy in the surroundings, but she started to feel a little isolated and vulnerable as the dark had closed in, she decided she would rather go to sleep.

'It's OK,' he said. 'I'm pretty tired, to be honest.'

She felt a little relieved and kissed him on the cheek and then closed her eyes.

'I love you,' he said. This made her smile, not that this was a phrase he didn't use very often, but still one that she was happy to hear, just as much now as when he'd first said it.

'I love you too.'

Debbie knew she'd be the first one to drift off to sleep, and moments later, she did.

Sometime later, Debbie thought she'd been asleep for maybe an hour or more, but she wasn't exactly sure, she drowsily woke up. She heard the sound of the zip on the sleeping bag being opened very slowly one notch at a time.

She thought she was dreaming and tried to ignore it; but then the rustling noise of Steve climbing out was too much disturbance to ignore. She presumed he was going to the bathroom and kept her eyes firmly shut. There were no more noises. Then she remembered that they weren't at one of the bed and breakfasts that they'd been staying at on their way through Devon; they were camping on Bodmin Moor.

Debbie forced her eyes open and sat up. It was pitch black inside the tent; she couldn't see what was happening. Then she noticed the light at the opposite end of the tent. It was Steve lay on his stomach in front of the door panel, still wearing only his boxer shorts; he was using his mobile phone to see what he was doing. She wondered why he was only using the light of the menu screen and not the torch that she knew he had on his phone.

'What are you doing?' she asked. She must've spoken too loud as he jumped up quickly.

'Shush,' he whispered.

'Sorry,' she said.

He put his finger up to his mouth to silence her, making a shushing noise as he did.

Now she was awake, now she was scared. Her eyes had

adjusted a little; she could see the seriousness on Steve's face in the glow of the light from his phone. 'What is it?' she whispered.

'There's something circling the tent,' he whispered back.

Her stomach turned, suddenly she felt sick with fear

He crouched back down towards the front of the tent and peered through the zip that he'd already opened slightly.

She hoped that he was going to say it was a sheep, or even a horse; but any animal that couldn't open zips on tents would be OK.

The light on the phone faded, he sat back up and pressed it on again. 'I'm going outside to have a look.'

She couldn't believe what she'd just heard. 'You're not going out there,' she said, in her most stern, whispering voice.

'It might be someone trying to steal my car.'

'So what, let them have it. There could be more of them than us.'

'I'm not letting anyone steal my car.'

She knew Steve could look after himself and he was big enough to scare away whoever it was, but for all they knew there could be four or five people outside of the tent.

He bent down again and looked through the flap of the tent which he opened a bit further. He then sat back again.

She knew he was going to go outside.

He unzipped the door of the tent slowly all the way to the opposite corner and let the flap fall to the floor.

She tried to look past him but she couldn't see anything but the darkness of the night.

He turned around to her. 'I'm going out; you stay here.'

'Please don't; I'm begging you,' she said.

He ignored her and crawled through the door of the tent. He then put the torch on his phone which was much brighter than the menu screen.

Debbie sat still with her hands over her mouth, trying not to breathe so she could hear what was going on outside. She saw him stand up; he then walked to the left out of view of the doorway. The cold suddenly hit her from the night-time coolness making its way inside the tent. Other than Steve's footsteps in the grass, she couldn't hear anything. Her heart was pounding hard in her chest as she tried to control her fear. Seconds felt like hours, but she couldn't bring herself to call to him. She could see the light from his phone through the canvas of the tent panel, but other than that, it was completely dark. She fumbled around the floor of the tent for her mobile phone so she could use it to see; she couldn't find it, she then pictured it in the passenger door well of Steve's car.

The light moved to the back of the tent as she listened to the faint footsteps in the long summer grass.

'What the...?' Debbie heard Steve say under his breath.

She listened for the rest of the sentence but it never came. The footsteps started again as he seemed to walk back around to the side of the tent. Suddenly there was a scuffling noise as Steve and whatever it was fell to the floor. His phone landed on the grass, she could still see a faint glimmer of light as it lay still on the ground. The scuffle was right next to the tent, the side panel shook as Steve seemed to be grappling with someone or something.

'Debbie!' he shouted.

She was so terrified she felt her heart was almost torn from its moorings inside her.

'Debbie, run!' Steve shouted.

She screamed, and frantically started to climb out of her sleeping bag.

He started to shout again, but his voice was then smothered into a horrific gargling sound.

Debbie froze with horror. The noise was like no other she'd heard before as Steve coughed and choked. He spluttered as some inaudible words came from his mouth as if he was drowning.

Debbie screamed again. A whistling and wheezing noise filled the night air as the breath left Steve's lungs. Then there was nothing but silence.

Debbie felt sick; she just sat there shaking with terror, still half inside her sleeping bag, tears running down her face. She had the ghastly certainty Steve was dead by the way his cry had suddenly stopped. She ached to get to him to at least try to help him; but she knew she couldn't get past whatever was outside of the tent. If Steve couldn't get the better of it, Debbie knew that she didn't stand a chance. She was so scared she could hardly breathe, and she couldn't see anything in the pitch black of the night. What could possibly have happened? Who or what had just attacked her boyfriend? The sound of her heartbeat thrashed in her ears as the sick feeling in her stomach had spread throughout her body. She didn't think she could even stand, let alone run. She knew she was totally on her own and miles from anywhere.

She heard faint footsteps making their way to the doorway of the tent. Her eyes were useless to her in the blackness of the night. Too terrified to even think, she lay down inside the sleeping bag and curled into a ball. She felt the tent move as whatever it was came inside. The sinking of the soft ground underneath the tent made her feel how close it was getting. She could hear it breathing slowly as she lay under the cover. Debbie was breathing short fast breaths that she tried hard to control so it couldn't hear her, but she knew whatever it was, knew she was there.

Nothing happened as she stayed perfectly still. She begged for it to end. She had never felt fear like this before. She almost hoped that it would kill her quickly and get it over with. The slow breathing became louder and she knew that it was only inches away from her. She slowly started to accept her fate as she just wanted it to be over, and no sooner had she pulled back the cover to look, she was overcome by a pain like no other she had ever felt before. Seconds later the fear seemed to leave her body, replaced by a numbness that spread throughout her. As she was dragged upwards from the ground, she struggled to fight for breath. As the moments passed she felt herself give up fighting. The pain then faded as she drifted away. The last thing she felt was falling to one side, and then nothing.

Chapter 3

Jo Green jogged along the road heading back into St Breward, the village on Bodmin Moor where she'd grown up and recently had moved back to. Jogging was something she did most mornings. A four-mile run normally took her forty minutes, but today she felt herself running a little faster. Dressed in her black running pants and purple T-shirt and sunglasses, she ran down the road that brought her back into the village. The road heading out of St Breward that overlooked Bodmin Moor was her regular circuit. Getting away from the houses and running high above the hills of the moorland was tough going, but the views and the calm feeling of seclusion made it worthwhile.

The date of Monday June the fifth had finally arrived, after being in her mind for the last few weeks, ever since she'd been accepted as a trainee detective constable. At twenty-five, after three years on the force as a police constable, she'd decided to apply for the job and she passed the interview and exam first time. She'd been reasonably confident about the interview; after all, everybody knew the name Jo Green.

She'd brought an end to the Bodmin Butcher murders back in January, when Cornwall was being terrorised by a serial killer. Jo acted on a gut instinct that she felt wasn't just luck. She knew that this was the perfect time to advance in her career while the newspapers were still taking about her; which was something she didn't enjoy, but she was sure it was helpful to her progress.

At first she welcomed the recognition for succeeding where others had failed. Knowing that this would boost her career was one thing, but she also wondered how many lives she'd saved and how long the murders could have continued. This brought her satisfaction as well as confidence that she'd chosen the right vocation. Her three years in uniform were the platform on which to build her detective career, and catching a serial killer was as good as it gets for a police constable. Except for the notoriety, she was still experiencing a euphoric sense of accomplishment; this was heightened upon passing her interview. This morning was her next step towards advancing her career.

Jo had always wanted to follow in her father's footsteps and become a police officer, but her teachers and college tutors encouraged her to stay in education. After college she was accepted at Lincoln College, Oxford and after her three years there she travelled in Europe with her boyfriend, David. They worked in cafés and bars and she loved it. But she knew, even though she didn't discuss it with David at the time, that once they'd returned to Cornwall, she would be applying to join the police.

She didn't imagine she'd get the approval of her father, which she would've liked. He used to say that one police officer in the family was more than enough. He died only a few days after they'd returned from Europe, before she'd told him of her plans. He was a uniformed sergeant. He'd been based at Bodmin Police Station, just eight miles from St Breward. This was where Jo spent the first three years of her police career and was now about to start her detective career.

Her father had been heading towards his retirement. Aged fifty-five, after thirty-two years on the force, he only had three years left before he could draw his police pension. But he died suddenly of heart failure. Jo applied to join the police a week after his funeral.

Running on a beautiful summer's morning like this was heaven to Jo; but today she had the added excitement of starting her new job. She had her mobile phone in a wallet that gripped onto her upper arm with Velcro, but she didn't use it to listen to music as she ran; she preferred the sounds of silence that came with living in such a remote area; except for her footsteps creating a metronome-like rhythm on the concrete road that weaved its way through the village.

She looked around at the beautiful green hills of Bodmin Moor that went on for miles. She was brought up in St Breward, but spent three years living in Oxford while at university, one year travelling Europe and the last three years in Liskeard in a rented cottage with David. Although she was happy to be back in the place she dearly loved, she often thought back to her three years living in Oxford as the most amazing times of her life.

She'd studied English Language and literature at Lincoln College, and she knew she'd worked harder than she ever had in her life, though she'd played hard too; acting in several Lincoln College Drama Society productions, and even playing Rosalind in the outdoor production of *As You Like It,* in the trinity term of her second year.

A vibrating sensation in her left arm told her that she'd received a text message. She tried to keep going and ignore it, but at seven in the morning, she was intrigued as to who it was and so stopped running to read it. She took her phone out and read the message.

It read, *Good luck on your first day, I'm sure you'll do great.*

That was typical of David, she thought.

She knew she'd unfortunately broken his heart by leaving him after a four-year relationship and he sends her a nice message like that. Why couldn't he be horrible? Why couldn't he shout? It would've made it easier for her, instead of him being nice and understanding and trying his best to leave the door open for them. She'd left him the cottage they'd been renting in Liskeard for the last three years.

They'd moved in together four months after they'd returned from Europe. Jo wanted to stay living at home while her mum came to terms with losing her husband, Jo's dad. Jo tried her best to comfort her through this tough time. She almost felt as though she'd put her own grieving to one side until her mum seemed to be coping with things and returned to some sort of normality. Once she'd started going to church again and the parish council meetings, Jo knew she'd be OK. St Breward was a close community where everyone looked after each other.

Her mum was somebody who was involved with everything in the village. She was the church verger, she organised events and fund raising projects and ran the Ladies Circle meetings. She was also in charge of the village calendar and arranged the local history group meetings. Once she'd become more involved with all those things, Jo felt it was all right to move out and leave her to it. Although Liskeard is only twenty miles away, so she still visited her on a regular basis.

After Jo's relationship with David came to an end, Jo had moved back home with her mum and younger brother Rick. This was a temporary arrangement while she saved up for a deposit for her own house. She hoped that a house in St Breward would come up for sale, but in a small village like St Breward, it didn't happen very often, and when it did, they were sold very quickly. She wanted to live close to her family and she'd missed living in a close community such as this. Also, leaving David the cottage instead of asking him to move out made her feel a little less guilty, but only a little. If only he knew the real reason why she'd ended things with him, she thought.

She returned the phone to the wallet on her arm without answering the message and then continued to run. She began to speed up as she entered the village. She ran past the gates of Hosken's Farm, when suddenly she heard a shout.

'Jo!'

She stopped. She then saw Teddy making his way towards her. Teddy Hosken was sixty-five years old, and had been a friend of Jo's father. Jo had worked on Teddy's farm as a child and still saw him at least once a week in the King's Head.

Teddy stood six feet tall and was of a stocky build. Jo had joked with him before that he was built more like a rugby player than a farmer. He was dressed in the shabby dark-blue overalls he always wore whenever he was working. His white hair looked to Jo like it needed cutting, as well as a comb putting through it, but he was clean-shaven.

'Morning, Teddy,' Jo said.

'Good morning, Jo. Lovely morning for a run, don't you think?'

'You could've come with me?'

He smiled. 'Maybe next time.'

'I'll hold you to that.'

'I was wondering if you had time to look at something.'

She did. It was only seven o'clock, but she didn't really want to be distracted before starting her first day.

'Can't it wait until later?'

'It could, but it'll only take a second; and it'll prove to you that I'm right about something.'

She gave in. 'Go on then; but we'll have to be quick.'

He turned around and they set off walking towards the front gates of his farmland.

She noticed his quad bike parked up and hoped it wasn't going to be needed, but sure enough, he went straight to it and climbed onto the seat.

'Come on, Jo,' he said. 'Hop on.'

'Teddy,' she said, putting her hands on her hips. 'Why do we need to go on that? How far are you taking me?'

'We're just going to the bottom of the hill, near the woods.'

'You're really serious? You want me to get on that thing?'

'It's perfectly safe. It's got four wheels, after all. We need to go a couple of hundred yards and will be quicker on this than on foot.'

'Wouldn't it be even quicker if you just told me now what it is you've found?' Jo asked.

'No. I want your first impression of what you're about to see. You need to see it for yourself rather than just hearing my opinion.'

'All right, you've made your point. Come on then, let's go.'

'No problem!' Teddy exclaimed.

Taking off her sunglasses as to make sure she didn't lose them, Jo climbed onto the quad and sat in the seat behind him. He turned the key to start the noisy engine and they set off through the gates and onto Teddy's land. Teddy drove alongside an old, wonderfully robust stone wall. The sunlight was so bright that Jo had to half-close her eyes as they headed down a rather steep grass hill towards a wooded area at the bottom.

'Beautiful day, don't you think?' Teddy shouted over his shoulder.

Jo thought the day would be even more beautiful if she could actually get on with it and get ready to go to the police station, but she was curious now to know what Teddy wanted to show her.

A few moments later Teddy brought the quad bike to a stand-still in the shadow of a large oak tree, just on the edge of a group of smaller trees. Jo climbed off the seat and walked around to the front of the bike. She stood there in front of Teddy and looked at the trees as if they might contain some fearful secret, but Jo couldn't see anything unusual.

'What exactly am I supposed to be looking at?' she asked.

'Come here, and I'll show you,' Teddy said, climbing off the quad.

Teddy marched towards the large oak tree, Jo followed closely behind. He then glanced up to a part of the tree about five feet above the ground before looking back at Jo.

Now she saw what Teddy wanted to show her. For reasons she couldn't entirely explain, a sudden coldness came over her, even though it was a warm summer's morning. She knew what Teddy thought it was, and although she had previously dismissed his obsession with this myth, she knew what he was thinking.

'Scratch marks, don't you see?' Teddy said.

'Yes, I see.'

She took a step closer and started to think of other explanations. The tree looked to Jo as if someone had made serious efforts to rip the trunk open, probably with a large knife. Some of the marks gouged into the bark revealing the white wood beneath.

Jo glanced back at Teddy. 'Don't tell me, you're convinced this is more evidence of the existence of the Beast of Bodmin.'

'Absolutely right,' replied Teddy with an enthusiastic nod. 'Completely indisputable proof, if you ask me!'

One of the amicable points of contention between Teddy and Jo was Teddy's fervent, even faintly obsessive belief that Bodmin Moor - eighty square miles or so of sparsely inhabited moorland in north Cornwall - was home to a creature Teddy routinely referred to as the 'Beast'.

Teddy seemed to regard this creature as some kind of mythical being and when Jo – who was sure the creature was non-existent – asked him what kind of animal it really was, Teddy, when pressed, said he imagined it was a puma or a panther. Teddy thought that such a creature might have escaped from a travelling circus or from being abandoned by an owner who had unwisely bought the pet and found they could no longer control it. But Jo had been trained, during her three years in the police, to look for evidence rather than lame fantasy, and she was sure that the Beast of Bodmin existed nowhere outside the elastic stretch of her good friend Teddy's imagination.

'As a police officer,' Jo said, quietly, 'I'd say you're looking at the work of a few idle layabouts who have nothing better to do than damage one of your trees. It seems to me a clear case of vandalism.'

'Well, you tell me why anybody would want to suddenly vandalise a tree in the middle of nowhere, when nobody can see the result of their labours?'

Jo didn't answer.

Teddy said. 'If somebody was going to go to all that trouble, they'd pick a tree more likely to be spotted, not one here on private land.'

'Well, you saw it,' Jo said.

'Ben found it this morning while he was looking for a couple of missing sheep, which he's found, by the way. But this is my land, you know that. Walkers don't come this way so nobody would ever come here, other than Ben or maybe my granddaughter. Damaging one of the trees wouldn't be something they would do.'

'Teddy, I take all those points but if you're saying that this is proof of the existence of the Beast of Bodmin, I don't agree with you.'

'I knew you wouldn't. But look, Jo, you've known me all your life. Also, you know how much stick I got when I announced in the King's Head what I saw on the moors that time.'

'Yes, I do,' said Jo.

Teddy had come into the King's Head a couple of weeks ago on a Friday evening and announced that he'd seen a big cat roaming on the horizon and that he'd run towards it but the animal had meandered off out of sight.

'I'm afraid what you said that evening made you a bit of a

laughing stock,' Jo said, as politely as she could, not wanting to upset him any more about that night than he already was.

'I know. So what I'm saying is, if you want me to keep this to myself, then I will. I think it's pretty obvious what did those scratches.'

'You could be right, but I don't think so. If you do tell people about this, you'll end up with people laughing at you again.'

'I take your point,' Teddy said. 'And I know you've got to get to work. But just tell me, in your professional opinion, strictly between you and me, who or what do you really think did that damage to my tree?'

Jo pulled her mobile phone from the wallet on her arm, and pressed the camera icon to activate the digital camera. 'What do I think? Well, it's either someone messing about...'

'Or?' Teddy asked.

Jo didn't reply immediately, but went up to the gashes in the tree and took several photographs of them, the camera on the phone clicking decisively as she took each photograph.

'Well?' Teddy asked.

Jo glanced at him. 'Or else maybe you're right. Maybe it's a bloody big cat.'

Chapter 4

Jo sat in her bedroom looking into the mirror on her dressing-table at the side of her single bed. She was used to putting her police uniform on before heading off to the station, which required no decision making whatsoever, but today, after trying on three different outfits, she'd settled on a dark-blue tailored-suit with a white blouse. She wanted to look as professional as she could, not wanting to show off the curves she was blessed with as to make sure she didn't encourage any untoward comments from her fellow officers. This wasn't something that happened very often, maybe because of her being tall - five ten - or maybe because it was well known that she attended weekly kickboxing lessons, but she finally settled on an outfit that she felt was appropriate for her first day as a detective.

She gave her shoulder-length brown hair one last brush, checked her makeup was just right and then she was ready. She then looked over to her bookcase on the opposite side of the room. The shelves were filled with an eclectic selection of classic stories. Jane Austen's *Pride and Prejudice* and *Mansfield Park,* Emily Bronte's *Wuthering Heights*, Charles Dickens's *Oliver Twist*, and Louisa May Alcott's *Little Women.* There was also a selection of more modern classics, such as *The Catcher in the Rye*, *Lord of the Flies* and George Orwell's *1984*.

The top shelf was filled with Rose Byron's crime novels; all of them set in London and them featuring the black Metropolitan Police Detective Inspector Toni Lincoln. Although Jo had thought of becoming a police officer for many years, reading those books had definitely contributed to her decision to join the police. Toni Lincoln was a fictional character, but to Jo she was very real, after reading all of the books over the last ten years or so. Jo often asked herself during situations throughout her police career *what would Toni Lincoln do now?* She wondered whether Toni felt as excited on her first day as a detective as she did. She was a fearless character that wouldn't let anything stop her from completing a case. This was a trait that Jo knew she showed when catching the Bodmin Butcher, and she hoped that her own fearless attitude would help her towards completing her portfolio and qualifying officially as a detective constable within the next twelve months.

As Jo came down the stairs and into the living room, the morning sun shone through the small window of the cottage as she headed over to the fish tank in the corner of the room. She'd bought the aquarium just after setting up home with David in Liskeard. She thought it would be something they would enjoy together, but David lost interest after a few months, whereas Jo found it an enjoyable and interesting hobby. She certainly enjoyed sitting watching the fish after returning home from a late shift. There was something very serene about sitting in the dark living room late at night with just the light from the aquarium, and the fish for company.

Jo reached into the cupboard underneath the tank and took out the tub of food. She lifted the flap and sprinkled the flakes across the surface. All the blue and red Cardinal Tetras bounced up at the surface to grab a mouthful before diving back down to the safety of the lower levels of the tank. She had a quick look around the sandy bottom for the loaches, but she rarely saw them on the morning feed. At this early hour, they were all tucked away behind the plants and bogwood. She closed the lid, watched them for a moment, and then she went through to the kitchen.

'Morning, love,' her mum said. 'Are you ready for your first day?'

'I certainly am,' Jo replied, gratefully taking the cup of coffee from her that she was more than ready for.

'Would you like some breakfast? I can boil you a couple of eggs and make some toast?'

'No, thanks. The coffee's all I need. I'm too excited to eat. I'll get something later.'

'I understand, love.'

Her mum, Mary, now fifty-one years old, sat down at the kitchen table. She was still in her light blue dressing gown, her dark curly hair as yet untouched as she looked over the Cornish Reporter that was lay open across the table. She was reading the story of the Bodmin Butcher.

'You're still the most talked-about girl in Cornwall at the moment,' Mary said.

'They'll be bored of it soon,' Jo said, sitting down opposite her. 'It'll be forgotten this time next week.'

She hoped this would be the case as it was now five days since the trial had ended. She wondered if the story would continue to be told until some other exciting news story happened. In Cornwall, that could be a while, she thought.

Although Jo was still happy she solved the crime, she didn't like the fame that came with it. She didn't like strangers coming up to her and starting a conversation about how she'd caught the Bodmin Butcher. To Jo, that was in the past, and she wanted to focus on the future, and this week, now that the trial was finally over, she hoped it could be a fresh start.

'Imagine having to spend thirty years in jail,' Mary said.

'Well, he deserves it.'

'He deserves more if you ask me.'

'I couldn't agree more,' Jo said. 'Is my name mentioned a lot?'

'Several times,' she said. 'I thought that after you were interviewed on the Southwest News programme, the story might've died down.'

'So did I, there's nothing else to say really. I told them the full story.'

Mary folded the newspaper closed and looked at Jo lovingly, the way she always did. 'Your dad would've been so proud of you.'

This wasn't the first time she'd heard her mum say this, but it still brought a lump to Jo's throat. 'I know he would.'

'He'd have been even more proud now you're a detective.'

'A trainee detective constable,' Jo said.

'Why aren't you a detective constable, or even a detective sergeant? You proved yourself by catching this monster,' she said, pointing to the paper.

'You can't just start a new job at a higher rank, Mum. You have to start at the bottom and work your way up. I have to spend a year as a TDC, and once I've built my portfolio, they'll decide if I qualify as a DC.'

'Well I'm sure you will succeed. You're capable of anything you put your mind to. Your dad always said that, even when you was at primary school.'

'I wonder what he'd have thought about me becoming a detective,' Jo said.

'He'd have been very happy for you,' she said. 'Although he probably would've told you to stay in uniform like he did. He always said that detectives were a different breed. They can't switch off at night as easily as he could.'

'That's true. I've been warned that it won't feel like a job from now on. It's more of a way of life, apparently.'

'Well, you're about to find out,' Mary said. She then turned around to look at the clock on the wall behind her. 'I'd better check Rick's up.'

She stood up walked back through to the lounge; Jo also got up and followed her, taking her coffee with her.

'Rick!' Mary shouted. 'Come on, you'll be late.'

Jo took another gulp of her coffee. 'I'm going to set off.'

'OK, love.' Mary said, taking the almost empty cup from her.

'I want to get settled before the day starts. I've no idea what'll be happening so I just want to prepare a little.'

'You'll do great, I'm sure.'

'Thanks.' She gave her a kiss on the cheek, and then turned to leave.

'What time will you be home?' she asked.

'I officially knock off at seven, but I don't think detectives always get out on time. I'll let you know.'

'OK.'

'Morning,' Rick said, as he came down the stairs in just a t-shirt and shorts. Even at nineteen years old, Rick was as tall as Jo, skinny, and had short dark brown hair. 'Look at you, Detective Green. You're looking smart.'

Jo smiled, but she wanted to get on her way. 'Thank you. Right, I'm going.'

'There's no chance of a lift to work then?' Rick asked.

'Sorry. I need to get to work early today; you know, with it being my first day. If you were ready now I could take you.'

'Yeah, I know,' Rick said. 'No problem. I'll walk. It's a nice day anyway.'

Jo quickly went back upstairs to brush her teeth, before she ran down the stairs again, grabbed her car keys and then left the house. She shouted, 'See you later,' as she closed the door.

As she left the cottage and headed for her dark-blue Ford Mondeo, it suddenly seemed to hit her that she was leaving a chapter of her life behind and starting a new one. Jo felt as though the trial of the Bodmin Butcher had been hanging over her since she'd arrested him six months before. She found the whole ordeal quite stressful, but today was a new beginning.

Jo had been in court many times during her career, but never for something as serious as the Bodmin Butcher murders, and never for something which attracted as much publicity as it did. But the Wednesday previous, seven men and five women found Vladek Boniek guilty of the murder of four innocent women.

Vladek Boniek, forty years old was a tall slim man with very short, neat brown hair. He was a Polish immigrant who'd moved to England eight years earlier. He lived in Tregoltha, a town just four miles from St Breward. He was a member of the Tregoltha chess club. The murder scenes were unusual because the murderer couldn't leave the scene without tidying up first. The first victim, Carol Forbes, also aged forty, was the treasurer of the chess club. The jury found that Boniek had stood behind her in her kitchen, reached around with a large kitchen knife and slit her throat. The prosecution said that he'd dragged her to the wall in her kitchen, laid her down neatly and folded her arms across her stomach. He used her towels to clean up the blood, before putting them into the washing machine and switching it on. He also washed the knife and placed it back in the drawer.

It was a similar story with Stephanie Newham, aged forty-five. Boniek knew her from the local pub and she lived a couple of streets away from him in Tregoltha. The jury found that Boniek had slit her throat before cleaning the kitchen as best he could and arranging her in the same way as he did Carol Forbes.

Claire Watts, aged thirty, was also a regular at the local pub. He'd been seen talking to her on several occasions and the jury decided that Boniek had also killed her in her own home in the same way as he did the others.

Christine Byrne, aged thirty-two, worked at the local petrol station and she was killed when she was walking home one night. The jury found Boniek guilty of stabbing her in the front of her throat, so Christine must've seen it coming. The prosecution case was that he'd pulled her to the side of the pavement and folded her arms across her body.

Jo was the first officer on the scene of Christine Byrne's

murder. She was driving through Tregoltha when an elderly man walking his dog found the body and knocked on the front door of the nearest house to get them to phone the police.

Jo was excited at being the first on the scene, but she was quickly brought down to earth when she saw the body. Christine was dressed in jeans and a woollen winter coat. She lay on the cold pavement next to a concrete fence at the opening of an alleyway.

She lay on her back with her arms across her stomach and her eyes wide open. Her face was white and her eyes seemed to stare up to the sky. Jo must've arrived at the scene pretty quickly because she saw steam rising from the open wound in the front of her throat. It was a frosty January night but her neck still felt warm as Jo felt for a pulse, but Christine was already dead. Jo moved people back from the area and handled the scene perfectly well, but her hands were shaking and she felt a little nauseous. This was her first dead body, and she knew she'd never forget it.

Vladek Boniek was known within the chess club for his obsessive personality. He wouldn't speak to anyone before a chess game. He only ever drank Evian water, from a 500 ml bottle, during a chess match. He wore the same faded green woollen jumper for every match, even in the height of summer. He also refused to begin a game of chess if there was anything other than the board, the pieces, the clock and a 500 ml bottle of Evian mineral water, on the table. He didn't like anything else cluttering up the area. If an opponent put their keys or mobile phone on the table, he wouldn't play until they were removed.

Boniek was considered a very good chess player and had helped the club win several tournaments. His speciality was playing well when he and his opponent were both short of time on their clock. He had the ability to see the board clearly and make quick decisions, putting his opponent under great pressure.

But it was the obsessive compulsive disorders that drew Jo's eye to him. The fact the killer cleaned up after himself made her think this could be the man they were looking for. After all, it's not like he was cleaning up to hide anything, the bodies were still there, the scenes were just a little neater than they were immediately after the murders were committed, Jo presumed.

As a police constable, it wasn't Jo's job as such to get involved in the investigation that was being run by the detectives from Bodmin Police Station, but she took it upon herself to go to the club and watch what went on there. Vladek Boniek stood out to her above all the others. Only one of the four victims was tied directly to the chess club, but two were regulars of the pub where the meets were sometimes held. Jo felt that with three of the victims being loosely connected to the chess club; that was a good place to start.

The detectives had already interviewed all twenty-two members of the club, including Boniek, but no one, even the other members of the club would have suspected him because he was so mild mannered. On the outside he seemed like such a gentle person. He might've shown signs of obsessive compulsive behaviour, but everyone was used to his unusual way of doing things, so nobody connected his behaviour with a murderer who tidied the murder scenes; no one except Jo, that is.

Jo decided to knock on Boniek's door one evening, just before the end of a shift. Vladek Boniek nervously allowed Jo to enter the house, and when she saw a large spacious living room, with nothing but a television, a chair, and a small table at the side of the chair, all arranged perfectly on the clean beige carpet, surrounded by bright white untouched walls, Jo began to feel that she was on the right track.

After cautioning a very nervous-looking Vladek Boniek as to why she was there, she then asked the question. 'Where were you on the night of each of the murders?' No sooner had she reached the end of this sentence, Boniek panicked and pushed her back against the wall before running from the house. He had banged her head hard, but she managed to recover enough to chase him. She tackled him to the ground a hundred yards from his house.

He confessed to the murders during his first interview, but changed his story a few days later, even though a blood-soaked handkerchief was found stuffed down the side of his armchair with blood belonging to Christine Byrne, and his fingerprints were found in the kitchen of Carol Forbes, the first victim.

It didn't take long for the jury to find him guilty. The judge sentenced him to Life was a recommendation that he serve thirty years, but there was talk that the Home Secretary would change this to a Whole Life Tariff. Jo won fame all across the country for bringing an end to these horrific murders. But she didn't enjoy the celebrity that came with catching a serial killer, even though she was sure that it was helpful to her career.

Now, she was hoping she could put this part of her life behind her; she was ready for her next chapter.

Chapter 5

Leaving David was a big decision to make, but Jo knew it was the right one.

She'd tried hard to live the life that she felt was expected of her, but enough was enough, it was time to be honest with herself, even if she wasn't ready to be honest with everyone else just yet. Her dad was a man's man, a traditional man, a man who was set in his ways and he wouldn't have understood why his daughter was gay. She wondered how long she would've kept up the pretence if he was still alive.

More than three years had passed since he'd died. Jo struggled to come to terms with this and threw herself into her career. She wondered what he would've said if she'd sat him down and told him about her sexuality. He was a kind, loving man and she was definitely a daddy's girl, so maybe he would've accepted it, but now, she'll never know.

She was blissfully unaware of the decisions that lay ahead of her during her time at St Breward Primary School. She loved her time there and was always awarded excellent report cards and parents' evenings always had a happy outcome. English was her favourite subject, but she found maths and history almost as enjoyable. When it came to school, she could do it all, even P.E. She was popular and had a close circle of friends and always thought back to that time, wishing she could do it all again.

She went to secondary school in Tregoltha. Tregoltha is a small but thriving community situated between Bodmin and St Breward. St John's was where Jo went to secondary school, and academically, she did just as well as at primary school, but in a large school surrounded by lots more people than the close-knit community she'd left in her previous school, she found it a little more exciting.

Jason Hendra, who was considered the best-looking boy in the year, showed an interest in her, so after being persuaded by her friends that this was a great fortuity, how could she say no? Her friends were envious of her and she enjoyed the popularity that came with being his girlfriend. The two of them were a couple for three months, but then she became bored of him. He might have had the nicest smile and been the tallest of all the boys, but she never really felt a connection to him. She enjoyed being with him when all her other friends were around, but when it was just the two of them, she felt as though there wasn't much to say.

She didn't show an interest in any other boys until a couple of years down the line when a new pupil arrived at the school. Anthony Pengelly was different to Jason. He was handsome but much more quiet and thoughtful. Jo was always reading crime novels, even as a teenager and she noticed that Anthony was spending his dinner breaks in the library and thought that she'd get to know him. He became her first love. From age thirteen to sixteen they were inseparable. She felt as though he understood her. They both enjoyed reading but they also shared other interests and she was completely comfortable in his company, even enjoying the silences. They spent most evenings and weekends together. She felt like they would be together forever, but just before her sixteenth birthday, everything changed.

He'd been pressuring her for sex, not in an aggressive way, just by way of suggestion and talking about it whenever possible. She'd told him that she wanted to wait until she was sixteen, but as the date drew closer, she began to feel that sex wasn't something she wanted to do. She had thought about it, and wondered what it would be like, but looking back now, she knew that she didn't really want to go down that road.

She felt guilty for making him wait so long, and wondered if he'd have stayed with her all that time if he knew he wasn't going to lose his virginity to her. There were plenty of other girls in the school and many of them already sexually active, Jo just didn't want to be one of them. But one night, about a week before her sixteenth birthday, they were in his house, and his parents were on a night out, Anthony thought that night was his night. He'd played the game, doing his best to prepare her a meal, albeit prepared in the microwave, he lit candles and played music, and Jo was beginning to be won over by his attempt at romance.

The kissing began on the sofa, and then they moved to his bedroom. She felt her heart race as they quickly began to undress. Although she was excited, she was also scared and it just didn't feel right to her. It wasn't as smooth as it was in the movies, she thought. The struggle to remove each other's clothes and putting the passion on hold as he fought with the little foil packet and the even longer wait as he applied the contents, it just didn't feel right. But then the act began. The pain quickly turned to pleasure as he made love to her, but it still felt wrong, she felt more guilt than pleasure. She turned her head away and tried to let him carry on, but then she couldn't go on any longer and she asked him to stop.

He didn't at first, but when she shouted, he stopped immediately and climbed off her. He asked her what was wrong.

She lay back against his pillow wondering what all the fuss was about. Was this what was on every man's mind twenty-four hours a day? Was this what thousands of songs are written about? Was this was what poems and stories are written about? And was this what she made Anthony wait so long for? She just didn't get it. Why was sex so important to everyone?

She wiped away the tears that had fallen down her face, dressed quickly and left the house after briefly apologising to

Anthony. She wondered what was wrong with her, she even wondered if she was frigid -a term she'd heard girls throwing at each other when discussing sex- but it just wasn't something she wanted to do.

That brought an end to her relationship with Anthony. He said all the right things to her, how he was prepared to wait until she was ready, but she didn't feel that she would ever be ready. Their relationship ended. Jo missed him, but the anxiety at the possibility of sex being implied again wasn't worth enduring, even though at the time she thought she might've loved him.

Jo stayed single all through college. She didn't really feel that she wanted to be in a relationship at that point in her life and just focused on having fun and doing well in her education.

A year before finishing college, she applied for Oxford. She successfully achieved the necessary grades and enrolled in the English Language and Literature course at Lincoln College, Oxford. English was something she enjoyed and she even considered writing for a living. She was reading three books a week by now, but was drawn to crime and detective novels.

It was late in her third year when she met David. She noticed his big brown eyes as soon as he walked into the pub where she and her friends were having a drink. He was tall and had dark hair in a side parting. He had a confidence in his stride that turned heads as soon as he entered the room. He caught her looking at him and smiled. She smiled back and she knew then that her plans of staying single were about to be cast aside.

He was from Barnstaple in Devon. They'd joked about how they were the only two people from the West Country that had made it into Oxford. This was certainly true for the time they had been there. They hit it off straight away. He was intelligent and funny and she found herself falling for him after only a couple of weeks of knowing him. He was there studying Philosophy, Politics and Economics and talked of becoming a politician, but after graduating he found himself a job working for an accountancy firm in Bodmin.

They had a great relationship and Jo was happy, they both were. After being an item for a couple of months, she finally had sex with him for the first time. She felt at ease with David, especially because he didn't actually ask her to have sex. She'd confided in him that it was something she wasn't comfortable with and he never pushed her to go any further. But one night, with the confidence from a few large glasses of wine, she and David finally made love.

She slowly began to understand what all the fuss was about. He was gentle, caring and intimate with her and suddenly, Jo felt as though she was over her anxieties and began to enjoy the passion and intimacy between them.

Things were great for the first two years of their relationship. The year they'd spent travelling was when she felt herself fall in love with him. She loved how outgoing he was and how nothing seemed to faze him, even arriving in countries where they didn't speak the language.

After they'd returned to England and Jo had lost her dad, she still felt her love for him grow. He helped her with the funeral arrangements, and showed his caring side as he helped her through what was certainly a difficult time. She was starting to feel as though they would be together forever.

It was after they'd been living together for a couple of years, that Jo started to feel a distance growing between them. He talked about having children, but she didn't want them. He wanted weekends together, but that wasn't always possible with her ever changing shifts. Jo wanted to talk about work; David didn't want to and always wanted to leave work at work. Although they weren't arguing, the connection between them was dying out. They even started to socialise in different circles.

One night, back in April, Jo and another officer, PC Laura

Trevilian arranged to go for a night out. Laura was a little shorter than Jo and had long blond hair and bright blue eyes. They'd been working together and had become good friends. They called at Laura's house in Tregoltha for a drink on the way back from the restaurant. She'd enjoyed a great night, letting her hair down on her night off. But she also discussed her problems with David. Laura was single and lived on her own, and didn't tell Jo what to do about her problems as such; she just listened to her, which Jo was happy with.

At the end of the night, as Laura opened the door for her to say goodbye after the taxi had arrived, she kissed Jo goodnight. It was on the lips, which Jo might not have thought anything of, but what was unusual was the length of the kiss. It was normally just a peck on the cheek from Laura, but this kiss went on for at least five seconds, and was followed by a long stare from her bright blue eyes that seemed to go on forever. She'd never asked Laura about her sexuality; she just presumed she was single, and straight, but that moment, standing in her doorway after midnight with the taxi's engine running would be the moment that everything suddenly made sense to her. The electricity that she felt between them just from this one kiss was more than she'd ever felt from David, or her other boyfriends. This was both magical and mysterious.

Jo turned to walk away and then turned back to look into Laura's eyes again. She wanted to kiss her again, but she also didn't want to ruin the most incredible moment of her life so far. She said goodnight again, and walked away. She smiled at her through the window of the taxi as it drove away. In that moment, everything fell into place.

She was awake for most of the night, her heart still pounding as she stared at the ceiling, wondering if that kiss was more than an accidently prolonged goodnight kiss. The look in Laura's eyes told her that it was meant as something much more. She was confused. As she lay there next to David as he slept, she sat up in bed and searched the internet for answers. Was it possible to get to age twenty-five without realising that she could be gay?

She typed into the internet on her phone *when did you realise you were gay?*

After clicking on the top link, she came onto a forum. As she read the posts, she found that many of the women had been drawn to other women since before they could remember, but there was one story that caught her eye. It was a woman who was aged twenty-seven before she first kissed another woman and suddenly realised that she was gay. She talked about how she thought that she had intimacy problems when she was in bed with men, and thought that it was normal for women to find other women attractive. It was only after a kiss with another woman that she realised that she was gay. Jo thought that she could've almost written this post herself. Everything started to make sense to her.

During the next shift she was on with Laura, three days later, there was a discomfort between them. She wondered if Laura felt as though she'd crossed the line, and neither of them mentioned the kiss. But an hour into the shift, Laura asked her if she wanted to come to her house for dinner that weekend. Jo quickly said yes and the tension seemed to lift as they both seemed to know that they were on the same page.

They enjoyed a quiet dinner, sat across from each other in Laura's dining room. Jo struggled finishing her meal as her stomach was fluttering with nerves and excitement.

Laura seemed to sense this and took control of the situation. She put her knife and fork down and walked around the table to Jo.

Jo looked up at her wondering what was going to happen.

Laura bent down to her and kissed her gently on the lips. This kiss was much longer than the first and much more passionate.

She took her hand and gently led her up from the table and they made their way upstairs, Laura in front of Jo, but still hand in hand.

As they went into the dark bedroom, Jo's heart was beating hard as her chest rose and fell with every deep breath. They slowly undressed and spent the rest of the evening making love in ways that Jo had never even imagined. Laura's utterly soft skin and gentle caresses showed Jo what making love really was. There was none of the haste and roughness of sex with a man. It was like they were in slow motion. The world seemed to stop spinning just for them. She was unaware of time, and guilt and the issues she'd experienced ever since that night with Anthony. She was in a state of pure heaven and didn't want it to end. She knew there would be decisions to make the next day, but at that moment, she was lost in a different world, a world she'd never before considered, not before that first kiss from Laura.

Chapter 6

Jo drove slowly through the winding narrow roads of the village of St Breward on her way to Bodmin Police Station. St Breward is situated eight miles north of Bodmin. This hidden village is home only to around nine hundred people. There is just one shop, a village hall, a church, a school and a pub and because of this, maintains the quiet tranquil and scenic ambience that Jo missed in the time she lived in Liskeard and Oxford.

As Jo drove through the village, it did occur to her that she lived in a part of the country where the crime and murder rates are low. She was aware that the homicide rate had increased from zero the year before last, to four the year after; although three of those victims were down to Vladek Boniek; the first three victims being murdered in December, the fourth in January. But violent crimes had risen along with rape and weapons offences. She knew that a similar percentage increase would mean a lot more in the cities like London or Manchester, but here in Cornwall these crimes were few and far between so a fifty percent increase in a crime could mean just one or two more incidents. Jo reflected that sometimes being a police officer in Cornwall was more of a matter of being a social worker than investigating major crimes, because there weren't very many major crimes to investigate.

She passed the grocery store on the left hand side of the road. The building stood out from the houses on that row, and had bright white walls with a green and white striped awning that kept the sun from reaching the two bay windows. Vinny Jackson, the owner, who was in his fifties and had a pale face from indulging in his hobby, which was smoking, was standing outside the front door of his shop, with a cigarette in his hand. He waved at Jo and Jo waved back. Vinny's shop sold not only almost anything you might want in a small village like St Breward, but Vinny was a fount of information about what was happening in the village and Jo was already experienced that as a police officer to know that people like Vinny could be invaluable to her, should the need for local information arise.

Twenty minutes later Jo had arrived at the station. Bodmin Police Station was a large three storey modern building that was surrounded by perfectly kept grass lawns. Set in its own grounds, the building was surrounded by lampposts and pathways, and young trees that hadn't yet reached their full heights. The large building was mostly glass at the front with white concrete walls on the sides and an overhanging roof that curved around the front of the structure.

Jo followed the road around to the back of the building where she parked her car and made her way inside. After getting buzzed in, and then signing in, she went up the staircase and to the top floor. She'd never been to the top floor before, and she didn't know what to expect. The door at the top of the stairs opened up onto a lounge area with four office-style couches set out in a square, with a large coffee table in the middle. This floor, like the others was covered by blue patterned carpet tiles that started as soon as she came through the staircase door.

Jo turned left and walked through the door that opened onto a long hallway. She knew that the office she was now going to be working in was third on the right. She walked down the corridor and stopped outside the door. Her heart was pounding, and now she'd arrived, she felt even more excited. She gave a moment's thought to how Detective Inspector Toni Lincoln would've felt standing outside the office door on her first day. She stood up straight and pushed her shoulders back, took a deep breath and then entered the room.

There were three detectives in there already. They were in the middle of what seemed to Jo like a serious discussion, so she stood there a moment; she wanted to witness the hustle and bustle of her new office. There were six desks all in symmetry along the sides of the room-three on each side-with one large desk in the middle. There was also an office with internal walls and windows with blinds in the back corner that she presumed belonged to DCI Collis. There were several white boards at one side of the room with photographs and scribbling in marker pens of black and red. There were countless shelves all around the room, and metal filing cabinets. Above the shelves, the walls were covered with maps and notice boards. The windows stretched all along the left hand side of the room, overlooking the car park, but covered by blinds that were partly open and allowed the morning sunlight to make its way through the gaps and lighting up the room.

Jo's first reaction was that this was what she'd been waiting for. This room was where she was going to spend the next several years of her career. This was where she could make a real name for herself.

'Jo Green,' she heard a voice say. One of the other detectives had spotted her. They stopped what they were doing and came over to greet her. One at a time they shook her hand.

'Welcome aboard, Jo,' DS Danny Hughes said. She knew them because of working in the same building when she was a police constable. She was involved with them in several situations.

'I haven't spoken to you properly since your rise to fame,' DS Hughes said. Jo was always impressed by Danny Hughes. He was good-looking and had a confidence about him. He wasn't a local, Jo thought his accent was a London one, but she hadn't yet asked in the few meetings they'd had previously. Jo thought he looked about thirty, but maybe slightly older. He was six feet four inches and had a physique of someone who keeps fit. Not like a body builder, but certainly like someone who either runs a lot or plays football regularly. He had short dark hair that was always perfectly set. He was wearing a very expensive looking suit and what Jo thought looked like an even more expensive watch.

'I'm hardly famous for passing a detectives exam,' Jo said modestly. She knew really what he was referring to.

'I'm talking about the Bodmin Butcher,' Danny said.

'Yeah, that was pretty impressive, Jo,' DC Bradley Dustow said. Bradley was medium build, possibly in his late forties with dark red hair in a side parting. He was wearing a light-blue shirt and a dark-blue tie.

Jo suddenly felt very welcome in her new job. 'It was just a case of being in the right place at the right time.'

'Come on, Jo,' DS Rachel Killik said. 'You're too modest. That was an amazing bit of police work.' Rachel was someone that Jo hadn't had as many dealings with as the others. She was older, possibly fifty, Jo thought. She had shoulder length blond hair and a slim figure, very attractive, and she also had a confidence in her that Jo admired. She'd heard that DS Killik was in line for a promotion to detective inspector, but didn't want to ask her about that just yet. Maybe once they'd all got to know each other a little better.

'I agree. How did you know...' Bradley was then interrupted by DCI Collis entering the room from his office.

'Right folks, let's get to work,' he said. He then made eye contact with Jo. 'Morning, Jo. Come through to my office; you too Danny.'

Jo let Danny walk in to the office first; she followed and then closed the door behind her.

DCI Collis sat behind his desk and offered a piece of paper to Danny. Brian Collis was a tall man, with a slightly greying beard to match his full head of hair. Jo thought that he looked like he was in his late fifties, but possibly older. He was friends with Jo's dad but she knew he was slightly older. He had a calm way about the way he moved, Jo thought, as though he couldn't be, and wouldn't be hurried. She'd met him several times before and had heard of his strict reputation. But she'd also heard Teddy talk of him in a more affectionate way; he and Teddy being friends.

'No time to even show you to a desk this morning, Jo. You're straight in at the deep end.'

'Not a problem, sir,' she said. She noticed over Danny's shoulder that the piece of paper had what looked like an address and a photocopied close up of a map fragment, with arrows written in pen.

'What's happening?' Danny asked.

'We've just had a report of a murder scene on the moors near Bolventor. A member of the public called it in.'

This made Jo's heart race. She expected to get some sort of induction before being sent out into the field, but it's better than nothing happening on her first day, she thought.

'Do we know any details?' Danny asked.

'Not many, just that it was somebody camping. Scenes of Crimes Officers are already there. I want you two to go there, right now.'

'Will do, sir,' Danny said.

'Yes, sir,' Jo added.

They both then left the office.

Chapter 7

Danny started the car as Jo put her seat belt on. The radio was playing, but Danny turned it down to a quiet level, number six. He then put his seat belt on and drove the car along the pathway, leading towards the main road.

'So,' Danny said. 'What's life been like since you shot to fame?'

Jo smirked. 'A little crazy, I have to say.'

'You must be pleased though, I mean, everyone knows your name now.'

Jo thought for a moment. 'That's not always a good thing.'

Danny drove slightly faster than the speed limit, as he took them through the town on the way to the carriageway.

'Strangers keep letting on to me like they know me, the locals that I thought were my friends seem to look at me like I think I'm something special, and although I'm excited about becoming a detective, I feel as though I've set the bar pretty high.'

'So,' Danny said. 'So you've set the bar high; clear it. You're good enough. You saw something in Vladek Boniek that the rest of us didn't see. You shouldn't be worried, you should be excited.'

'I suppose you're right. I can't have asked for a better result. It's just that...'

'What?' Danny asked.

'I don't know. It's almost like I would feel if I'd won the lottery. I feel like some people are happy for me, and others look at me differently. It's not like they're jealous, it's more like they think that *I* think I'm above them. I can't explain it.'

'Well, you know what I think?'

'What's that?'

'Stuff them.'

Jo laughed. That wasn't the answer she was looking for.

'If they can't deal with the fact that you've become famous for catching a serial killer, then there's something wrong with them.'

'Maybe you're right. They seem to think that I've become a detective because of catching him, but it's not like that, is it? I still had to pass the exam and the interview.'

'True, but the panel that interviewed you would've known your record. The Bodmin Butcher would have made a good difference to your chances, but why shouldn't it?'

'I suppose you're right.'

'Also, becoming a detective constable isn't a promotion; it's more of a side step, even after you've finished your probationary period.'

'That's a good point. I don't get a pay rise, do I?'

'Not until you become a DS like me,' Danny said, smiling.

They drove for a few minutes in silence.

Then Danny said, 'You are happy that it was *you* that brought an end to the Bodmin Butcher murders, aren't you?'

'Yes, Of course I am. Why would you think otherwise?'

'You seem a little embarrassed about it, almost like you wish it didn't happen.'

She thought for a moment. 'No. I'm not embarrassed as such. It's just that my life has been a bit of a roller coaster since I caught him. I broke up with my boyfriend a few months after, and moved back home to my mum's house; and waiting for the trial to come around was arduous. I'm glad it's over to be honest.'

'That's understandable. It's a long wait and you'd have been gutted if he'd been found not guilty.'

'That was worrying. The whole world would've known that I was wrong.'

'Well, luckily, you were right all along.'

'David didn't think so,' Jo said.

'David?'

'My boyfriend, well, ex-boyfriend, he thought Boniek was innocent.'

Danny turned to her and looked shocked at this comment before turning back to watch the road. 'Really?'

'He said that he thought he seemed too meek and mild to be a killer.'

Danny laughed. 'What was he expecting, a man in a striped jumper with knives for fingers?'

She laughed. 'We didn't agree on much towards the end.'

Danny said. 'I know how you feel. I've broken up with my girlfriend recently.'

'Have you?' she asked.

He grabbed his mobile phone from his inside pocket. He then pressed the gallery icon and flicked through his photos, while sporadically looking back at the road.

'What are you showing me?' Jo asked.

He found the photo he wanted. 'Here, look at this gorgeous creature.'

Jo looked at the picture of a beautiful young woman, possibly late twenties, light brown hair and big brown eyes. She was smiling in the photograph, and Jo thought she was stunning. 'Wow,' she said. 'Who's she?'

'I was going out with her for a few months, but it didn't work out.'

'That's a shame. She's gorgeous.'

'Gorgeous she is, but she has issues.'

'Really?' Jo asked.

'Yes, but that's a conversation for another day.'

Jo was a little surprised that Danny had a girlfriend. He had a bit of a reputation for trying his luck with female officers at the station. Laura told her to watch him when Jo had told her about her becoming a detective and working in the same department as him. But so far, she was quite comfortable in his company.

Jo knew the scenery of the moors like the back of her hand but she never ceased to admire it. But right now there was something automatic about her admiration of the view; she was thinking about where they were going. She'd seen dead bodies before but it was never something she got used to and she didn't imagine that if she ever got used to it that would be any good for her, for her career, or for anybody else. She certainly wasn't in the mood for any more chit-chat. She was now braced for seeing more bodies, more mayhem, more evidence of the cruelty at the heart of life.

They came off the road and parked up on the grass next to all the other vehicles. There was a police car, a black Vauxhall Opel and a white unmarked van. As they parked up, Jo saw that the area had already been taped off by the Scenes of Crime Officers. There were also several members of the public watching from behind the tape.

'There's always an audience,' Jo said.

'Part of the furniture; I don't even notice them anymore,' Danny said. He then opened the boot and passed Jo the protective clothing that was still in the cellophane wrapper. After putting the light-blue coveralls on, they then walked over to the scene.

'I don't need to tell you, don't be shy of getting stuck in, Jo,' Danny said. 'If there's something you want to ask, me or them, just ask.'

'Thanks, Danny,' she said.

Danny showed the officer standing guard at the tape his identification before ducking under and zipping his suit up. Jo nodded to the officer and then climbed under the tape herself.

Jo could see four people in the investigation team; three standing on the grass to the right of the tent and one inside the tent visible through the open flap. All four were dressed in light blue polythene coveralls that only left their eyes visible and at that distance Jo couldn't be sure what the gender was of the four people, although it looked as if the team member in the tent was female as she was shorter than the others, who Jo thought were probably all men.

The team member from inside the tent now came out to greet them. 'Good morning, Danny,' the SOCO said. It was a woman's voice. She pulled her mask away revealing a thoughtful and intense face and large brown eyes.

'This is Detective Sergeant Sara Mulfra,' Danny explained to Jo. 'Sara, meet the famous Jo Green. It's her first day as detective constable.'

'Not *the* Jo Green?' Sara asked.

'The very same,' Danny said.

'They didn't give you an extra promotion to detective sergeant?' Sara asked.

'If only it was that simple,' Jo said.

'Well, I'm very impressed,' Sara said.

As always, Jo felt herself starting to get embarrassed by this. 'I just had a lucky thought about some of the evidence and we got him,' she said with a brief shrug of her shoulders.

'Best not to be too modest, Jo,' said Danny.

Jo cleared her throat. 'So what's the situation here?'

Sara smiled. 'Well, now that Jo Green's arrived I'm sure we'll have the murderer within a few hours.'

'Let's hope so,' Danny said.

Jo raised her eyebrows to Danny, almost as if Sara had just backed up her story of fame from their journey.

'All right,' Sara said. 'We're pretty sure we've got two murders.'

'Pretty sure?' Jo asked.

'Well, we don't have any bodies.'

This surprised Jo.

'No bodies? Then what have we got?' asked Danny.

'Come with me,' Sara said.

Jo and Danny followed her to a place at the right hand side of the tent. As they approached, Jo saw that the grass there was black with dried blood.

'When there's as much blood as this showing on the grass's surface,' Sara said, 'there'll be a much larger amount soaked through to the soil beneath. I'm not sure how much there would have been altogether, but I don't think they could have survived. Also, there are blood spots on the side of the tent.'

'What about inside the tent?' asked Jo.

'Inside there's at least two pints of blood, and a smudged area where the body was dragged out.'

Jo was thinking of this morning's trip to Teddy's farm.

'We're treating this as a double murder,' Sara said. 'There was a pair of folded up jeans with a driving licence for a Steve Roberts and a purse in the bag with a provisional driving licence for a Debbie Rowland. They each have separate London addresses.'

'Is there any money?' Jo asked.

'Yes. There's a couple of pounds worth of change in the purse, and over two hundred pounds in cash in the male's wallet.'

'I see.'

'Any footprints?' Danny asked.

'There are lots of indentations in the grass, but nothing distinguishable as yet.'

'Has anyone checked the surrounding areas?' Jo asked.

'Not yet,' the SOCO said. 'We're still trying to work out what might have happened.'

Jo turned away and walked back to the uniformed constable standing at the tape.

Danny followed her.

'I'm sorry; I don't know your name.'

'PC Shields,' he replied.

'Thank you, PC Shields; can you please arrange for a team to search the surrounding moors and woodland?'

'Yes, of course.' PC Shields began talking through his radio.

Danny pulled Jo about ten yards away from PC Shields.

'What are you thinking, Jo?' Danny asked, keeping his voice down so that only Jo would hear.

'Well,' said Jo, 'I'll reserve judgement until we get more evidence but...well...has it occurred to you that it might not necessarily have been a person who did this?'

'What do you mean?' Danny asked.

'Some big cats are known for killing their prey and dragging them away. Leopards are known for carrying animals up into trees out of the way of other predators.' She could tell by Danny's face that he wasn't impressed by what she was suggesting.

'Surely you're not serious, Jo,' Danny said. 'Do you really believe in all that Beast of Bodmin nonsense?'

'Well, we don't know for definite that it's nonsense,' Jo said.

'Come on, it's just a story made up for the tourists, just like the Loch Ness Monster. I'm sure that legend makes the cafes and restaurants near Loch Ness a few hundred thousand pounds every year and maybe the Beast of Bodmin does something for our area as well.'

'I've got a friend, Teddy Hosken, who fervently believes in it and he's quite a pillar of the local community. A few weeks ago...'

'I know Teddy Hosken,' Danny said, 'or at least I know of him. I don't think we should be too influenced by what he says. But anyway, Jo, the woods will be searched, that would have been the next step anyway. But please, you've got an amazing track record and I don't want you to lose any of it. Please don't suggest this Beast of Bodmin theory to DCI Collis or you'll run the risk of being back in uniform before you've been given a desk.'

'I wasn't planning to suggest it to DCI Collis,' Jo said. 'I won't suggest it to anybody unless there's more evidence.'

As they drove back to Bodmin, Jo thought about her conversation with Teddy at the farm earlier that day and whether there really was anything in Teddy's theory. Jo seriously doubted it, but she'd already learned in her police career that you don't dismiss any possibly believable theory until there's enough evidence for doing so.

Chapter 8

Jo was given a desk, the middle one of the three on the left hand side of the room next to the window. There was nobody else in the office as she sat contemplating the case. The room felt eerily quiet to her as she tried to get herself comfortable at her desk. There was a phone and a computer, and basic stationary, an untouched A4 notepad and a pack of ball point pens with black, blue, and red pens inside. But that was all.

The desk in front of hers had family photographs and personal items like a miniature golf bag that was also a pen holder, an obvious gift, Jo thought, nobody would actually go into a shop and buy themselves such an item. She wondered if this was Danny's desk because of this. She presumed that DS Rachel Killik's desk was the tidier one on the other side of hers. The other desk on the opposite wall was cluttered. There was stationary scattered all across it, piles of paper and cardboard files, and a coffee cup. It was unorganised but she thought that maybe whoever the desk belonged to, possibly knew where everything was.

She moved a blank whiteboard which was on wheels, a little closer to her desk. She used a black marker pen to list the facts of the case so far. She wrote the names of the victims in the top left hand corner, *Steve Roberts and Debbie Rowland*. She then wrote, *both presumed dead, no bodies*, underneath. And then she added, *on holiday from London, money not taken*.

As yet there were no distinguishable footprints or a conclusive sign of a third person. She was half-expecting the crime scenes team to find big cat foot prints but it hadn't happened, or at least not as yet.

Danny came into the room, talking on his phone as he

entered. He walked quickly over to Jo and gestured for her to give the pen to him. He then wrote on the board underneath the notes Jo had just made, *Jamaica Inn.*

'OK. Thanks, Sara. Speak to you later.' He then hung up the phone.

'Was that the SOCO?'

'Yes. She says that she's found a meal receipt for Jamaica Inn for just before nine.'

'Well, we need to go over there and ask them if anything unusual happened.'

DS Rachel Killik then walked into the room. Jo was surprised when she walked over to the desk with the golf bag pencil case and sat down.

'DCI Collis has left a message for you two,' Rachel said.

'Has he?' Danny asked.

'He wants you to meet him for lunch over the road.'

Jo looked at Danny. 'What does that usually mean?'

Danny said. 'It's likely that he wants to discuss the murder scene. Did he say when, Rachel?'

'Twelve o'clock.'

'OK,' Danny said.

'Oh, I've been in touch with Ealing Police Station,' Rachel said. 'They've got someone on their way to tell the parents of the young couple and try to get a recent photo and DNA samples from their relatives. They'll send everything to us once they've got them.'

'OK, thanks.'

'It's an exciting start to your first day, Jo?' Rachel said.

'I suppose so,' she said. 'Good timing if I want to work on a homicide case.'

'That's true. We don't get many murders around here.'

Jo then turned to Danny. 'Have we time to get to Jamaica Inn before we meet with DCI Collis?'

Danny looked at the clock on the wall near DCI Collis's office. 'I don't think so. We'll have a coffee, fill out the whiteboard and then go and meet him.'

Rachel said. 'We might have the images of the victims by the time you've finished your lunch.'

'That's true,' Danny said.

Jo started to walk over to the door to go and get them each a coffee, but then curiosity got the better of her.

'Rachel,' she said. 'Do you play golf?'

Rachel looked confused and took a moment before looking at the pencil holder and realising why she asked her that question. She laughed. 'No. I bought it for my husband, but he never uses it, so I brought it here to keep my pens in.'

This made Jo smile.

She then asked Danny. 'So, which is your desk?' She was thinking it was fifty-fifty. His was either the ridiculously tidy, or the ridiculously cluttered?

'That one,' he said, pointing to the tidy one behind Jo's desk. So DC Bradley Dutson had the untidy one, Jo thought.

Half an hour later, Jo and Danny made their way through the front entrance of the station. Walking along the path from the car park was PC Laura Trevilian. Jo's first reaction was to be uneasy, but she knew that Laura wouldn't cause an uncomfortable scene, so she smiled at her.

Laura smiled back, revealing, Jo thought, her beautiful white teeth. Her blue eyes smiled as she stared into Jo's. Her blond hair was tied back as it always was when she was in her uniform.

'Morning,' she said, briefly looking at Danny before steering her gaze back to Jo.

'Morning, Laura,' Danny said.

'Hello, Laura,' Jo said. 'How are you?'

'I'm fine,' she said. She then turned to Danny. 'Is there any chance I could just have a quick word with Jo?'

'Yes, sure,' he said. 'I'll go and get the car.' He then walked onto the car park.

'So,' Laura said. 'First day.'

'Yes. First day,' Jo said. She was hoping that it wasn't going to be uncomfortable between them, but this wasn't a good start.

'How have you been?' Laura asked.

'I'm OK. I hope you are too.'

'I've missed you. We haven't even been on the same shift since...' She didn't finish her sentence.

Jo didn't want to play any games and so she came straight to the point. 'Since we broke up?'

Laura nodded. 'Broke up.'

'I'm sorry, Laura. I had everything packed up in my car when I left David, I even drove to Tregoltha. I parked up and sat there for half an hour trying to decide what to do.'

Laura took a step closer to her and spoke quietly. 'Look, Jo. If you want to stay in the closet a little longer, then that's OK with me. I just...'

Jo interrupted her. 'It's not that.'

'Well, what is it then?'

Jo took a step back. She didn't want Danny to think that they were talking about something so personal. She heard the engine start and knew he'd be alongside them in a moment.

'My life is just a little complicated at the moment. I chose to move back to St Breward with my mum and Rick to just get settled and decide what I want. I'd been with David for four years and I was leaving him and moving straight in with you. We'd only been seeing each other for six weeks. It was all just too fast and complicated.'

'If time is what you need...'

'I don't want you to wait for me. We had an amazing time together, but I don't want another relationship, not yet.'

'We don't have to live together to be together.'

'I'm sorry,' Jo said.

Danny pulled the car up next to them.

Laura seemed to shake off the disappointment and tried to smile past it. 'OK. Look, I'll let you go. Give me a call if you want.' The smile wasn't as genuine as a few moments previous. It was now the air hostess smile that people use to try and convince others that they are happy when they're not.

Jo smiled a sympathetic smile. 'OK.' She turned to leave but then turned back. 'Our time together was very special, and I'll never forget it.'

Laura, still smiling said. 'I know.'

Jo then turned around and walked over to the car. She felt a lump in her throat. She knew she would always have feelings for Laura, but she also knew that Laura wasn't someone she wanted to spend the rest of her life with. Laura helped her realise who she was and listened to her pour her heart out over David and how confused she was at the fact that she loved him, but had to leave him. Laura would always be special to her, but Jo wanted to be on her own. She felt as though a serious relationship would get in the way of her career. But she also didn't want to commit to anybody when she'd just ended a four year relationship.

As Danny drove the car away from the entrance, Jo could see from the corner of her eye that Laura was still standing there. She decided to look the other way, and not give her any false hope. The lump in her throat was still there, but she knew she'd made the right choice.

Chapter 9

Jo followed closely behind Danny as they entered the pub-restaurant. He held the wooden framed glass door open for her as they walked in. They were quickly greeted by a young waitress with long dark hair tied back into a ponytail.

'Welcome to...' she started. She then seemed to realise who Danny was and pointed into the restaurant area. 'Oh; usual table,' she said, smiling politely.

'Thanks,' Danny said, as he briskly walked past her.

Jo smiled at the young girl as she followed him.

The room was filled with wooden tables and there was crimson-red upholstery on the chairs and benches. Framed paintings of the Cornish scenery hung on the walls, all with a price tag underneath. The bar was to the right of them, behind the salad bar, and the carpet was crimson and beige.

The place wasn't very busy. There were only a few tables occupied. Jo thought it might be because it had only just turned twelve o'clock. The table where DCI Collis was waiting for them was a long way from the other diners, possibly a request of his so they could speak without the public overhearing their discussion. The table was in front of a large window that overlooked the fields behind the building.

Jo could smell a mixture of different foods that would normally send her appetite into overdrive, but not today. She still wasn't hungry, even though she'd burnt off several hundred calories on her run that morning.

DCI Collis was sitting facing them and gestured for them to take a seat as he was talking on his mobile phone. There were three large glasses of orange juice already on the table.

'Yes, they're here now, so let me know.' He then ended the call before waving the waitress over to them. He then spoke to Jo and Danny. 'Can you make a quick decision,' he said, pointing at the menus. 'I only have half an hour.'

'Yes,' Danny said. 'I'll have the burger.' Jo presumed he'd eaten here often enough to know what he wanted before they'd even arrived.

Jo still wasn't hungry, but knew she'd have to order something. You can't be invited to lunch by your boss and not order anything, she thought.

'I'll have the tuna baguette, please.' This was the first thing she spotted that she found remotely appetising.

'Fish and chips for me,' DCI Collis said.

The waitress then promptly left them to their meeting.

'OK. DS Mulfra has just brought me up to speed. So, what do you both think we're dealing with here?'

Jo thought very briefly about her suggestion of wild cats roaming the moors, but pushed it to the back of her mind for now.

'Well,' Danny said. 'I can't get my head around the fact that the bodies have been taken.'

'Why's that?' DCI Collis asked.

'Well, Jo and I were discussing this earlier. Why would you go to the trouble of removing the bodies? It can't have been an easy thing to do, even if they were less than average size and height.'

'They're from London and are obviously on holiday,' Jo added. 'But if it was somebody who knew them, surely they wouldn't have followed them all the way to Cornwall before murdering them.'

'So what could've happened?' DCI Collis asked.

Jo thought that he probably had his own ideas, but wanted to see if they were on the right track without his prompting.

Danny then said. 'It's not a robbery, because the male had over two hundred pounds in his wallet.'

'And they never took the car,' Jo added.

'Well taking the car would've been like carrying around a smoking gun,' DCI Collis said. 'It would've given away their movements if it turned up later. Also, the murder scene is a long way from anywhere, so the murderer was most likely in a vehicle. What else?'

'Jo had a good theory,' Danny said.

For a moment, she thought he was referring to the Beast of Bodmin discussion, but then she realised what he meant.

'Oh, yes. I thought it might've been a road rage incident.'

Collis raised his eye brows. 'That's possible.'

'Possible,' Jo said. 'But I'm not that sure now I've had time to think about it. Road rage incidents are very hot bloodied. If it was road rage, they calmed down and waited until the couple had set the tent up before attacking them.'

'Unless they couldn't catch them and maybe spotted them on the moors after the incident,' Danny said. 'You know, after recognising the car.'

'How do you think they were killed?' Collis asked.

'There was a lot of blood, inside and outside of the tent,' Danny said. 'I think it's possible that one of them came out of the tent, possibly to relieve themselves, and they were attacked first. The killer then went into the tent to kill the other one. Which way around that is, I don't know.'

'It must've been the male who was killed outside of the tent,' Jo said.

Collis seemed to smile a little as if he was waiting for one of them to realise this. 'Because...'

'If the female was killed outside of the tent, the male would've come out to help her, and he probably wouldn't have let her go out on her own either.'

'That's a good point,' Danny said.

'So, sum it all up for us, Jo,' Collis said.

'The male left the tent, to either go to the car for something or to relieve himself, like Danny said. He gets murdered, probably with a knife or something similar. DS Mulfra said there would be a more sporadic spray of blood if the victims had been shot rather than stabbed. After killing the male, the killer then goes into the tent where the female is possibly trying to hide, he then kills her. After that, he carried the bodies away, one at a time. Maybe he had a vehicle parked on the road. There aren't any footprints, but apart from the longer grassy areas, the ground is reasonably hard because it hasn't rained for weeks.'

'Why would he remove the bodies if he doesn't know them?' Danny said. 'It's not worth the risk of getting caught unless you're linked to the victims.'

'I'm struggling with that myself,' Collis said. 'We need to search the surrounding areas.'

'Jo asked uniform to start a search,' Danny said.

DCI Collis took a sip of his orange juice before continuing. 'Well, if you hadn't already guessed, I'm assigning the case to you two.'

'Thank you, sir,' Danny said.

'Danny, you'll obviously be in charge, but I want you to help Jo as much as you can. She has a year to build her portfolio and I think a case like this is a good start for her and something that will look good on your record too, if you ever decide to go for a DI position.'

'Yes, sir,' he said.

'Use all the resources you need to catch this murderer. I want this dealt with before the press start talking about there being another serial killer on the loose. Cornwall has always had a reputation for being a safe place to visit. We're in danger of losing that if this goes unsolved.'

'We'll do our best, sir.'

'Visit petrol stations, camp sites, anywhere you feel necessary to build a picture of their journey, maybe starting with Jamaica Inn. Then organise a wider search of the moors, possibly a five mile radius around the scene.'

'Will do,' Danny said.

'Now, this case would normally be given to a DI or an acting DI. So as you can imagine, I came very close to giving this to DS Killik as she is on the verge of qualifying as a DI. But she is still bogged down with other cases at the moment, so I decided to give it to you.'

Collis then turned to Danny. 'Jo is going to make a great detective, Danny. So use her to your advantage. If she's half as intelligent as her father, she's going to be very useful to us. She did very well at solving the Boniek case. You didn't do anything wrong Danny, but you interviewed him at his home and didn't realise he was the killer. I'm not saying that you should've known with the evidence we had, but Jo obviously had a good instinct at the time, so maybe she'll get lucky again.'

'Hope so,' Danny said.

'I'm hoping you can work well together on this. And I want it to be brought to a conclusion before I get pressured into bringing in outside help.'

'Yes, sir,' Danny said.

The food was then brought over by the waitress.

'Right, let's tuck in, then we can get back to it,' DCI Collis said.

Chapter 10

Jo waited in the car as Danny went back into the police station. She was feeling very excited about being assigned the murder case. Murders don't happen very often in Cornwall so she felt very honoured to be asked to be a part of the investigation. Danny was a detective sergeant, so Jo knew he would be in charge, but she still felt as though this was her chance to show that she was capable of advancing in this field. She hoped she could prove that catching the Bodmin Butcher wasn't a just a fortunate guess.

Jo began to think about the case. She had never before thought that the Beast of Bodmin was real, but she couldn't think of any reason why a person would go to the trouble of moving the two bodies. What would they have to gain by doing so? How much time did it waste? Was it worth the risk of being spotted by a passing motorist? And more importantly, where did they take them?

She spotted Danny come through the door of the station and he quickly made his way to the car. He got in and handed Jo two pieces of paper. She looked at the pages which were the scanned images of Steve Roberts and Debbie Rowland. She saw a stocky, well built young man who didn't look easy to overpower, and a petite young woman.

'Rachel is going to call the uniformed sergeant,' Danny said. 'She's going to ask him for as many PCs as he can spare to meet us at the crime scene in one hour. That gives us time to get to Jamaica Inn and see if anyone knows anything about these two.'

He then started the engine and headed away from the station and onto the main road.

'He looks like a big lad,' Jo said, looking at the image.

'I was thinking that. He can't have been easy to carry.'

A few moments later they were heading out of Bodmin. Once they'd reached the carriageway, Jo thought she'd try to get to know Danny a little more.

'So, when did you move to Cornwall?'

'A year ago next month,' he said.

'What made you choose to live here?'

He seemed to think carefully before answering. 'It's a beautiful place to be. The scenery is amazing, the people are great and its really laid back compared to London. Also I'd broken up with my girlfriend and just thought that a new start would be best.'

'The lady you showed me a picture of?' Jo asked.

'No, I met her in Cornwall. I'm talking about the love of my life back in London.'

'I see. So you moved here on your own?'

'Yes. Just me.'

'Cornwall must feel like a lonely place compared to London. I'm surprised you moved here on your own. Did you find it hard adjusting, coming from a busy city?'

'I have to admit, it was very hard at first, but I threw myself into my work and made some new friends and I'm very happy now?'

'Have you family in London?'

'I don't have any family.'

'Really?'

'No. I wasn't always a nice person.' He stopped again, as if he was thinking about sharing his story or not.

Jo didn't push; she just left the silence to see if he wanted to continue.

Danny then said. 'I spent a bit of time in a young offenders' institute when I was a kid. My mum died when I was ten, and I drifted from foster home to foster home.'

'That must've been hard, losing your mum so young.'

'I was off the rails and mad at the world for a long time, but the young offenders' institute helped me find my feet. I got into fitness, and played lots of sports, rugby, football, and cricket. I started to see more to life than just getting into trouble all the time.'

'What sort of things did you get up to?'

'It was just petty stuff really, like shop lifting, fighting, and being a mouthy little sod to anyone that looked at me. I grew out of it, eventually.'

'So when did you decide to become a police officer?'

'I was in my early twenties when I started down this path, and I've never looked back.'

'I find that quite a fascinating story. You've obviously turned your life around.'

'The old me is a distant memory now. I've got a great career, I have great friends, all I need now is to find the future Mrs Hughes and everything will be perfect.'

Jo smiled. 'I don't want to shatter your dreams, but I don't think this job always suits having a partner.'

'I think you might be right.'

Danny drove into one of the few remaining spaces on the car park at Jamaica Inn. They got out and walked around to the front of the building where there was a cobble stone yard at the front of the large coaching house. The large grey slate building which had stood for over two hundred and fifty years surrounded the yard that was home to six wooden picnic tables and benches. The sun shone brightly in the early afternoon sky, so most of the tables were filled by families enjoying drinks or a meal. Some of the families had dogs with them, most were tied to the table legs, and there were several children running around and enjoying the large courtyard. There were four lantern style lampposts across the centre of the yard, and the famous Jamaica Inn sign hung next to the stone wall.

Jo and Danny entered through the front door which led them

into one of the bars. Danny walked straight through the bar which was just as busy as it was outside, and into the next room and headed for the reception. The old public house smelled like real ales and log fires. Jo glanced at the impressive stone fireplace as they walked past it. It wasn't lit today, of course, with it being such a hot day, but it was still the impressive centrepiece of the room.

Jo had been to the inn on many occasions. Although it was always busy, especially in the holiday season, she still thought of it as one of her favourite places. There was a magic about this pub, Jo thought. Stories of smugglers and murder, and the ghosts that reside there, make for many a story from the local patrons. She even took the time to read Daphne Du Maurier's novel a few years earlier when she was at Oxford. And now, her first day as a Detective, she was about to conduct her own investigation inside this fascinating and historic building.

They approached the reception, there was a woman standing behind the desk. She was in her mid-thirties; light brown short hair, she wore glasses and was dressed in a white blouse that had a bronze name tag on the breast pocket that read *Karen Mellin*, and had the words *assistant manager* beneath it.

'Can I help you?' she asked.

Danny showed her his badge. 'I'm Detective Sergeant Hughes, this is Detective Constable Green.' He then put the pieces of paper with the scanned images of Steve Roberts and Debbie Rowland onto her reception desk. 'Have you seen this couple before?'

She held up the pages and studied them. 'Yes. They were in here last night.'

'Can you tell us anything about them?' Danny asked.

'I think they were from London. They both had a London accent, like yours,' she said to Danny.

'How long were they here for?' Jo asked.

'I think it was mid-evening, possibly later. They asked for a room, but we're full at the moment. They stayed for a while and had a meal in the restaurant. They probably left after about an hour, I'd say.'

'Did you serve them in the restaurant?' Jo asked.

'No. I was out here, but I dealt with them when they arrived and said goodnight to them when they left.'

'Is there any staff here now that served them?' Danny asked.

'Yes.' She came around the reception desk and walked towards the restaurant. 'Follow me.'

They walked up to the bar in the next room and she called the barman over, 'Paul.' She did this quite discreetly. She either knew to be discreet because of it being a police matter, or she didn't want her customers to know that she had two detectives asking her and her staff questions.

Paul was tall with spiky blond hair and a slight acne problem. He put down the bottles he was carrying and came over to them.

'Do you remember this couple from last night?' she asked.

Danny offered the pictures to him; he took them and looked closely.

'Yes. I served them with their drinks and their food. It was quite late you see. It must've been after nine because the waitresses had knocked off for the night.'

'But you were still serving food?' Jo asked.

'Yes,' Paul said.

'We try to keep the late comers happy; it's usually ten-thirty before the kitchen closes altogether,' Karen said.

'Well, can you tell us anything about them?' Danny asked.

'They were from London, and they were travelling through Devon and Cornwall on holiday. They said they wanted to stay here but they hadn't booked. I think they were heading towards St Austell from here.'

'Have they gone missing?' Karen asked.

71

Danny looked at Jo, but then he answered the question. 'They were both murdered last night after setting up camp on the moors.'

Jo saw the shock on their faces. From one point of view, they had in fact gone missing, with their bodies being removed from the crime scene that is, but Karen and Paul didn't need to know that.

'Really?' Karen said.

'So what we're asking you is if there's anything you can tell us that we need to know?' Danny said.

They looked at each other, but didn't speak as they were thinking.

'Did they mention getting into an argument with anyone?' Jo asked. 'Like a road rage incident or something like that.'

'No,' Paul said. 'They were both really happy. He moaned about not being able to get a room, but he was annoyed with himself for not booking. He was still quite upbeat.'

'They were both very polite when they left as well,' Karen said.

'We'll need to see the CCTV of the carpark,' Jo said.

'Only the manager can access that,' Karen said. 'She'll be in later today. I can get her to email the file to you if you like?'

'Yes, please,' Danny said. 'As soon as possible.'

'Will do.'

Danny seemed to concede to the fact that there was nothing more to ask. 'Well,' he said, offering a card. 'My number is on there, plus the department email address. Send the file addressed to me. Anything comes back to you that you might think is helpful to us, no matter how trivial you think it is, give us a call.'

Karen took the card. 'I certainly will, and I hope you get to the bottom of what's happened.'

'Thank you for your time,' Danny said.

Chapter 11

As they pulled the car to a stop on the grass near the murder scene next to all the other vehicles, Jo quickly counted the police officers that were standing there waiting for them. The crime scene was still taped off and the Scenes of Crimes Officers were still working on the area. The police officers waiting to help with the search were all standing this side of the tape.

'Eighteen,' she said.

'Should be enough,' Danny said. 'There will be a few new faces. Some of them are from Newquay and Wadebridge, apparently.'

The officers were all dressed in black trousers, black tee shirt and some were wearing black baseball caps. They also each had a walking pole of some description to help them search through the long grass. She knew some of the officers, but there were several of them she hadn't seen before.

They exited the vehicle and made their way to the crowd of officers. Danny then called them all to attention.

'Right, ladies and gentlemen.'

They all stopped talking and turned to face him.

'I'm DS Hughes, this is DC Green. Some of this information you might already know, some of it you might not.' He held up the two pieces of paper with the victims pictures on. 'The tent behind you belonged to Steve Roberts and Debbie Rowland. They are both presumed dead. The scene was found early this morning and there are two large areas of blood which we are waiting for confirmation of identification. What makes this murder scene unusual is the fact that the bodies have been taken. We don't know why as yet and obviously we don't know where they've been taken to. A small group of officers searched the surrounding areas this morning, but found nothing. We have around eight hours of light left, and there has to be something out there on the moors to help us build a picture of what happened. Look out for blood and tissue traces, clothing, shoes, disturbed ground and anything resembling footprints or vehicle tracks. If you find anything, radio it in with your location and do not disturb the scene. The DCI wants us to cover anything up to a five mile radius so keep going until it goes dark, then make your way back here. DC Green and I will check the areas this side of the scene, so I want you all to spread out and head onto the moors, trying to cover all directions as you go. OK let's get going.'

The officers all turned around and slowly started walking side by side over the moors, using their poles to search through the longer patches of grass as they walked.

'Shall we start?' Jo asked.

'Yes. Let's just check around this area, and then we'll cross the road and check there,' he said, pointing back across the road they driven from.

'You've sent everyone over the moors, why's that?' Jo asked.

'To be honest, I don't think we'll find anything this side. The SOCOs said there were no signs of another vehicle, so I'm pretty sure the bodies would've been taken over the moors. We can cover this side in the time that they'll be gone. And we're near to the car if we're suddenly needed elsewhere.'

'I see,' Jo said.

They then proceeded to check the area heading towards the road.

After several of hours of searching, Danny suggested to Jo that she should drive from Bolventor heading back towards Devon to call at the petrol stations to see if anyone would recognise the pictures of the victims.

She did so and asked at the station on the A30 towards Launceston but they hadn't seen them. She then drove all the way to Okehampton, but it was the same there. They hadn't yet constructed the journey that the young couple had taken. Jo knew that the next morning would start with a meeting to discuss the full facts of the case so far. She hoped that they could come up with some ideas then.

She didn't feel as though this was a typical murder. The bodies being removed was the biggest question that was hanging over them. If it was a person then they must've been of considerable strength to carry two bodies away for that distance. Unless there was more than one killer in which case they would've been able to remove the bodies quicker. But most murderers work alone and it must've taken several hours to carry one body away before returning for the next. Jo didn't feel that she was going to work out the full timeline of events until more evidence came to light. She hoped that the search of the moors would reveal something interesting that would help them begin to put it all together.

Chapter 12

That night, Jo walked to the King's Head. The pub was normally a very quiet place to be, but as she arrived at the door, the noise from inside sounded like there was a party was going on, with lots of shouting and laughing. She thought of turning back, but she'd arranged to meet Danny there. She then realised that maybe she'd have more chance of getting a quiet table and sneaking past everyone if it was a busy night, so she went inside.

The walls were still the original bare stonework with dark wooden beams stretching across the ceiling. The Inn was dimly lit by the wall lights and had lit candles on each of the wooden tables. There were pictures on the walls of country scenes and wildlife and the wooden benches that surrounded the room had patterned cushions scattered along them.

As Jo went into the noisy pub, she was surprised to see a crowd of people all standing around a table in the middle of the room. Dorothy, the landlady, was standing next the table with a large birthday cake full of lit candles. Everyone was singing happy birthday to Annie. At the end of the noisy rendition, Annie tried her best to blow out the fire hazard of candles. Jo laughed as all the other people standing around Annie bowed down to help. Once the fire was extinguished, one at a time they all gave her a kiss and wished her happy birthday. Even Jo's brother Rick hugged the person from the village who Jo thought was possibly getting closer to a message from the Queen.

Jo smiled at her brother before going to the bar to order a glass of wine.

After getting her drink, she looked around for a place to sit; she then noticed at the far said of the pub, the table in front of the log fire was free. The fire wasn't lit; it rarely was in the height of summer. It always made her smile at how some of the older patrons would get there as early as they could in winter to claim the best seats in the pub, but in summer the area was always clear.

She sat down and sipped her wine. Drinking wasn't something Jo did on a regular basis, especially through the week, but after a reasonably successful first day, sipping a glass of wine felt like the right thing to do.

'How did it go today, Jo?'

She looked up and saw Teddy standing there with his coat on and his border collie at his side.

'Very well, thanks. Are you going to have a drink with me?' As she said this, she then saw Danny enter the pub and make his way over to the bar.

'No, I'm off home now. I just wanted to check that you'd had a good first day.'

'That's very kind of you, Teddy.'

'Is there anything new on the campers?'

Jo smiled at him. She used to discuss certain things with Teddy about the events of the day, but she knew that now she was a detective, her days of discussing crimes with Teddy were over.

'Nothing I can discuss.'

'That's fair enough.'

'Are you OK, Teddy?' Jo asked. He seemed a little quieter than his usual self. Almost as if he was distracted.

'Yes, I'm fine. Early start tomorrow so I'm turning in.'

'OK. Don't work yourself too hard.'

Danny then came walking over with a bottle of lager in his hand. He then sat down at the table opposite Jo.

'Teddy, this is DS Hughes,' Jo said. 'This is Teddy Hosken.'

Danny acted like a gentleman, stood up again to shake his hand. 'It's nice to meet you, Teddy. I've heard a lot about you.'

'Don't believe anything Jo tells you. It's all lies,' Teddy said, smiling.

'Not from Jo; from DCI Collis,' Danny said.

'Oh, I see. How is the old fellow?'

'Same as always.'

'That bad, eh?'

Danny smiled.

'Tell him I said Hello. Anyway, I just wanted to congratulate you on your first day, Jo. I'll leave you to it. Come on, Sam.'

'Nice to meet you,' Danny said.

Teddy and his dog then left the pub.

Jo and Danny both took a sip of their drinks.

'So, this is your local?' Danny said, looking around the room.

'It is. It isn't always this lively, but it's Annie's birthday.'

'I see. How far away do you live?'

'I live on the other side of the village. It's about a twenty minute walk from here.'

'Well,' he said, taking another sip of his drink. 'I had a phone call just after I'd left the search.'

'Really?' Jo asked.

'An officer found some torn clothing on some nettles in the woodland near the scene. It's being examined as we speak because it looks like there's blood on it.'

'So the killer must've taken the bodies, or at least one, into the woods.'

'The piece of clothing was about the size of a pound coin, but if it is one of the victims, we can start to piece things together. Any luck with the petrol stations?'

'No. Nobody recognised them.'

'Oh well. Rachel and Bradley want to speak to us first thing in the morning. Think they have more of a story from the parents about where they'd been and where they were heading. So we'll know more then.'

'Has the CCTV arrived from Jamaica Inn?' Jo asked.

'Yes,' Danny answered. 'I sat and went through it from before they arrived to after they had left.'

'And?'

'Nothing. They seemed in a good mood when they turned up and the same when they left. And there weren't any other cars hanging around and nobody followed them off the carpark.'

'Oh well, it was worth checking,' Jo said.

Jo noticed her brother Rick leaving the pub. He was just waving as he was leaving so Jo called him over. His friend Lucy was with him.

'I didn't want to interrupt,' Rick said.

'It's OK,' Jo said. 'This is my brother, Rick, and his friend Lucy.'

Danny stood up again to shake their hands. 'Nice to meet you, Rick.' He then turned to Lucy. She was nineteen, the same age as Rick. She was a petite young girl with shoulder length blond hair.

'Didn't you just serve me at the bar?' he asked.

'Yes. I've just finished my shift. Rick's going to walk me home.'

'Well that's very gentlemanly of him.'

'How was your first day?' Rick asked.

'Very eventful,' Jo said.

'Are you involved with the murders?' Lucy asked.

Jo looked at Danny as if to ask whether she can admit to being assigned the case or not.

'Yes,' Danny answered. 'Our DCI thought that Jo and I were the right people for the job.'

'Excellent. Well I hope you manage to catch whoever did it,' Rick said.

'We will; don't worry,' Danny said.

'Right then; we'll leave you to it,' Rick said. 'Nice to meet you, DS Hughes.'

'Danny, Please,' he said.

After they'd left, Jo turned to Danny. 'Very confident, aren't you?'

'There's no point in doing this job if you don't think you can do it,' he said. 'Is Lucy his girlfriend?'

'No. They did become a couple a while back, but they've known each other since primary school. I think that's why she ended things with him.'

'That's a shame. She's a lovely looking young girl.'

'She is that. She's a really nice person too. I just think that they've known each other too long to be anything other than friends. Everybody always thinks they're a couple, because they spend a lot of time together, but no, they're just friends.'

'Is Rick hoping to change that?'

'I don't know,' Jo said, 'Possibly. But I don't think so. I think they're happy with things as they are.'

'What happens if she meets the man of her dreams, will Rick just be pushed aside?'

'I doubt it. I think if Rick ever got married, he'd have Lucy as his best man, or best woman.'

Danny only stayed for another five minutes or so before he said it was time for him to head home. Jo thought it wasn't really worth his journey for how long he stayed, but at least he made the effort to come and see her, and see her local pub.

Danny said goodnight to Jo, and then left.

Jo stayed for one more glass of wine and sat at the table on her own going over the events of the day in her mind. She knew she'd struggle sleeping if she didn't relax for a while before heading home to bed. This was her way of winding down before getting ready for the next day.

Chapter 13

Rick walked with Lucy along the winding road through St Breward. The road was only lit by the occasional street lamp on every turn. Lucy linked his left arm as he held his mobile phone in his right, using his torch to light the way. It was dark by now and a little cooler than the previous evenings and Rick was beginning to wish he'd brought a jacket as they headed home.

'Your sister seems to have settled back into the village,' Lucy said.

'What d'you mean?' Rick asked.

'She's been in the pub a little more often; only a once or twice a week, I'd say. But she just seems a little more settled now. When she first moved back here, she seemed a bit distracted, like she wasn't sure if she belonged here or not. Now though, she seems to be getting back to her old self.'

Rick thought about this for a moment. 'I suppose she was a little distracted after breaking up with David. I think she wants to buy a house here, so she must be happy.'

'She must be.'

They walked a few more minutes in silence before Lucy finally said, 'I like Jo.'

'Do you?'

'Yes. I wish I was more like her.'

'In what way?'

'Well, she's confident and ambitious, and she doesn't put up with any rubbish off anyone. You know full well that if that other detective or anyone else ever tried it on with her, she'd give him a right-hander.'

This made Rick laugh. 'He seems all right though.'

'Yes. He was a gentleman, and very handsome too.'

'Sure, if you go for that type,' Rick said.

'He's not as handsome as you, Rick,' Lucy said.

Rick smiled. The truth was, Rick was still a little confused about Lucy. They had been friends all their lives and he was positive that he loved her. He just wasn't sure what kind of love it was. Last year he approached the subject of them being a couple and Lucy was all for giving it a go. But the relationship they had seemed to disperse into awkward evenings where neither of them spoke. They seemed to struggle finding things to say to each other. It just didn't feel right to him.

After they'd broken up and promised to stay friends, the barriers appeared to drop and he felt he could relax around her again. Now, a year had passed and he was thinking about talking to her again about the idea of becoming a couple. She was beautiful to him and he felt very protective over her, but he wasn't sure why. Did he think of her more like a sister? Or was he just bad at relationships? If so, maybe a discussion about this in a frank and open manner might get to the bottom of it. Maybe she feels the same, he thought. He was scared of ruining what they had, but if they could get it right this time, maybe it would be the best thing they ever did.

They walked along the road approaching Vinny's grocery store. It was a hundred yards or so to Lucy's house. His phone beeped as a text message came through. He read it as they walked.

'Who is it?' Lucy asked.

'It's Matt. He's in the pub now. He's wondering where I am.'

'You go back if you want. It's still early.'

Rick thought for a moment. 'Yes, I think I will.' He then text him the response and put the torch back on the phone.

Lucy stopped walking. 'Well go on then.'

'I'll walk you home first.'

'I've only got a bit to go. I'll be fine.'

He thought about turning around. He then decided to go

another way. 'I'll walk a little further with you and cut back over the fields.'

'You can't do that. It's pitch-black.'

'I've got my phone.'

Lucy frowned at him with a disapproving look, but Rick insisted on staying with his plan.

'It'll be fine. I'll run. I'll be there in five minutes.'

They reached the corner of Lucy's street and stood beneath the lamppost. There was a row of terraced cottages on the left. Lucy's house was at the next block, about twenty yards from where they were standing.

Rick pointed to the left where a track led between the houses that led onto the moors. 'I'll head through there. It'll be quicker than going back the way we came.'

'I really wish you'd go back that way. Especially considering what happened on the moors last night.'

'That was at Bolventor; it's miles away.'

'I'd still be happier if you went back the way we came.'

Rick conceded. He thought it was silly when there's a perfectly good short cut available to him. But he was flattered that she cared so much.

'OK. I'll go that way.'

'Thank you. And be careful.' She gave him a kiss on the cheek and turned around.

He almost stopped her to start a new conversation. A conversation about how it might be a good time to consider them trying again. But even though he knew what he wanted to say, he withheld, just like he did the night before, and the night before that. Maybe they should just stay friends, he thought. But he struggled to stop thinking about her and had countless text conversations throughout the day, especially when he was on a quiet day at work. He just didn't know what to do. What he did know was that Lucy was gorgeous to him and if he didn't act soon, he could easily miss his chance; a girl as pretty as Lucy wasn't going to stay single for much longer.

Rick loved the time they spent with each other and the fact that they both have lots of free time to be together. But he knew that she wouldn't be a barmaid forever and he knew she wouldn't live with her mum forever. He'd seen it before with Jo's friends. As nice of a place St Breward is, people who grow up there tend to be drawn to other busier places. He knew that Lucy was clever enough to do anything she wanted. Although she wasn't always as confident as she should be, sooner or later she would be one of the ones that got away. Maybe if she met someone from somewhere other than the village of St Breward that might be what would happen.

Rick knew things couldn't stay like this. He needed to come up with a plan. A plan of how he could convince Lucy that they're relationship was something special, and that it might be even more special if they try one more time.

'You too,' he answered. 'Good night.'

'Text me when you get there,' she shouted over her shoulder. 'Will do.'

Once Lucy was out of sight, he made a sharp right and headed over the moors. This was something he'd done many times before, and it did scare him, but it scared him in a way he liked. He didn't really think that anything would ever happen, but walking over the moors in the dark of the night was something he enjoyed. As he started over the field, he used his phone to light the way. There was no moon to help him that night and what few street lights there were soon disappeared behind him as he headed over the grassland in the direction of the King's Head.

He put his thoughts of him and Lucy being a couple to one side for the moment. His stomach turned with excitement as he turned off the light from his mobile phone. This was a game to him, a game he might not have played if he didn't have a couple of pints of lager inside him. He headed towards the small spinney he knew was close to the edge of the moorland and close to the road where the King's Head resided. The silence of the night was almost deafening to his ears. All he could hear was his own footsteps on the hard dry grass.

As he reached the wooded area, the gentle breeze caused the leaves and branches to move in the night air. The rustling sound deceived him with every movement that they could be being caused by something other than the wind. He didn't have to enter the woods, the path led alongside the area. His eyes began to play tricks with him as he watched the dancing shadows turn into different shapes.

His heart was pounding as he finally gave in and turned his phone light back on.

He walked a little faster as the excitement filled his stomach. He couldn't decide whether he was still enjoying the venture across the dark moors, or whether he should've listened to Lucy and stayed on the road.

He tried to send his thoughts back to the situation with Lucy. He wondered if there was a right time to approach the subject or if he should plan some romantic gesture, like taking her to a nice restaurant or sending her flowers, or even sending flowers anonymously to see if she would guess that it was him. He wasn't sure if this...

What was that? He heard a thumping sound in the woods, as if somebody had just jumped down from a tree. He froze and listened for the next noise.

Nothing.

It felt like he was standing there forever. He almost felt as though he couldn't move. His legs felt like jelly and his stomach turned. He could feel his hands shaking as he tried to hold the light on his phone still. He couldn't hear any more noises, other than the movement of the leaves in the gentle wind but he was certain he'd heard the noise.

Then something occurred to him. He and Matt were always playing tricks on each other, and Matt knew he was on his way back from walking Lucy home, and it would've been a good bet that he'd walk back over the moors. That was it, he thought. It was Matt trying to scare him.

'Nice try, Matt. You almost scared me for a second.'

Suddenly there was a disturbance in the bushes as something moved. He then heard a low grumbling noise, it didn't sound like a noise Matt could make; it was too deep. His legs still felt like jelly, but he quickly bolted into a fast sprint as he ran as fast as he could in the direction of the pub. He ran and ran and even though the pub was getting closer and closer, he was still scared, more scared than he'd ever been before. His calf's ached and his chest throbbed. He struggled to breathe but he somehow continued to run, faster than he'd ever ran before. He felt sick, but he kept going. As he got closer to the pub he hoped he could outrun whatever it was. He kept running at top speed and never looked back to see what followed.

Chapter 14

Jo didn't feel as though she'd had much sleep by the time she heard her mobile phone ring. She forced her eyes open and reached for it from the small chest of drawers at the side of her bed. She saw that it was Danny, and she also saw that it was 6.30 am. She answered the phone.

'Hello.'

'Jo; it's Danny.'

'What is it?' she asked, sitting up and switching her lamp on.

'We got another murder. It's in St Breward so I'll collect you on the way there. What's your address?'

'Number thirty-six, Church Lane.'

'I'll be ten minutes.' He then hung up.

Even though Jo felt dazed, she quickly stood up and walked over to her bedroom door and opened it. She was surprised to see her mum standing on the landing.

They both jumped as they gave each other a fright.

'Why are you standing there?' Jo asked, a little snappishly.

'I heard your phone go off. Is everything all right?'

'No, Mum,' she said. The events from the night before were spinning around Jo's head. Rick walked Lucy home, but Jo never saw him again. She had another drink after Danny went home, but she didn't see Rick, even though she stayed up for an hour after she'd arrived home.

She quickly pushed past her mum and made her way to Rick's bedroom door. She felt sick, partly because of being woken up and jumping out of bed so quickly, but mostly because of the fear that she might've lost her younger brother.

'What's wrong, Jo?' her mum asked.

As she pushed open the door, she was relieved to see Rick curled up under his covers and fast asleep.

She leaned back on his door frame and breathed a sigh of relief, banging her head as she did.

'Jo, will you tell me what's wrong.'

Jo gently closed the door. 'Look. Don't say anything to Rick, or anyone else, but there's been a body found in the village.'

Her mum covered her mouth as she was shocked at this news. 'No!'

'Don't upset yourself, Mum. We might not know who it is,' she said, heading back into her bedroom and opening her wardrobe.

'We know most people around here.'

'I know. Look, let me get ready. Don't tell Rick until I know any more. And certainly don't tell anyone else. I'll phone you in a bit, OK?'

'All right, love,' she said. 'I'll let you get ready.' She then closed the door. Jo noticed her mum's hand shaking as she held onto the handle.

Jo was beginning to regret telling her mum, but she wasn't thinking straight after being woken up so suddenly. She wondered who the victim was and where it had happened. She got dressed quickly, brushed her teeth and then waited outside of her front door for Danny.

Jo quickly jumped into the passenger seat. Danny then spun the car around and headed back through the village. Jo wasn't feeling the excitement of the previous day's journey to view a murder scene. Today she was nervous about what they were about to see, and more importantly, whether she knew the victim. She knew the chances of it being somebody she knew was pretty high.

'You need to show me how to get to Vinny's. Is that a newsagent or something?' Danny asked.

'It's a grocery store. Rick works for him.'

Danny turned to Jo. 'Is Rick at home?'

'Yes.'

'I had to ask.'

'Don't worry; it was my first thought as well.'

'Do you think it might be the girl?'

'I doubt it. Rick walked her home,' Jo said. 'Where exactly is the body.'

'Outside the shop, apparently.' He then paused for a second as he turned the corner. 'But there is no body.'

'What?'

'I presume this Vinny is the one who found the scene. It sounds very similar to the camp site; a blood bath, but there isn't a body.'

'Just here on the left,' Jo said, as they approached the shop.

As they parked up on the curb, Vinny came through the doorway of his store.

Jo could see by his face that he was still a little shocked at what he'd found. He was always very cheerful and greeted her with a smile, but today he looked even more pale than usual and whatever expression Jo saw on his face, it was anything but cheerful.

Danny showed his badge and introduced himself. 'DS Hughes. Are you Vinny Russell?'

'Yes.'

'I'm guessing you know DC Green?'

'I do.'

'Right, show us what you've found?'

He didn't answer. He just nodded before pointing over the road towards the bus shelter that was twenty yards or so further down the road. They had driven past the bus shelter but they were looking towards the shop and hadn't noticed anything.

Jo and Danny turned around to look. Over the road from

89

where they was standing was a metal framed bus shelter with a row of four detached houses situated behind with long gardens of about twenty feet in length behind slate garden walls.

The sun was up by now and it was another cloudless summer's morning. Jo felt as though they had the street to themselves, for now. But she knew that it wouldn't be long before people would be leaving the houses and walking past whatever it was that Vinny had found.

They walked over to the scene. Jo saw Vinny go back into the shop from out of the corner of her eye. She stayed focused on the scene as they walked across the road. She could see a pile of something, but couldn't make out what it was. As she got closer, she realised that she was looking at a women's shoe, a mobile phone, and what she could only describe as someone's insides.

The pile of flesh was scattered on the ground in a large area of dried blood which covered about four square feet. The flesh was only a small pile, but enough to make Jo think that the victim must be dead, and enough to make her feel very sick. As she stood staring at the scene of horror, Vinny tapped her on the shoulder. He offered her a small bottle of orange juice. She took it from him and drank a couple of big gulps.

Danny was crouched down looking closely at the area.

Vinny passed another bottle of juice within Danny's vision. He took it from him before standing back up.

'Thanks. The body was dragged that way,' he said, pointing in the direction away from the shop.

'Because of the shape of the blood stain?' Jo asked.

'Yes, it seems to smear that way a little. Not much to go on, but we'll get an I.D. off the phone, and a more positive I.D. off the tissue.' He then turned to Vinny. 'You don't have CCTV, do you?'

'Just one camera that points inside the shop; that's all.'

'There wasn't much need for CCTV in a village like St Breward, until now that is,' Jo said.

'Who do you think it is?' Vinny asked.

'We'll not speculate at this stage,' Jo said. She couldn't be certain, but she was thinking that it could be Lucy. She recognised the shoe and the phone, but it was more of a subconscious recognition. She hoped it wasn't her. But if it was, what had happened? Rick walked her home. How come he got home safely if Lucy didn't?

Jo looked up as a van came around the corner.

'Right, let's step away,' Danny said. 'They'll accuse us of contaminating the crime scene.'

'I'll be in the shop if you need me,' Vinny said, before walking away.

The van pulled up in front of Danny's car, a man and a woman got out. Jo recognised the passenger from the crime scene on the moors. It was DS Mulfra. The man went to the back of the vehicle to get ready for the investigation.

'Good morning,' Sarah said. 'What have we got?'

'Similar to yesterdays only this time there's some flesh,' Danny said.

'Right, well I'll get a tent around the scene and get started.' She walked back to the van to put the coveralls on and help unload the equipment.

'Danny, should we have a walk around and see if we can find anything?' Jo asked.

'Good idea, come on.' He then said to Sara, 'We're going to have a look around.'

'No problem.'

They slowly set off walking down the road, looking at the ground as they went. Jo hoped that if they could find anything, they'd be able to deal with it before any of the locals saw. Police cars with uniformed officers inside drove past them with their lights flashing, but no sirens. Jo knew that they would tape off the scene to keep the public away. Once word got out that there had been another death, Jo was sure that everybody would be out of their houses.

They had only walked twenty yards or so from the scene when Jo heard a shout.

'Jo!'

She looked up and saw Mrs Webster, Lucy's mum standing at her door in her dressing gown a few houses down from where they were.

'Has something happened?'

Jo didn't think it was wise to panic her just yet. 'Good morning, Mrs Webster. Nothing to concern yourself with, you go back inside.'

'It's just that Lucy didn't come home last night. I'm just a bit worried that's all.'

Jo and Danny looked at each other. Her stomach sank as this news confirmed in her mind that it was Lucy. She wouldn't have stayed out all night without letting her mum know. Lucy was a sweet young girl who missed out on her rebellious stage and never gave her mum any ounce of trouble throughout her short life.

'Mrs Webster, you go back inside,' Danny said. 'We'll get someone to come and speak to you in a moment.'

Danny didn't know her or her daughter like Jo did, so Jo presumed that he thought it better to take over.

Jo was thankful for this.

Mrs Webster nodded and went back inside and closed the door. Jo could tell she was worried but didn't think she'd connected the dots to realise why two detectives would be walking slowly past her house so early in the morning on the one day her beloved daughter isn't in her bed.

They headed back to the crime scene.

'What now?' Jo asked.

'We get Sarah to try to switch on the phone, and if not, we take a photo of it, and the shoe, and show them to Mrs Webster.'

'I really hope it's not her,' Jo said. But she knew that it was. She was clinging to a very small chance that it might be a coincidence, but she didn't feel it was likely to be anyone else. Jo knew she'd have to comfort Lucy's mum, and then she'd have to go home and break the news to Rick. She wondered how anyone could do such a terrible thing to such a sweet young girl. She hoped that she was wrong and it wasn't Lucy, but she knew it was unlikely to be anyone else. She hoped and prayed that it was all just a coincidence.

Chapter 15

Jo wanted to be involved as much as possible in anything that came up during the investigation. But she was quite happy to let Danny be the one to tell Lucy's mum what they'd found and tactfully ask her to identify the shoe, as the phone found at the scene was dead. After she'd stopped shaking long enough to look at the photo on Danny's mobile phone, she screamed a painful gut-wrenching cry that hurt Jo's ears. Jo tried to be professional, but she had to drop to her knees and hug her as she sat on the edge of her armchair crying at what Jo and Danny then knew was a positive identification of the victim.

Jo fought her own tears back, but she failed. Mrs Webster's husband had died when Lucy was very young and so Lucy was all she had. There was nothing Jo could say to take away what she was feeling. All she could do was embrace her and share in the tears.

Danny then left the room.

Within the hour, the family liaison officers turned up, and Jo rejoined Danny at the crime scene. They couldn't be one hundred percent certain that the murder victim was Lucy, and they couldn't be one hundred percent certain that she was dead. But it wasn't looking like there was any other possible outcome to what they'd found.

Danny was standing next to the tent talking on his mobile phone when Jo slowly walked back to the scene. He ended the call.

'You OK?' he asked.

Jo felt as though she could cry again at any moment, but she managed to control her tears. 'That was tough,' she said. Her voice quivered a little as she wiped her eyes. 'Thank heavens for waterproof mascara,' she joked.

Danny put his hand on her shoulder. 'Do you need a minute?'

'No. I'm OK.' She then tried to focus on the job in hand. 'What's next?'

'Well. I think we need to speak to your brother first.'

Jo knew that this was something that had to be done, but she wasn't looking forward to telling Rick about Lucy's death. She also knew that he would be considered a person of interest to the investigation with him being the last person to see Lucy alive.

'Should we go there now?'

'I don't think you should go at all,' Danny said, as politely as he could.

'I won't be in the room for the questioning, but I'd like to be the one who tells him.'

'That's fair enough,' Danny said.

They both got in the car and Danny started the engine.

Jo knew there was no legal reason why she couldn't be there for the initial questioning. It was just an inside rule that the police always follow in situations like this. Officers keep away from their relatives so that if the case goes to court at some point, the fact that the officer is related to the person in question doesn't come into the equation. This is good practice for all who are involved, whether guilty or innocent. Jo just wanted to be there to tell him about the loss of his best friend.

Rick was sitting on the couch watching television and eating a bowl of cereal when Jo and Danny walked in. He was still dressed in a white T-shirt and shorts that he'd slept in. He looked around at them as they entered. He instantly looked a little confused as to why they were both there.

'Hello,' he said, after swallowing his mouthful before turning off the television.

Jo and Danny didn't speak. She walked around and sat next to him on the couch. She could feel the lump in the back of her throat. She was exhausted from the last hour she'd spent with Lucy's mum, and she now felt as though she was about to go through it all again.

Jo nodded to Danny to take a seat in the arm chair by the fish tank.

Her mum then came down the stairs, now dressed in her beige pants and blue jumper. She looked nervous as soon as she saw Jo and Danny there. 'What's going on?'

'Mum,' Jo said. 'Please just go in the kitchen.'

Her face dropped as she put her hands over her mouth. She obviously realised that the victim was somebody they all knew.

'I'll come through in a minute,' Jo said.

Mary went into the kitchen and closed the door.

Rick still looked confused. Jo took the half empty cereal bowl from him and put it on the coffee table.

'Rick,' she said. She then took a hold of his hands.

'You're scaring me,' he said.

'I have some bad news.'

She couldn't hold off any longer. Bad news like this was going to be devastating to him, but she had to just spit it out.

'Lucy was killed last night.'

'What?'

Jo nodded.

'She can't have. You must be wrong.'

'We're not.'

His eyes were wide and his bottom lip trembled. Tears quickly formed as he pulled his hands away from Jo's and covered his face.

'I'm sorry,' she said.

He didn't speak. He then began to silently cry as his shoulders bounced up and down. Jo pulled him to her and embraced her younger brother as he wept. A loud sniff broke the silence and he stood up and walked over to the chest of drawers under the stairs where there was a tissue box on top. He wiped his eyes and nose with his back to them. He then turned around and came back to the couch and sat next to Jo.

'What happened?' he asked.

'Well, I can't talk to you about it, so I'm going to go in the kitchen with mum. DS Hughes is going to ask you about last night. Is that OK?'

He wiped his eyes again and then nodded.

Jo just gave his hand a gentle squeeze and then got up and left the room closing the door behind her.

Jo noticed that there were four cups sat out ready next to the kettle. She also saw that her mum was standing next to them looking even more anxious than she did that morning.

'Who is it?' she whispered.

Jo walked over to her and spoke quietly as not to be overheard in the living room. 'It's Lucy.'

Mary looked shocked. 'Lucy Webster?'

'Yes.'

'I can't believe it,' Mary said. 'Poor Janice. She lost her husband all those years ago, and had to bring up Lucy on her own, and now she's lost her as well.'

'I know. It's terrible. And I don't know how Rick's going to be after this. She was his best friend.'

Jo started making the drinks.

'Why is that man talking to him?'

'That's DS Hughes who I'm working with. Rick walked Lucy home last night so he's just asking him a few questions.'

'You don't think Rick had anything to do with it, do you?' Mary said, a little too loud for Jo's liking.

'Shush,' she whispered. 'No, of course not, but as far as we're aware, Rick was the last person to see her. He walked her home.'

'Are you going to arrest him?' she said, her eyes welling up.

'Not at this stage. But he will most likely be taken in for questioning at some point, but that's just normal practice. We don't think he had anything to do with it, but we need to know what happened.'

After Jo made the drinks, she passed two of the cups to her mum.

'Here, Mum. Take these in for me. This one is Rick's and that one's Danny's.'

She took the cups from her, even though her hands were still shaking a little.

Jo knocked on the door before opening it. 'But don't say anything. Just give them the drinks and come straight back.

She did as she was told.

Half an hour later, Danny opened on the door to the kitchen and walked in. Jo and her mum were sat at the kitchen table.

He came over to Mary and shook her hand. 'Sorry. We haven't met properly. I'm Danny Hughes. I'm working with Jo on this case.'

'Well I'd say it's nice to meet you, but I'm not sure it is in these circumstances.'

'I quite agree,' he said smiling. He then sat at the table with them. 'Rick is just getting dressed. We're going to have to take him to the station and get his story on record.'

'You're arresting him?' Mary said, loudly.

Danny put his hands up. 'No. Mrs Green, it's OK. We just have to follow procedure. Everything Rick says seems valid to me, but at the end of the day, he is still the last person to see Lucy alive, well, that we know of.'

'Except for whoever killed her,' Mary said.

'That's right,' Danny said. 'We'll get him to the station and interview him properly, and he'll be home for dinner.'

'He's supposed to be working?'

'Vinny knows all about it,' Jo said. 'He said to tell Rick to have the rest of the week off.'

Chapter 16

That afternoon, as Danny and DS Killik were interviewing Rick, Jo sat at her desk in the large empty office. She had written all the new information onto the white board. She wasn't happy about writing her brother's name onto the board, but she couldn't leave his name off just because of him being her brother. She had to look at the whole picture just as she would if she didn't know the people who were involved.

She thought back to what Teddy had shown her the day before. There had been three murders and no bodies. Could it be a big cat? From one point of view, the idea sounded ridiculous. There had been stories of wild cats roaming Bodmin Moor ever since Jo could remember. She even remembered having to write a poem about the Beast of Bodmin when she was at primary school, but she always thought of it as nothing more than folklore and legend. But, big cats are very real, so could one have escaped from a zoo or a circus? It was something that was always laughed at. If you believed in the Beast of Bodmin, then there was something wrong with you. But why would a murderer go to the trouble of removing the bodies from the scene? And why would a murderer carry a body through the built up area of St Breward? And whoever or whatever had done this awful crime, why hadn't anybody seen anything?

She went onto the search engine of her computer. She typed in the words Beast of Bodmin.

Wikipedia came up at the top of the page. She read it from top to bottom. She read of how the Beast of Bodmin is a phantom wild cat that supposedly roams the moors of Cornwall, and the stories of slain livestock and numerous sightings.

She also read of how scientists have rejected the claims because of the numbers needed to support the breeding population.

After reading the page, she clicked on a video of a supposed sighting. The night time shaky video wasn't worth sitting through as Jo could easily tell that the animal in question was a domestic cat.

She went back to the search engine and this time she typed the word panther.

She read of how panther is a short term for panthera, which is the family name for most of the big cats, including lions, tigers, jaguars, and leopards. She put her ability to read fast and take in information to good use and read all about their breeding and feeding habits, where they all come from and how they behave.

After about half an hour of reading, she felt as though she knew a lot more about what they could be up against. She was beginning to feel that it was possible that the deaths were down to a big cat and that it wasn't actually that farfetched. They are secretive animals that are hard to spot in the places that they actually live, so it could be possible for one to live in the eighty square miles of Bodmin Moor without being spotted.

She was undecided, but she was certain that it was still too early to discuss this idea with DCI Collis. She wasn't prepared to lose face with the team she'd just joined by suggesting something most consider to be a fantasy.

She clicked on a picture of a large black cat. It was a black leopard and it was standing on a cliff top with green hills in the background. Its black fur revealed the rosette markings beneath as the sun shone on its coat. It's piercing green eyes looked in the direction of the camera. It was a beautiful creature that Jo couldn't fail to be impressed by.

'Is that our suspect?'

Jo almost jumped out of her skin. She quickly turned around to see DCI Collis standing behind her.

'Sorry, Jo,' he said, patting her on the shoulder. 'I didn't mean to frighten you.'

'It's OK, sir. I was just...'

'You were just researching our case,' he said.

She didn't know how to backtrack from what he'd seen. 'I was just waiting for Danny and Rachel to finish interviewing Rick, so I thought I'd do a little research.'

'And?'

She thought for a second, but then she decided to opt for honesty. 'I don't know. I thought I'd research big cats just in case. I don't necessarily think this is what we're up against, but I keep wondering why the killer would remove the bodies? It doesn't make sense. And I know that big cats are known for dragging their kills to quieter places before eating. It sounds ridiculous, but I'm just looking at all options.'

DCI Collis pulled a chair out and sat down. 'So you think it is possibly a big cat?'

'I don't know. I think we need to look into the possibility, while being careful not to be too distracted by it and taking our eye of the fact that we're most likely looking for a person.'

'One option for the bodies being removed would be a cannibalistic killer.'

Jo hadn't yet thought of that scenario. 'That's a possibility, but it sounds even more like the plot from a movie than a panther being on the loose.'

'True. It isn't something you would think of happening in Cornwall, but neither is the idea of three murders being committed in just two nights.'

'I don't know what to think at the moment. We'll have to consider the chance of the killer being a cannibal. I'll mention it to Danny.'

'I spoke to Teddy this morning,' DCI Collis said.

Jo was pretty sure where this was going.

'What's your opinion on what he showed you?'

She paused for a moment before saying, 'I've never seen big cat scratches on a tree, so I don't know if they are genuine or not. I doubted it at the time and told him that I thought it would've been vandals.'

Collis gave a short laugh. 'I bet that didn't go down too well.'

'Not really.'

'I know he's been obsessed by this myth for years.'

'I know. I was in the pub when he came in shouting that night,' Jo said.

'The night of the sighting?' Collis said in a slightly mocking tone.

'Yes.'

'What are your thoughts on that?'

'Well, I've known Teddy all my life. He might tell the odd tall tale for the sake of getting a laugh, but he was never a liar. He thought he saw something that night. He could've been wrong. The moors can play tricks on you at night. It might've been shadows of something that looked like a panther. But my point is, he thought he'd seen it. Whether he did or not, I don't know. Everyone was laughing at him. It wasn't nice.'

'I've known him for most of my life too. I know how eccentric he can be. But he was very serious when he told me about that night. He isn't serious very often, so I knew he was telling the truth, or like you say, he thought he was telling the truth.'

'I just don't know whether we'd be going down the right road by discussing this as a possibility.'

'Well, I've called a meeting for two o'clock. We'll discuss everything then and see how far we get.'

'OK.'

Jo felt a relief come over her that she could discuss the Beast of Bodmin idea with her boss without causing trouble, as Danny had previously thought. DCI Collis was obviously opening his mind to the possibility as well.

Jo sat at the large desk in the middle of the room with Danny to her left. DCI Collis was sitting in the end seat, at the head of the table. DS Rachel Killik was sitting opposite Jo. Bradley Dutson hadn't arrived as yet but DCI Collis decided to start the meeting without him.

'Right, Danny,' Collis said. 'Take it away.'

Danny took a deep breath and then began to recap the events of the last two days. 'Sunday night, Debbie Rowland and Steve Roberts travelled from a campsite in Devon and tried to get a room at Jamaica Inn. There weren't any rooms available, but they decided to stay for a meal. After they'd eaten, they left at around nine-thirty and headed south, but they didn't stay on the carriageway due to the road works. They came off at the next junction and after driving for a couple of miles, they decided to set up camp on the moors. They had a couple of bottles of lager and sat out on camping chairs for a while before taking everything inside and climbing into their sleeping bag. At some point between ten-thirty and the next morning, they were disturbed, and the male left the tent to investigate. There is a possibility he just went outside to relieve himself, but we don't know. He was then murdered, possibly with a knife or something similar, the killer then went into the open tent and killed the girl. Both bodies were removed from the scene. We don't know why, but what we do know is that it can't have been easy, because although the female was only small in stature, the male was six feet two inches, and quite a stocky young man.'

DS Killik was scribbling some notes on a pad as Danny spoke.

'The following evening, Lucy Webster, a nineteen-year-old barmaid from St Breward finished her shift at nine, and was walked home by Rick Green, Jo's brother. He walked her as far as the shop which is only about fifty yards from her house. Rick had a text from his friend Matt...'

He looked through his notes. 'Matthew Hunter, asking him to meet him back at the pub. Rick wanted to cut across the moors to get back to the pub, Lucy asked him not to, so he waited until she was out of sight and cut over the moors anyway. The next morning, Lucy was found, well, some remains were found, but again, no body. Forensics has proven the identification of all three victims, but no DNA evidence of a third party.'

'OK,' DCI Collis said. 'Has anyone got anything else to add?'

A moment's silence filled the room. Jo wanted to ask something, but waited to see if anyone else spoke first. When nobody did, she then said, 'I presume we're treating this as a serial killer?'

DCI Collis raised his eyebrows. 'I'm hoping that the press don't call it that just yet.'

'But the two scenes are obviously connected,' Danny said. 'Two murder scenes and the bodies removed from both. It must be.'

'You're right, Danny. But I don't want this becoming another Bodmin Butcher frenzy. Let's get thinking and see what we can come up with; any ideas?'

Danny leaned forwards with his hands clasped together and let out a sigh.

'What is it?' DCI Collis asked.

'There's something else that Rick told me,' he said. 'After DS Killik left the room and the interview had finished.'

Jo wondered what had Rick would keep to himself only to share it with Danny after the interview?

'He said he was chased by something.'

This was met by a confused expression from DS Killik and DCI Collis.

Jo was just as puzzled. 'By what?'

'He said that he heard a grumbling noise, almost like a growl.'

'Where was this?' Rachel asked.

'He said he was near the woods close to the pub.'

This caused the room to fall silent.

Jo didn't know what to say. She knew Rick didn't believe in the Beast of Bodmin, and she also knew Rick always told the truth.

Just then, DC Bradley Dutson entered the room at a fast pace and made his way over to the television that was suspended in the top corner of the room.

'Sorry, sir,' he said. 'But when you see this, you'll understand why I was late.'

He pulled a roll of wires from the top of the television and plugged them into his mobile phone. He then plugged the other ends into the small slots beneath the screen.

'What's going on, Bradley?' Danny asked.

'Just watch.'

He took a few minutes to find the right channel. 'A bloke has just stopped me on the way in and showed me a video he'd filmed while walking on the moors; he sent it to my phone.'

Everyone turned around to watch as the screen came on.

Jo was intrigued at what she was about to be shown, she presumed it was important to the case if Bradley had interrupted the meeting for it. She looked up at the screen as the unsteady amateurish footage came onto the television. It was footage of the moors just before nightfall as the man doing the filming narrated.

'There it is,' he said.

'Have you got it?' another voice said over the whistling noise of the wind. The camera focused on a black shape in the distance that looked like a black cat that was laid down near a cobble stone wall.

'As you can see, that is a very large black cat, possibly a panther,' the voice said.

This was met with groans from the people in the room.

'Come on, Bradley, don't waste our time with this rubbish; it's obviously a domestic cat.' Danny said, sounding irritated.

'Just wait,' he said.

The walkers crept towards the animal slowly, still holding it in shot. They were about thirty yards from it when suddenly it stood up.

'Bloody hell,' the man doing the filming said.

Danny, Rachel and DCI Collis all looked at each other, suddenly with an obviously different opinion of what they were watching.

Jo thought the same as Danny at first, that it looked like a pet cat, but when it stood up next to the wall, she could tell by its shape, size and by its long tail that this was indeed a panther. The animal then seemed to be nervous of the approaching men and leapt over the wall and out of shot. They ran down the hill towards the wall, when there they steadied the camera again on the animal that was now running over the fields towards the woodland. It then disappeared from view.

'Well,' he said. He then slowly turned the camera in a full circle to show where he was. 'As you can see, we are at the north end of Colliford Lake, though the lake is out of view, it's just over those hills. And that way leads to River Loveny. Those of you who walk regularly on Bodmin Moor will recognise this spot and you'll see that the animal was at least the size of a panther or black leopard. There's no way that it was anything else.'

The friend of the man then stood next to the wall to show the scale, and Jo was convinced that it was definitely a panther.

Bradley then stopped the video and the screen went blank. The room was silent for a moment.

Jo didn't want to be the first to give an opinion but she did think that the footage looked real.

'When did that happen?' Danny asked.

'Last night at about eight o'clock,' Bradley said.

'How far is that area from our crime scene?' Danny asked.

'About a mile,' DCI Collis said. 'Maybe slightly more.'

'It looks real, but we need to interview them,' Jo said. 'Make sure this isn't a set up or a hoax.'

The room was quiet again. Jo felt as though everything they had been thinking about the murders had just been turned upside down. She didn't want to be the one to say it after what Danny had told her the day before. Nobody else seemed to be forthcoming in giving their opinions either.

DCI Collis then broke the silence. 'Right, Bradley, ring the fellow who's phone it is, tell him not to discuss it with anyone and ask him to come in so we can speak to him.'

'Yes, sir,' Bradley answered.

DCI Collis sat in silence again as he weighed up the new information.

Jo felt as though the silence was going to carry on forever; but she waited for her boss to speak.

'Right,' he said. 'This is something we all need to take on board, but not get too carried away with. That looked very real, and the location was right, and judging the sun's height as best we can, the timing looked right. But what other options are there?'

'It could be a hoax,' Rachel said. 'People can do amazing things with home computers these days.'

'Or it could be someone's pet panther?' Danny said.

'Pet panther?' Bradley scoffed. 'Who would have a pet panther?'

'People do keep private collections of dangerous wild animals,' Jo said. 'I was reading about it before.'

Bradley looked puzzled. 'Were you already thinking that it might be a panther?'

Jo looked at DCI Collis. 'Not really. But I had some time to kill earlier, so I was looking on the internet.'

'I think we have to accept the fact that there could be a so called Beast of Bodmin,' DCI Collis said.

'It is possible,' Jo said. 'It gets categorised with things like the Loch Ness Monster and the Chupacabra, and Bigfoot, but panthers are real creatures. It isn't that farfetched for one to be on the loose on Bodmin Moor.'

'But the Ministry of Agriculture did a survey of the moors a few years back, and they proved that there weren't any wild cats on the loose,' Rachel said.

'Sorry, Rachel,' Jo said. 'But that's not quite true. They couldn't prove that there were big cats living on the moors. That doesn't mean that there definitely aren't any. They just couldn't find evidence of them.'

'OK, let's just think about this for a moment,' Bradley said. 'Let's say that this panther footage is real. What do we do next?'

Nobody answered.

'Do we announce it to the press and tell everyone to stay off the moors?'

'If we do that, we'll have people from all over the country coming down here to try and catch it on camera,' Danny said. 'You know what these strange mysteries geeks are like.'

'Right,' DCI Collis said. 'Here's what we're going to do. We're going to carry on with our investigation without sharing this footage with anyone. Bradley, you get this amateur filmmaker in as soon as you can. Danny and Rachel go and interview the locals from St Breward and see if anything useful comes up. Jo, I want you to do a special assignment.'

Jo was intrigued.

'I want you to go to a zoo, probably Newquay Zoo, and talk to a big cat expert. Keep it under the radar though. Pay at the door and try to be discreet.'

'Will do, sir'

'Find out properly if it's possible to have a panther roaming the moors, and if it's possible that it's our killer, and more importantly, any tips they have on catching it. Any information they can give you that might help us.'

Chapter 17

Jo held the map of the zoo above her head to shield the sun from her eyes as she tried to find the lion enclosure. She walked by the large parrot aviary to her right. She didn't stop to admire the deep-blue coloured Hyacinth Macaws which she knew would've grabbed her attention had she had more time on her hands and didn't have a job to do. It felt strange being in a zoo when she was in work's time. It was late in the afternoon and she presumed that zoos mustn't be very popular at this late hour on a week day as the place didn't seem to be too busy.

After navigating the concrete pathways through the zoo and following the signs, she finally found the lion enclosure. She was amazed at the large male that was prowling the perimeter. A year or two had passed since Jo last went to a zoo. Although lions are an animal that she'd seen on television many times, she couldn't help but be overwhelmed at the large muscular creature that was only six feet away from her. The metal mesh didn't look thick enough to contain the lion should his mood suddenly change. She felt her heart race a little as he snarled before carrying on with his stroll.

A young man in a dark green polo shirt and matching green trousers was walking past and Jo saw the opportunity to find the person she needed.

'Excuse me,' she said.

The young man stopped. He looked about eighteen and was a little scruffy in appearance with dark untidy hair.

'Yes,' he said.

'Can you point me in the direction of your big cat expert?'

'All the information is on the boards,' he said, in a polite way.

Already Jo felt like she was in the way, not that she was going to take no for an answer. She knew the badge in her inside pocket could get her into any conversation she wanted, but she hoped it wouldn't come to that. 'I need a little more than that.'

'OK,' he said. He paused a second, then he used his radio to find the person in question. 'Helen.'

'Yes,' the crackly voice said a few seconds later.

'There's a lady outside the lions who wants to speak to our big cat expert.'

'Who is it?' she asked.

He looked at Jo for the answer.

'It's important,' she said.

The young man turned away before speaking quietly into the radio. 'I don't know, she's very smartly dressed; looks official.'

'Ah, right. I know what this is. I'll be there shortly.'

The young man turned back to her. 'She's on her way.'

'Thank you very much.' Jo then went back to watch the lions as the young man walked away. Three females were laid down in the sun as the male still walked around the enclosure. As Jo waited to meet the keeper she searched through her pockets for her notebook and pen. No sooner had she found it, a lady came around the corner dressed in green, the same as the young man; only with shorts on instead of long trousers. Jo's first impression of her was that she was a person in charge. She had a confidence in her stride as she walked towards her, which made Jo think that she was higher up the chain of command than some of the other zoo keepers. She had long dark-red curly hair tied into a loose pony tail, and her eyes were the greenest eyes Jo had ever seen. She instantly found her attractive; something she hadn't experienced since breaking up with Laura. Jo was determined not to be distracted by this as this lady was going to be very useful to her case.

'Good afternoon,' she said. 'This way.'

She walked fast and Jo had to set off quickly to keep up with her. 'Don't you want to know who I am?' she asked.

'It's pretty obvious. After that news report at dinner time, I knew it wouldn't be long before one of you came knocking.'

'News report?' Jo asked.

'The footage of the panther on the moors,' Helen said. She then looked at her with a confused expression. 'Didn't you see it?'

'I've seen the footage; I just didn't know that it was out there. We could've done without that,' she said.

'Do you not think it's better if people are scared enough to stay indoors at the moment?' Helen asked.

'Possibly.'

'It might save a few lives then.'

Jo liked her directness, but hoped that she wouldn't talk like this throughout the discussion. Jo liked to control conversations; she didn't feel as though Helen was going to let her do so.

Helen unlocked the metal door to the building that was attached to the lion enclosure. Once inside she closed the door behind them. The room was like a large kitchen with a sink, cupboards and a large table with four chairs around it in the centre. There was a metal panelled door on the other side of the room that Jo presumed led to the inside part of the lions sleeping quarters. There was also a large thick glass window that looked out into the confinement where she could see the lions. The room smelled like raw meat, so she presumed that this was where the keepers prepared the lions' food.

'Take a seat,' Helen said.

Jo walked over to the window first to look at the lions once more before they got down to business.

'Coffee with two sugars I reckon.'

'How did you know?' Jo said, without turning around.

'Your job must be too stressful to drink anything other than that.'

Jo laughed. She almost told her that she was only on day two of the job, but decided against it. She then sat down at the table as Helen prepared the drinks. She put her map down on the desk and opened her notebook at the ready.

'I'm DC Jo Green,' she said. 'I heard the young lad call you Helen, but what's your last name?'

'Thomas.'

'What's your position here?'

'I'm head of the big cats.'

'Have you been in the job long?' she asked.

'I left school at sixteen and worked at the Welsh Mountain Zoo. I then moved to London Zoo and I went through my animal management qualifications there and got my degree in biological sciences. I did a three month work placement in Nairobi National Park and have been the head of big cats here for two years.' She spoke very quickly with her back to Jo. 'So if you're wondering whether you're talking to the right person or not, you are.'

Jo didn't feel as though she was being confrontational by the way she was talking to her. It was more like she was getting straight to the point and didn't have time to beat around the bush. This also made her a little more attractive to Jo.

'I heard you say through the radio that you were expecting me, why's that?' she asked.

'That footage looked very real to me, and I spoke to my superior who grew up near Bolventor and he knew where the video was shot.'

'You're convinced it's real then?' Jo asked.

Helen gave her the coffee cup and sat opposite her. 'It was on Bodmin Moor, and it was a real panther. Either it's on the loose there or it was someone's pet that they've filmed,' she said.

'Is it possible for people to keep big cats without being found out?'

'Possible; but it doesn't belong to the people filming because it ran away.'

'That's a good point,' Jo said. 'A pet wouldn't run away from its owner like that.'

'Definitely not; it looked startled.'

Jo needed to know more. 'So do you think it's possible that the people killed have been eaten by this cat?'

'I think it's possible, but I would've thought that you'd have found a body or a skeleton. Although they are strong and are known for carrying their kill up into trees or to a secluded place, I really think you'd have something more than a puddle of blood; unless the news isn't telling the full story.'

'The campers were dragged a long way, clothing fragments were found in the woods about two hundred yards from the scene. Lucy from the bus shelter, well there was just a pile of insides, for want of a better word.'

'Can they not tell from the examination of the remains if they had been bitten or torn?' she asked. Jo wondered if Helen was very clever, or just a regular viewer of crime dramas.

'I was hoping so, but they said there isn't enough flesh to tell how it was extracted from the body.'

'I see.'

'Do big cats eat bones as well?'

'Yes, on smaller prey they do.'

'So the panther in the film could be doing the killing?'

'I think it's possible,' Helen said.

Jo took another gulp of her coffee. 'Well, could a big cat carry a human body two hundred yards, then eat them, including the bones, and would they kill two people and carry them away one at a time?'

Helen leaned forwards across the table. 'That's the bit I'm struggling with,' she said. 'Yes they sometimes eat the bones, and yes they can carry them that far, but would they kill two prey and then take them away one at a time? That is unusual behaviour.'

'I've built a picture of the scene in my mind. Is it possible that the male needed the toilet, and so went outside? The cat killed him, and the girl inside the tent screamed or even came outside. She saw the cat and ran back inside and the cat left the male and then went after her.'

Helen was nodding as Jo spoke.

'Then after dragging one away and eating him or her, or storing them somewhere, then comes back for the other.'

'That is all possible,' Helen said. 'Big cats do gorge themselves when they haven't eaten for a while, but I don't think it's likely to eat three whole people in just two nights.'

'They wouldn't do that in the wild?'

'No,' she paused. 'But in the wild they eat creatures that are very fast; they couldn't catch them with a full stomach, but a human wouldn't take much running after.'

They sat back and pondered the situation.

'So what do you think then?' Jo asked.

'It's just a little farfetched; attacking and eating three people in such a short time.'

Jo was busy scribbling down notes as Helen spoke. She didn't know whether or not she would find his trip to the zoo helpful, but now she felt as though she knew more from talking to Helen than she'd read on the internet. But Jo was thinking that it didn't look likely that the panther has eaten three people in two days. In a strange way Jo found herself excited at the thought of searching for the Beast of Bodmin out on the moorland surrounding her home town; but above all, she hoped they could solve the problem before any more people lost their lives.

'Is it possible that the panther has killed all three victims, but not eaten them?' Jo asked.

'I suppose so, if the animal was disturbed in some way before eating. But I would've thought that it would've gone back to the first kills rather than catching another meal.'

'But again, as you said, people are easier to catch,' Jo said.

'True,' Helen said. 'I don't know if you know this or not, but in 1976, the government introduced the Dangerous Wild Animals Act. Before then, you could buy and own any big cat. You could actually go into a department store and buy a lion or a tiger. When it became law to get a licence to own them, people had to make the choice; either have them put to sleep, or find a home for them. Adding another lion or panther to an existing collection isn't that easy, they couldn't just phone the local zoo and ask them to take them. So the theory is that rather than having their beloved pets put to sleep, they released them into the wild instead.'

'Was the licence too expensive?' she asked.

'It wasn't the cost of the licence; it was the criteria for owning one. People didn't have the space, money or resources to build the enclosures that the licence required. So being given no option but to put their pets to sleep, people released them and hoped for the best; again, this is all theory.'

'How long do they live for?' Jo asked.

'Well that's a good point; they only live for fifteen to twenty years. So the original cats that were supposedly released would've died of old age by now.'

'Unless they're breeding,' Jo said.

'Unless they're breeding,' Helen repeated. 'But if they were breeding, there would have to have been a bigger number of them to keep the family going. They might be elusive, but with a couple of generations living out there, there would have been sightings all the time.'

'I see.'

'There are other ways it could've ended up on the moors. It could've escaped from a travelling circus or possibly escaped from a zoo. This would be unlikely but the laws haven't always been as strict as they are now, and several zoos have closed over the last decade or so. There were some reports of animals being illegally sold when zoos have closed down.'

'There are a lot of grainy films on the internet. Would we not have had concrete proof before now?' Jo asked.

'Well, like I say, they are very elusive animals that are hard to spot in the places that they actually come from. Bodmin Moor covers eighty square miles, with a large portion of it woodland. It is possible they've been living out there for years, but I think it's more likely that the cat in the film is a more recent escapee.'

Jo stood up and walked back over to the window to look at the lions. She wondered whether or not they were getting carried away, but she needed to make sure that she didn't ignore the possibility that this could be what's been happening.

'So how do we deal with this?' Jo asked.

Helen got up and walked over to the window and stood next to Jo. 'You can get on the phone and arrange a team of marksmen to patrol the area looking for it.'

'I would've thought an animal lover would've wanted to keep the panther alive,' Jo said.

'I could get a tranquiliser gun and go looking for it, but it's not that simple. There are laws to be followed with things like this, permission from the Ministry of Agriculture, and when you dart an animal you have to have a vet with you, although I'm not sure if that applies when catching an animal in the wild; especially one that's alien to this part of the world.'

'Maybe we should we try to arrange that first,' Jo said.

'If the footage is real and there is a panther on the loose, then it needs to be caught quickly before someone gets hurt; if they haven't already.'

Jo nodded. 'You're right.'

'Maybe I could go out early morning and look for it. I'll speak to my superior, see what he thinks.'

Jo couldn't fail to be impressed by her. She felt as though Helen already knew this day was coming and was prepared for suggesting this all along. She wondered if it was the extreme lengths that an animal lover would go to in order to stop a creature being senselessly killed or if she was a little bit adventurous and found the whole situation exciting. All Jo knew for sure was the fact that she liked her. She liked her quick talking attitude and the intelligence and the confidence Helen exuded. She came across like somebody who doesn't take no for an answer and somebody who gets what she wants. Maybe this was what Jo liked about her.

'Well, here's my number,' Jo said, as she gave her a card. 'Anything comes to mind that you think we need to know, just give me a call.'

'I will,' Helen said, looking at the card. 'Do you live in Bodmin?'

'St Breward; a village on Bodmin Moor,' Jo answered.

Helen raised her eyebrows. 'You'll want it caught quickly then with it being so close to home.'

'I do, whether it's killed our victims or not, it needs to be caught.'

Jo then thanked Helen with a hand shake and headed back to Bodmin.

Jo felt as though she'd learnt a lot from Helen, but above all, she hoped she would get to see her again.

Chapter 18

Jo was relieved when she came downstairs that evening to find she had the house to herself. Her mum had gone to her weekly parish council meeting at the church hall, and Rick at eight-thirty on a Tuesday evening was most likely in the pub. She was surprised that he'd gone out with what had happened to Lucy the night before, but she was glad that he had. It'd been a stressful day for Rick and although Jo didn't think that getting drunk would be any help to him, she thought it was better than him staying in his room and being on his own. At least he'd be with his friends.

Jo sat down in the armchair next to the fish tank. She hadn't put any of the room lights on so the tank looked nice and bright in the mid evening light that showed dimly through the small cottage window. She put her drink down; then she opened the cupboard and took out the tub of tablet food. She dropped two into the tank before resting back in her chair. At first, she could only see the tetras swimming towards them, pecking at the small round pill sized food. But then all the loaches and catfish suddenly appeared to join in the feeding frenzy. The black and white loaches pushed their way towards the food. She was impressed at how much they'd grown and coloured up. The aquatic store owner was right; he said that they would be impressive once they'd fattened up and their colours started to develop. Even though they were black and white; the black seemed deeper and the white was a vivid pearlescent white. Jo remembered researching them on the internet while they were mixing in the polythene bag before she released them into the tank. She didn't always make the effort to learn the Latin names, but for some reason, Botia Histrionica was one that stayed in her head.

The mixture of Corydoras catfish all arrived at the scene moments later. She enjoyed watching them all tussling over the food, swimming in and having a nibble before spinning around whilst the others have a go. It was almost like they were taking turns and sharing the food with each other.

She sat back in her chair and relaxed for a moment. She then noticed a new photograph that her mum must've put on the wooden mantelpiece; a picture that was taken while on holiday in South Wales. Jo was fourteen and Rick was nine. They were standing in front of the holiday cottage; her mum and dad were standing behind them. She remembered her dad asking the lady who gave them the keys to the cottage if she'd take a photo of them before she left. It was a nice photo that opened up a lot of memories for Jo. She loved to go fishing with her dad and Rick; this was something that they did quite a lot on that holiday.

She realised she was starting to be drawn into thoughts that she hadn't allowed herself to go into throughout the last three years since her dad died. After the funeral, she didn't allow herself to think about him; good memories like family holidays and other fun things that they had done, or bad things, like visiting him in hospital after his heart attack. She remembered how shocked she felt when her mum rang her while she was house hunting with David.

Seeing her usually fit and healthy father lying on a hospital bed was a shock to Jo, she was fighting back the tears as soon as she walked into the room. Your dad is the one who looks after you, protects you and will always be there when you need him. To see him looking tired, pale and obviously scared - even though he tried to cover it up with a smile - was a complete shock to Jo.

Jo, Rick, and her mum all sat with him for an hour before

they was told it was OK to leave. The doctor told them that it was a massive heart attack, but he was stable, and in the best of hands. He said that he will have to take it easy for a while and possibly need surgery, but they would know more over the next couple of days once they'd done a few more tests. The nurses told to them to go home, and said they would ring them if anything changed.

What they didn't say was to make sure you say goodbye to your dad properly, because at two-thirty in the morning we will ring you to tell you to get back here quickly because he's just had another massive heart attack and died before we could help him.

Jo wasn't angry with anybody, the doctors didn't know that was going to happen, he was stable when they left. But she thought that somehow, her dad knew. The way he looked her in the eye as he said goodbye to them, it was like he knew. The nurse told them as soon as they had arrived that he'd already passed away. Jo presumed that they weren't allowed to tell you over the phone, perhaps it was a rule that they had to tell you in person; she didn't know.

A single tear ran down Jo's cheek. She hadn't thought about her dad for a long time. She felt guilty about this, but she couldn't bring herself to think about him, not without crying. She almost felt like if she started, she wouldn't be able to stop.

It was two weeks after her dad died that she applied to become a police officer. She'd read somewhere that when you lose a parent, you can suddenly start to question your own life, and wonder if you're going down the right path. She'd been pushing aside her calling for far too long.

There was a loud knock at the door that startled her. She wiped away the tears before getting up from the chair and opening the door.

'Teddy,' she said.

'Evening Jo; fancy a drink?' Teddy said, smiling at her. It

wasn't unusual for Teddy to knock on and ask her to join him at the local pub.

Jo thought that an hour in the pub would do her good. Much better than sitting alone and thinking about the past, she thought.

She smiled at Teddy. 'That's the best offer I've had all day.'

Chapter 19

Once at the pub, Jo and Teddy sat down at the table in front of the fire. The pub was busy, especially for a week night. Most of the patrons were locals but a few holiday makers were also sat at the tables enjoying a meal. The pub was busy, but it was much quieter than the night of Annie's birthday, which Jo was happy about. A quiet drink with her old friend Teddy was what she wanted. But no sooner had Jo taken the first sip of her drink, a text message came through. She looked at her phone. She didn't recognise the number, but opened it anyway. It read, *Hi Jo, great to meet you today. I'm passing through Bodmin and was wondering if you fancied a chat. Thanks, Helen.*

This message made Jo's heart race a little. She didn't hesitate in answering it straight away, telling Helen to come to the King's Head in St Breward.

'What's made you so happy?' Teddy asked.

Jo was a little embarrassed at her lack of poker face. 'Nothing,' she said. 'It's the zookeeper I met today. She wants to come to the pub for a chat.'

'Why did you meet a zookeeper?' Teddy asked.

'It's because of the footage of the panther,' Jo said. 'DCI Collis thought we should get some advice from an expert.'

'Was it useful to your investigation?'

'Yes. She was very helpful.' Jo wondered what Helen wanted to talk to her about. She hoped she had some information for her, but she also hoped that she just wanted to see her.

There was a moments silence as Jo and Teddy both took a sip of their drinks.

Jo then saw a smirk on Teddy's face, the kind of smirk he

always struggled to hide before coming out with one of his witty remarks.

'I forgive you by the way,' he said.

This comment confused Jo. 'Forgive me for what?'

'For not believing me when I said I'd seen a black panther on the moors, and for not believing me when I showed you the scratch marks.'

Jo smiled. 'Oh, that.'

'It's OK, Jo. I accept your apology.'

'I haven't given you one yet,' Jo said.

'Well, when you're ready, I'll be listening.'

Although Teddy was joking, Jo knew how embarrassed he was the night he saw the panther, and she knew how relieved he must feel for being proven right by the recent events.

'Look, Teddy,' Jo said. 'This is something you've believed in for many years, but you have to admit that nobody else around here believed in the Beast of Bodmin.'

'I know, but I thought my good friend Jo Green would've believed me.'

'Well if it makes you feel any better, I defended your actions to DCI Collis today.'

Teddy's eyes widened. 'You told Brian that you believed me?'

Jo smiled. 'Not exactly.'

'What then?'

'I told him that you either saw something, or thought you saw something.'

Teddy leaned back in his chair. 'So in others words, you believe me but you think I'm cuckoo.'

Jo couldn't help but laugh. But she'd known him for long enough to know he wasn't really offended. But she also knew the relief he'd be feeling at the footage of the panther coming to light.

Twenty minutes later, Jo looked up to see Helen walk into the pub. She was still dressed in her green zookeeper's uniform.

Jo waved to catch her attention.

As Helen reached the table, Jo introduced her to Teddy, who stood to shake her hand.

'This is Teddy,' Jo said. 'He's a local farmer and family friend.'

'Nice to meet you, Teddy,' Helen said. 'I'll just get a drink.'

'No,' Teddy said. 'You sit down, love. What can I get you?'

'Thank you. I'll just have an orange juice, please.'

As Teddy walked over to the bar, Jo asked, 'So, what brings you here?'

'I had a few errands to run after work so I thought I'd see if you fancied meeting up. Is there any news on the murders, or any more sightings of a big cat?'

'Nothing as yet. We had a meeting late afternoon. I told my boss and the team of detectives everything we discussed. I told them what you'd said about how the panther wouldn't have eaten three people whole. So we're set on looking for a person and seeing the two situations as separate.'

'I think that's the most likely scenario,' Helen said.

'Did you speak to your boss about the tranquiliser gun idea?'

'I did. He's not happy about the idea of doing it on the quiet, but he said if the police ask him to he'll provide the equipment and let me go out and try to dart the animal, but he doesn't want to break any laws.'

'Understandable. I'll mention it to my DCI.'

Teddy arrived back at the table and placed the orange juice in front of Helen and a glass of wine next to Jo's nearly empty glass.

'Thank you,' Helen said.

'No problem at all,' Teddy said, picking up his half empty pint of bitter off the table. 'I'll leave you to it.'

'You don't have to go on my account,' Helen said.

'No. It's fine. I wanted to go and speak to Kenneth anyway. He's over at the bar. I'll see you later.'

He then began to walk away when Jo suddenly realised something.

'Teddy,' she said.

He turned back.

'Where's Sam?' she asked. 'I think this is one of the first times I've seen you in the pub without him.'

'Well you'd better get used to that, Jo.'

'Why?'

'I lost him today.'

Jo was shocked at this. 'What do you mean?'

'I was working on the wall near where the scratches were. Part of it had collapsed. Anyway; he was there one minute, gone the next.'

'Have you looked for him?'

'Me and Vicky have been out all day. We gave up just before nightfall. We'll go out again at first light.'

'Sorry,' Helen interrupted politely. 'But who's Sam?'

'My collie,' Teddy said.

'As he ever run away before?' Helen asked.

'No; he's a well trained working dog.'

'Why didn't you tell me?' Jo asked.

'Well, I was going to, but with all the talk of the panther...' He then choked up and couldn't finish his sentence.

'I'm sorry, Teddy. Maybe he'll be sat on your doorstep when you get home,' Jo said, knowing full well that this wouldn't be likely. Sam was a border collie that never needed a lead he was so well behaved. And a dog that had the freedom he had certainly wouldn't run away from home.

'Maybe,' Teddy said, turning away and walking over to the bar.

Helen then leaned over the table and said quietly, 'It doesn't look good, does it?'

Jo shook her head.

'Will he be OK? Dogs aren't just pets, they're one of the family. It can be a terrible thing losing a dog.'

'He's been through worse.'

'Really?'

'Much worse. He lives in his farmhouse with his granddaughter Vicky; she's eighteen now. When she was eight, ten years ago, Teddy's wife and daughter, Vicky's mum, were both killed in a car accident. He's raised Vicky ever since.'

'That's really sad. I don't know how he's managed to deal with that and carry on,' Helen said.

'Well he hasn't had much choice, but he's a tough old goat.'

'I hope his dog turns up. Are you sure he's OK?'

'He'll be fine.'

After a moment of silence as they took in what Teddy had just revealed, Jo decided to try to get to know Helen better. 'So, tell me about you. How come you ended up living in Newquay?'

'Who said I lived in Newquay?' Helen asked.

'I just presumed you did with you working at Newquay Zoo.'

'No, I live in Tregoltha.'

'Really?'

'Yes. I wanted to leave London. I enjoyed working at London Zoo, but after I broke up with my partner, I just thought I'd have a fresh start. There are plenty of zoological parks in Cornwall and Devon, and I sent my CV to most of them. Newquay Zoo was one of the ones who showed interest, I've been working there ever since.'

'I see. Was it a bad break up?' Jo wasn't sure if this question was too personal, but asked it anyway.

Helen didn't answer straight away, as if she was contemplating how much information to reveal.

'She didn't turn out to be the person I thought she was.'

Jo wasn't sure until that point whether Helen was gay or not.

She was hoping so and she was hoping that Helen paying her a visit was because she was interested in her.

There was a silence for a moment and then Helen smiled at Jo and said, 'You can ask me about it if you want.'

'Well, I don't want to be too nosey. I'm interested, but I don't want to upset you if it's difficult to talk about.'

'It was difficult, but I'm OK now.'

'How long ago did it end?'

'About two years ago; it was just before I left London. We'd been together for about nine months. She was perfect. We had lots in common, we liked the same films, the same books and she worked at a stud farm, so both being animal lovers, I thought she was the one.'

'But she wasn't?'

'We moved in together after only a few of months of being a couple, it was soon after that her true colours started to show. She started with little jealous comments and asking where I'd been or checking up on me, and ringing me at work all the time for stupid things. It was as if she was checking that I was actually at work and that I hadn't lied to her about where I was.'

'That's no way to treat the person you love,' Jo said.

'Well, it just got worse and worse. One day the battery died on my phone and she actually paid at the entrance of the zoo to come and check I was there.'

'And you shouted at her, I'm guessing?' Jo asked.

'I didn't want to cause a scene, so I quietly snapped at her and told her to go home and told her we'd talk later. But that wasn't what happened. As soon I got home, we started talking but it very quickly blew up into an argument and she asked me who the girl was that she saw me flirting with. I presumed she saw me talking to another keeper, but I wasn't flirting, I couldn't even remember who I was talking to.'

'Did you tell her that?'

'No. I thought why should I have to defend myself? I just told her she was being ridiculous and then refused to talk to her. That's when it got out of hand.'

Jo sensed this story was about to get worse. 'Did she hit you?'

Helen nodded. 'She gave me one hell of a beating. I was black and blue by the time she'd finished.'

'That's terrible.'

'She begged for my forgiveness the next morning and told me she'd get help. But I wasn't staying around for that to happen again.'

'Good for you. Most people stay after the first one and give them another chance.'

'Not me. The thing is, I can look after myself. She was smaller than me so I'm sure I could've got the better of her, but I never fought back. It was like I was frozen with disbelief that she would do this to us, so I just stood there and took it. We had such a good thing going. We were deeply in love, but she ruined it.'

'Have you spoken to her since?'

'She rang many times and sent texts but I never answered her. After a few months she gave up. I made a point of not responding to any of them as to discourage any thoughts she might've had about me changing my mind.'

'Well, I hope you're OK now, and I hope it's not left any lasting damage on you.'

'I've been happy being single since I moved down here. It's not stopped me trusting anyone else or anything like that; I've just been concentrating on my career.'

Jo considered hinting at them going on a date at some point, but she thought it would come across as insensitive to make an advance after hearing such a sad story. Jo wondered if Helen knew she was gay and also wondered if she knew that she was still in the closet. Jo kept her eyes focused on Helen, her beautiful smile and gorgeous green eyes. She knew that she was finding her more and more interesting with every conversation they had. Even at this early stage in their friendship, Jo was wondering if Helen was somebody she could fall for. She hoped this was mutual, but she wasn't sure as yet.

Teddy arrived back at the table, followed closely by Kenneth. 'Sorry to interrupt, but Kenneth has something to discuss.'

Kenneth begrudgingly stood behind Teddy. Kenneth was in his late sixties, his hair was long on top, much like Teddy's, only he was very thin and pale and a lot shorter than Teddy. He was a writer of Cornish history and folklore, quite a successful one too, but since his wife died five years earlier, he hadn't released anything new; not to Jo's knowledge anyway.

'Tell her what you told me, Kenneth,' Teddy said.

Kenneth shook his head. 'It's probably nothing. I wouldn't want to waste your time, Joanne.'

He was very well spoken, and had barely a hint of Cornish in his accent. He was also the only person who ever called her Joanne. She'd noticed that he does this with everyone else, including calling Rick, Richard. But that wasn't on Jo's mind at the moment. What information did he have that Teddy thought was important enough to bring him over to her?

'Why don't you let me be the judge of that, Kenneth; take a seat.' She pointed at the chair next to Helen.

Teddy moved around and pulled the chair out, before almost pushing Kenneth into the seat, leaving a hand on his shoulder.

'Go on, Kenneth, tell her.'

Kenneth looked up at Teddy before looking back at Jo and rolling his eyes.

Jo smiled.

Kenneth leaned forward with his hands on his lap.

Jo was intrigued at what she was about to learn.

'All it is, you know the gentleman from London who lives at Carsten Farmhouse?'

'I've never seen him, and I didn't know he was from London to be honest. But I'd heard that someone bought the house a year or two back,' Jo said.

'Well, he has a long driveway leading to his house, but my house is on the opposite side of the road to his entrance. I can't see his house from where I am, because his house is probably two hundred yards or so from mine and trees are blocking the view.'

'OK.'

'Well anyway, I saw him in Tim's Butchers' shop in Camelford a few weeks back. And after he'd left, Tim told me that he buys meat off him on a regular basis, in quite large amounts by all accounts. A couple of carrier bags full at a time.'

'Right,' Jo said, still wondering where Kenneth was going with this.

'He'd told Tim that he breeds bull mastiffs, but I've never heard any barking coming from his property. And, the last three nights, I've seen him coming and going every couple of hours. He seems distressed, as if in some kind of a hurry. Through the daytime he keeps coming and going in his car, but at night, he's on foot; just the last three nights.'

'Kenneth, what is it you're getting at?' Jo asked.

'Well,' he said, looking slightly embarrassed.

'Tell her,' Teddy said impatiently.

'I'm getting there,' he snapped.

This almost made Jo laugh, and she noticed a smile appear on Helen's face too.

'He carried a dog lead when he came out last night. He swung it so as to wrap it around his hand as he walked away from the entrance to his driveway. It was a metal lead, like a heavy choke chain.'

'Perhaps one of his dogs has escaped,' Jo said.

'Well as I say, if he has dogs, I've never seen or heard them.'

Jo leaned forward over the table. 'Are you saying that you think he has a pet panther?'

'It sounds ridiculous, I know. But if you could see the way he was behaving, you'd know what I mean.'

'No, Kenneth. It's fine. I'm glad you told me and we'll look into it.'

'OK,' he said. He then nodded politely and left the table, still looking a little embarrassed, and headed back to the bar with Teddy.

Helen raised her eyebrows. 'There could be something in it. That panther had to come from somewhere.'

'This is St Breward, Helen,' Jo said. 'You can't keep a panther in St Breward, and keep it a secret.'

Jo then thought about it for a moment before looking back to Helen and saying, 'Can you?'

Helen didn't answer. She just smiled before taking another sip of her orange juice.

Chapter 20

The next morning, Jo was driving through St Breward on her way to work when she spotted Vinny standing outside his shop, smoking as usual. Only today, instead of just waving, he stepped into the road and raised his hand for her to stop. As Jo pulled the car over, she took her sunglasses off and wound down the passenger window.

Vinny came over to the car and leaned down to her. 'Here Jo,' he said, passing her a disc in a plastic case.

Jo took it from him. 'What's this?'

'It's the disc from my CCTV. My nephew installed it for me so I didn't realise you could see a little through the window, but he called here last night and said it would be worth a look so he put the disc in the DVD player.'

Jo's heart raced a little.

'It might be nothing, but it's worth you looking at.'

'What can you see?' Jo asked.

'Fast forward to eight-thirty and you'll see Rick and Lucy, or at least I think it's them. A few moments later, someone else walks past.'

'Really?'

'Yes. I say eight-thirty because we didn't reset the clock on the machine when the clocks went forward. It'll actually have been nine-thirty.'

'Excellent. Thanks for that, Vinny.'

'No problem. Sorry I didn't realise sooner, but I don't really know how to use it properly. I've just been changing the discs every morning and rotating them like he told me too.'

'Well, we'll have a look when I get to the station.'

With that, he smiled and tapped on the car roof before turning back to his shop.

Jo was surprised to walk into the office and see a meeting already in progress. DCI Collis was sitting at the head of the table, DS Danny Hughes to his right, and DS Rachel Killik and DC Bradley Dutson to his left. Jo looked at the clock to see if she was late. She wasn't, she was twenty minutes early.

'Morning, Jo,' DCI Collis said. 'Take a seat.'

She sat next to Danny as the meeting continued.

'All I'm saying is,' Rachel said, 'we can't presume that a panther has done the killings.'

'But we have to be open minded about the possibility,' Bradley said.

'Until some more evidence comes to light we're going to be going back and forth like this,' Danny said.

'Well, I have something that might be a matter of interest,' Jo said.

'What's that?' Danny asked.

'Actually, I have three things that might be of interest.'

'Go on,' DCI Collis said.

'First of all, Teddy was working on his farm near where he showed me the scratch marks on his tree.'

'Yes.'

'His border collie, Sam was with him when he started work, but when he'd finished, he'd gone. He and his granddaughter spent the day looking for him and he hasn't shown up.'

'You think the panther has killed him?' Danny asked.

'Well, he's a very well trained sheepdog that has never disappeared on him before.'

'It's a possibility then,' DCI Collis said.

'Secondly,' Jo said, holding up the DVD that Vinny gave her. 'As I was driving to work, Vinny stopped me and gave me this.

He has one CCTV camera focused on the inside of his shop, but he said you can see a little of what went on the night Lucy was killed.'

The detectives all looked surprised.

Bradley stood up from his seat and took the disc from her. He then took it over to the television in the corner of the room and put the disc in.

'Vinny said the time hasn't been altered so forward it to just before eight-thirty,' Jo said.

It took Bradley a few minutes to fast forward it with the remote control. Once he'd got to eight-thirty, he stopped and let the disc play at normal speed.

Jo saw a black and white scene of the inside of Vinny's grocery store. She could see through the window but not very well. The detectives all stood to get a closer look at the screen. Moments later, two pairs of legs came into view, but only up to the thigh as they were standing on the opposite side of the road. Jo thought it could be Rick and Lucy, but she couldn't tell properly. They both stopped walking and faced each other, obviously mid-conversation. After a moment or two, they stepped towards each other as if to kiss goodnight, then they parted with what looked to Jo as Lucy heading to the right and Rick to the left, back in the direction of the pub. After no more than ten seconds or so, the figure of what looked like a man started walking from left to right. The camera could see him up to the centre of his back because he walked from the side of the road where the shop was, opposite to where Rick and Lucy were standing. He then crossed the road quickly before going into a jog, heading in the direction of Lucy.

Bradley rewound the disc and pressed pause on the part of the footage where the man was in shot.

The room was silent as they all took in what they'd just seen.

'That's a bit of a game changer,' Danny said.

'It did look menacing,' Rachel said. 'Especially the way he appeared before running after her. It looked as though he was waiting next to the doorway of the shop, watching them.'

'Right,' DCI Collis said. 'Let's sit back down and discuss where we go from here.'

They all sat back in their seats before Danny started the conversation.

'I think, sir,' he said, addressing DCI Collis, 'that we need to put that image out to the press and concentrate on finding a person.'

'You think so?' DCI Collis said.

'Yes. I know there could be a panther on the loose, but we have marksmen out looking for it so we should concentrate on finding whoever that is,' he said, pointing up at the screen.

'Hang on,' Bradley interrupted. 'Jo, you said three bits of information, the dog, the CCTV, what's the third?'

Jo sat back and folded her arms. 'The third one goes against what you just said, Danny, but it is a matter of interest.'

'Go on,' Danny said.

'Local writer and historian, Kenneth Trent,' Jo started. She then turned to DCI Collis. 'I believe you know him, sir.'

'Yes, of course.'

'Well he lives opposite Carsten Farmhouse, and he says the owner of the house buys meat from the butcher in Camelford in quite large amounts.'

'What and you think he has a panther?' Rachel asked.

'Kenneth said he's seen him leaving the house frantically the last few nights on foot, and he saw him carrying a dog lead.'

'Carston Farmhouse?' DCI Collis asked.

Jo nodded. 'In St Breward.'

DCI Collis then turned to Bradley.

Without being asked, Bradley said, 'I'm on it.' He then stood and left the room.

Jo said, 'Sir, with your permission, I'd like to take Helen Thomas, the zookeeper I met yesterday. She might be helpful in this situation; if he is a big cat enthusiast. He might have more of them for all we know. It sounds farfetched but that panther had to come from somewhere.'

'I don't see a problem with that,' DCI Collis said. 'You go too, Danny.'

'Shouldn't we be leaving this to uniform, sir? We need to concentrate on finding whoever that is in the footage.'

'I understand your point, Danny, but let's follow up on Jo's lead first. We can hand it over to uniform once we know what's what.'

'Yes, sir.'

Moments later, Bradley came back into the room holding a piece of paper.

'Find a name, Bradley?' DCI Collis asked.

'I found more than that, sir.'

'How do you mean?'

'The owner of this house is an ex-con from London.'

'Really?' DCI Collis asked.

Bradley held the paper in front of him as he started to read. 'Lester Hamilton, from Rotherhithe...'

'What?' Danny shouted.

Bradley stopped reading and looked at Danny.

'Lester Hamilton?' Danny asked.

'You know him?' Bradley said.

'Know him? I spent most of my career in London trying to put him away.'

'Really?'

'Yes. Lester was a very clever local villain that always managed to find his way out of the things he'd done. Extortion, money laundering, arms dealing, to name but a few.'

'You're kidding?' Bradley said.

'Getting witnesses to come to court was very difficult, and do you know the only thing we managed to prosecute him for?'

'What?' Jo asked.

'Keeping illegal animals.'

'Seriously?' DCI Collis asked.

Danny nodded.

'What kind of animals?' Bradley asked.

'Poisonous snakes, lizards, that sort of thing.'

'This is starting to add up,' Rachel said.

'Is he really living in Cornwall?' Danny asked.

'Afraid so,' Bradley said, handing the piece of paper to Danny.

'Well, I'm definitely coming now, Jo.'

Chapter 21

Less than an hour later, Jo and Danny turned into the private road that led to Carsten Farmhouse. The road that Kenneth referred to as a driveway was at least two hundred metres long and was lined with hedges on both sides. The road was more than wide enough for one car but two would struggle to pass. It was more like a country lane than a driveway as it weaved left and right. As the house finally came into view Jo couldn't help but be impressed by the large sandstone-bricked building that was fronted by a large grassed area with a paving stone path leading up to the solid wooden front door. The house was old fashioned but very well maintained. There was ivy growing up the left side of the front wall, working its way around the large windows. Jo felt as though this house would be anybody's dream home, only a few rooms short of being referred to as a mansion. There was a car parked in front of the house, a black Mercedes, but with the story Kenneth had told her the night before, Jo didn't expect anybody to be home.

Danny rang the doorbell. It was a loud chiming sound that should've been heard from anywhere inside the house, but nobody answered. He rang it again, and waited. Then he tried the handle on the door. It opened. At first Jo thought perhaps Lester Hamilton was home, but in St Breward, it wasn't unusual for people to leave their doors unlocked.

Before Jo could say anything, she heard a car coming up the driveway.

Danny obviously heard it too because he closed the front door again.

Jo watched as the silver Citroen Picasso came around the corner. She then saw a hand waving at her from behind the wheel. Jo couldn't see who it was at first because of the reflection on the windscreen, but as the car got closer to her she saw that it was Helen. She couldn't help but be excited to see her again. She wasn't going to let this distract her from the job they were there to do, but she was definitely pleased to see her again.

'Good morning,' Helen said, as she got out of the car and walked over to them.

'Morning, Helen,' Jo said. 'This is DS Hughes; DS Hughes, this is Helen.'

They shook hands.

'Danny; please,' he said.

'Nice to meet you,' Helen said. She then stood back and looked up at the house. 'This is a house and a half.'

'It is,' Danny said. 'It's also unlocked.'

He then opened the door again. He walked straight in and then Jo, followed closely by Helen.

'Is it OK to just walk in?' Helen whispered to Jo.

'He's a person of interest to our investigation,' Jo said. 'It's fine.'

'Lester Hamilton!' Danny shouted. 'Are you home? Police!'

Nobody answered.

They walked through the hallway and turned left into a very large living room. The room had a beige carpet and large corner-shaped couch. There was also a very large television, fifty inches at least, Jo thought.

They then walked back through to the hallway.

Jo's heart pounded a little. Although it didn't appear that anyone was home, Jo knew that she needed to be on her guard, especially with Lester Hamilton being a known criminal.

'I'll check upstairs,' Danny said.

Jo walked through to the large modern kitchen with black marble worktops and oak cupboard doors and all the modern and expensive looking appliances.

'Jo,' Helen said.

Jo turned to look at her.

Helen pointed through the large patio doors and into the garden. There was what looked like a large zoo enclosure towards the bottom of the garden.

'Upstairs is clear,' Danny said as he rejoined them.

Jo walked over to the large glass door and turned the key that was already in the lock before sliding the door open.

As they walked along the path that separated the two large areas of lawn, Jo could see what looked like a very professional looking enclosure.

There was a large red brick garage-like building with green metal posts and wire mesh up against it. It looked to Jo like Lester Hamilton had the building constructed as sleeping quarters for the panther and the large metal cage was attached to the wall. It was a very professional job. There was a large tree trunk on its side and lots of other branches and some living bushes planted around the pen that was part grass and part soil. The soil had been flattened over time to a dry mud floor. The top of the cage had clear plastic corrugated roofing fixed to it for half of the cage. The other half wasn't covered. Jo presumed that this was so the animal could decide if it wanted to stay dry or sit and enjoy the rain.

Jo was impressed. It looked like a well made enclosure. And Jo now knew for sure that they were in the right place. Kenneth's suspicions were right.

'This isn't a homemade enclosure,' Helen said.

'No?' Danny asked.

'This is made to a very high standard. It wouldn't look out of place at Newquay zoo, apart from it not being very big.'

'It's definitely for a big cat though,' Jo asked.

'Definitely,' Helen said. 'You can see the scratch marks on the tree'

Jo looked at the marks and thought of Teddy's tree. They looked similar, only there were many more on this tree and Teddy's scratch marks showed more of the white wood as though they'd been done that day. These marks had been done over a long period of time because they were covered by algae from the rain.

Danny banged on the door of the cage, obviously checking that there wasn't an animal inside sleeping.

'There's nothing in there, Danny,' the loud deep voice said in a broad London accent.

Jo turned quickly to see a man standing in front of the open patio doors. He then started walking along the path. He had dark hair combed backwards. He was medium height, but stocky and walked with a confidence that this was a person who wouldn't be easily intimidated. Jo saw a man who looked very confident for someone who'd possibly caused the deaths of three people. He walked slowly, with a strong posture and his shoulders back. He looked like he was in his fifties, and was casually, but smartly dressed. He looked like he had money, and he didn't look as though he was nervous about finding the police on his property.

'Lester,' Danny said.

'Whatcha, Danny,' he said, offering a hand to be shaken.

Danny folded his arms, looking him in the eye as he did.

'Don't be like that, Danny. I thought you'd be pleased to see me.'

'Pleased to see you?' he said.

Lester was smiling, but Danny wasn't.

'I believe you both know each other,' Jo said.

'Our paths have crossed on a few occasions,' Danny said.

'Yeah, back in Rotherhithe, Danny was always trying to blame me for something or other that I hadn't done,' Lester said, in a slightly smug tone.

'Not quite true, Lester,' Danny said before turning to Jo. 'Lester was a very clever at finding his way out of the things he'd done. And everyone was too scared to give evidence against you. Extortion, money laundering, arms dealing...'

'Danny,' Lester said, trying to cut him off. 'That's all in the past. I'm on the straight and narrow these days. Why do you think I moved to Cornwall? St Breward isn't a place for a life like that. And I didn't know you'd follow me here either. And more importantly, why have I come home to find you on my property?'

'Look,' Jo started. 'I'm DC Green, this is Helen Thomas, a big cat keeper from Newquay Zoo. We're here about your panther.'

'Who says I have a pan...' he started, but Danny cut him off.

'Come on, Lester. It's obvious what you keep in here. It's not a chicken coop, is it? Don't waste our time.'

'OK, OK,' he said, raising his hands. He took a deep breath. 'She's called Raven. I've had her for two years.'

Danny smirked at this.

'What?' Lester said.

'How can you keep a panther for two years without being found out?'

'It's not something I brag about. I don't want people coming around trying to get a glimpse of her, so I keep it to myself.'

'You live on your own?' Jo asked.

'Yes.'

'Where did you get her from?' Jo asked.

'I bought her from a zoological park in Devon that closed down. I also bought the enclosure from them. Paid them to move it and construct it on my property and then they brought the panther. It's a proper enclosure with snap-shut safety doors, so I'm not sure how she got out.'

Danny shook his head and said, 'You say you're on the straight and narrow, but then you go and do something like this. People like you think you're above the law.'

'Why do you say that?' Lester said, defensively.

'Dodging jail all your life and you're still keeping illegal animals,' Danny shouted.

'Whoa, Danny, hang on a minute,' Lester said, raising his voice. 'There's nothing illegal about it. I have a licence.'

This news shocked them all.

'What?' Danny said.

'I have a dangerous wild animals licence.'

'How did you manage to get a licence?' Jo asked.

'It isn't unusual. There's about forty big cats kept in the U.K.'

'Really?' Danny asked.

'Yeah. I have to have my property inspected every year and keep up with maintenance, and if the inspectors aren't sure about something, they'll bring a vet in to check on the animal's welfare, but yes, it's all legal and above board.'

'But you've been prosecuted for keeping illegal animals,' Jo said.

'Look,' Lester said, holding his arms out. 'I applied for the licence and they gave it to me. What can I say?'

Jo was sharing Danny's embarrassment. It hadn't occurred to any of them that somebody in the area could be legally keeping an animal like this. All they had to do was pick up the phone. Jo was still shocked that somebody could keep a dangerous animal like this as a pet, but she believed Lester was telling the truth.

'I didn't know there were any big cats being kept privately in Cornwall,' Helen said.

'Well, I think I'm the only private collector. But if you think about it, Devon and Cornwall has loads of animal parks of all sizes. The smaller ones are owned by individual people or families. The only difference between them and me is that they are open to the public, but as I say, up and down the country there are many private big cat enthusiasts.'

'Tell us how it got out,' Jo said.

'I found her cage door open Sunday morning. I don't have a lock on it. I didn't think I needed one, so I don't know if I've left the door open by mistake or if someone's been in my garden. They're snap-shut doors you see.'

He then walked over to the door and opened it before swinging it shut. The metal clasp locked the door and Lester had to pull the lever down to open it again.

'Why would someone open it?' Helen asked.

'Well, she's very friendly...'

'Very friendly?' Jo asked.

'Very,' he answered. 'Look, to be honest. I'm ashamed to admit it, but I had a lot to drink Saturday night and I went in with her and sat with her for a while. I then fell asleep and I can't remember leaving the enclosure. I did though because I woke up in my bed, but I suppose if I'm honest, I could've left the door open.'

'Why didn't you report her missing if you're keeping her legally?' Jo asked.

'I've been out looking for her since. It was only when a friend of mine rang me to say that people had been killed and there was footage of her on the moors that I thought I'd better report her missing. I was going to come to the station this afternoon. I've only come home to see if Raven had found her way back here.'

'So you think she has killed those people?' Jo said.

'No, not at all. She's very friendly with me, and she isn't too bad with other people.'

'What do you mean, isn't too bad?' Jo asked.

Lester seemed to think for a second before disclosing his answer. 'She gets a little jealous, that's all.'

'Jealous?'

'Yes. She sometimes growls at other people if they stand too close to me.'

'Is that normal?' Jo asked.

'I'm a member of a closed forum for big cat keepers. I've asked on there and a few other people have experienced the same thing.'

'So you have friends that go into the enclosure with her?' Danny asked.

'Occasionally, but not without me.'

'I'm going to be honest with you, Mr Hamilton,' Jo started. 'I'm going to have to check with the council that you're telling us the truth, but above all, we need to capture your pet before it kills anyone else.'

Lester raised his hands. 'No, no, hang on, DC Green. My panther hasn't killed anyone and she wouldn't. I don't know what happened to those three people, but Raven didn't do it.'

'How can you be sure?' Helen asked. 'Even a tame big cat still has the wild instincts it was born with. That's nature.'

'Even if she was out there attacking people, she wouldn't have eaten three people in that amount of time. It's not possible. And you'd have found half a body. The news said the bodies have been taken.'

'You're just protecting your pet,' Danny said.

'Believe me, I wouldn't forgive myself if anything happened, and I want her found before she does get her wild instincts back, but I think it's more likely for her to hunt for sheep or some local wildlife rather than attack people.'

'Either way, we've brought marksmen in to try to stop it,' Danny said.

Lester looked flustered. 'No, please. Let me go back out there and carry on looking. I'll find her, I promise. I know you and I have a history, Danny, but honestly, I've left that life behind. Let me try to find her.'

'Mr Hamilton,' Jo said. 'If we do nothing, and somebody gets attacked, we'll have blood on our hands. We have to try and stop her, one way or another.'

'Well can't you go out looking with a tranquiliser gun?' he said pointing to Helen. 'Surely zoos are equipped for that.'

'Possibly,' Jo answered. 'But we'll still have to have marksmen out there.'

'Right,' Lester said, taking a deep breath and trying to calm himself down. 'OK. Let your marksmen carry on looking, but let me go too. I'll give you my number and if you see her, let me come to the scene wherever she is and I'll get her on a lead, or even into a cage.'

'There is more chance of Lester catching her than anyone else,' Helen said. 'She might not run away from him like she did in the footage.'

Danny seemed to think about it for a moment. He then said, 'OK. You get back out there looking, but if you see it, you report it to us first before you try to catch it.' He then passed him a card with his number on.

'Here's my number too,' Jo said. 'Also, I'd like to see your licence before we go.'

Lester - who'd so far seemed very confident - seemed to pause for a moment before saying, 'Yeah, no problem.' He then led them back into the house.

They waited in the hall at the bottom of the stairs. After a minute or two Lester came down stairs holding a piece of paper.

Jo took it from him and saw that the document had Bodmin Metropolitan Council as the heading. A third of the way down the page was Lester's name and address, and the words Dangerous Wild Animals Licence. Jo was surprised to see that the licence was only three hundred and thirty-seven pounds, but she remembered Helen telling her in their first meeting that the cost of the licence wasn't the main criteria; it was the enclosure and the safety that was the important part of the permit.

'I'll need to take a picture?' Jo said, removing her mobile phone from her pocket.

'Certainly,' Lester said.

As they all left, Lester was the first to drive away, obviously eager to continue with his search.

Jo and Danny then thanked Helen for her time before heading back to the station.

Chapter 22

That evening, Jo and Danny made their way to the King's Head in St Breward. During the meeting that afternoon, the detectives agreed to turn Lester's missing panther over to uniform so they could concentrate on looking for the murderer. Although a panther being on the loose and three people being killed seemed as though there would be an obvious connection, they decided to believe Lester in the fact that his animal was tame, and that it wouldn't be capable of killing and eating three bodies whole in just two nights. The detectives wanted to put all their focus on the man from the CCTV footage.

DCI Collis had asked Jo and Danny to talk to some of the locals, so they decided to use an hour in the pub to find out if anybody had any useful information for them.

They sat at the table in front of the fireplace. Jo had a glass of wine; Danny had a bottle of lager. She presumed he was only going to have the one as he'd driven them there. The pub was busier than usual. Jo wondered if the news of the recent murders was having the reverse effect of keeping people indoors and bringing them all out to the pub to discuss with each other the different possibilities of what was happening.

Everyone knew about the three murders. Everyone knew about the footage of the panther that the walkers had filmed. But so far the news of a pet panther escaping had been kept under wraps. Jo wasn't sure if it was a good idea to hide this information. But DCI Collis decided to keep it from the public for one more night and give the marksmen, who were working through the night, a chance to catch the animal.

There was a sense of excitement in the pub that Jo thought was subconsciously tactless of the villagers. But she also understood that in a small village like St Breward something like this brings the locals together. She knew that people were upset at the recent events, especially after losing Lucy who was well known in the village. Jo just felt as though the locals were talking about the events with a little more excitement than they should be. They were obviously discussing whether the murderer was another serial killer like the Bodmin Butcher, or the panther from the footage.

'Who's the best person to speak to?' Danny asked.

'Dorothy is probably the best bet; the landlady.'

'Where is she?'

'I haven't seen her yet. She must be upstairs.'

'I'll go and ask,' Danny said.

He walked over to the bar and spoke to Marcus, the young barman. Jo could see him nod before going through to the back. Danny then came back to the table.

A few moments later, Dorothy came walking over to them.

Jo could see that she was holding back tears, obviously upset at losing Lucy. Jo hadn't spoken to her since Lucy had died.

Jo stood and greeted her with a hug. 'I'm sorry, Dorothy.'

Dorothy didn't speak. She just made a few sniffing sounds as she tried to keep from crying. She then sat down next to Danny, opposite Jo.

She had a tissue in her hand and wiped her eyes.

'I hope you've got some idea who did this dreadful thing,' Dorothy said.

'Unfortunately not,' Danny said. 'But we're working on it.'

'We were hoping you could give us some information about the night it happened,' Jo said.

'What kind of information?' Dorothy asked.

'We have nothing in mind,' Jo said. 'We were just wondering if anything unusual happened, or if anyone was behaving differently, or even if you had any customers in that you hadn't seen before.'

Dorothy sat back in her chair as she pondered. 'Well as I said to those other detectives, DS Killik I think her name was, I can't remember the fellow's name.'

'DC Dutson,' Danny said.

'It was Annie's birthday. The place was packed, but I don't remember seeing any new faces; apart from yours of course,' she said to Danny.

'Nobody had a disagreement with Lucy?' Jo asked.

'Not at all. How could anyone have a disagreement with Lucy? She was the most pleasant mild mannered young girl you could ever wish to meet.'

Dorothy dabbed her eyes again.

'She did seem like a lovely young girl,' Danny said.

'Oh, she was. She'd do anything for anyone. She's never given me an ounce of trouble, or back-chat. I don't ever remember her coming to work in a bad mood.' It then seemed to dawn on her that Jo's brother was her best friend. 'How's Rick doing? He was in last night. He hardly spoke. He just sat at a table with Matt, staring into his glass.'

'He's obviously a little shell-shocked,' Jo said, knowing that she was under exaggerating somewhat.

'He must be gutted.' She then turned to Danny. 'They were very close. They've been best friends all their lives.'

'I believe so,' Danny said.

Jo decided to steer the conversation back towards the investigation. 'So, you can't think of anything out of the ordinary that happened that night?'

'I can't; I'm sorry.'

'Can you remember her leaving that night?' Danny said.

'She knocked off at nine, but then she had a chat with a few people before leaving, which wasn't unusual.'

'Yes,' Danny said. 'She spoke to us. She came over to our table with Rick.'

'Did she?' Dorothy asked.

'Yes. We just spoke to Teddy before he went home, and then Rick and Lucy came over to say hello,' Jo said.

'Maybe we should speak to Teddy; just in case he saw anyone hanging around,' Danny said.

'That's a good idea. He would've walked home that way,' Jo said.

Dorothy had a look over her shoulder. 'I don't think he's in tonight; but Ben is over there.'

'We'll speak to him and see if he knows anything,' Jo said.

Dorothy got up from her seat. 'Well, let me know if you need me. I'll be behind the bar.'

Jo managed to catch Ben's eye and gestured for him to come over to them.

Ben was only eighteen years old. He had short, light brown hair and was always dressed a little untidily. He was quite well suntanned from working outside on Teddy's farm. He wasn't a confident person and Jo could see as he awkwardly walked over to their table that he was a little nervous.

'Sit yourself down, Ben,' Jo said.

He sat next to Danny in the chair where Dorothy had been sat.

'Have I done something wrong?' Ben asked.

'No, not at all,' Jo said, smiling. 'We just wanted to speak to Teddy about the night Lucy died. Do you know if he's coming in tonight?'

'I don't know. He didn't say he was. I'm sure he didn't do it.'

This made Jo laugh. 'I didn't say he did.'

'Oh,' Ben said, looking a little embarrassed.

'We just wanted to talk to him because he left the pub just before Lucy did,' Danny said.

'We're wondering if he saw anyone or anything unusual on the way home,' Jo added.

'He didn't say anything to me. Except for the scratches on the tree, but I think he showed you them, didn't he?'

'Yes. He showed me on Monday morning.'

'Did you think it was a big cat that did them?' Danny asked.

'I don't know,' Ben said. 'I haven't seen them yet. And I wouldn't know what real big cat scratch marks look like anyway.'

'What do you mean?' Jo asked.

'I don't know what they...'

Jo then interrupted. 'No. What did you mean when you said you hadn't seen them yet?'

'Well, Teddy said he'd take me to them after we'd finished for the day, but I said I wanted to go straight home. I had a bit of a headache you see? It happens when you're working in the sun all day.'

Jo was confused and didn't know what to say.

'Jo. What is it?' Danny asked.

She decided to end the conversation with Ben first.

'Err...Thanks, Ben. You can get back to your friends now.'

Ben got to his feet. He looked a little dumfounded at the sudden end to the conversation, but he accepted it and returned to his table on the opposite side of the room.

'What's wrong, Jo?' Danny asked.

'I'm trying to work out why Teddy has lied to me.'

'How has he lied?'

'He told me that Ben found the scratch marks. Ben just said that he hasn't seen them yet.'

Danny didn't answer. He seemed to disappear into a deep thought.

Jo did the same.

Chapter 23

The next morning, Jo arrived at the station. As she walked into the office, she was greeted by an atmosphere that wasn't as pleasant as it usually was. DCI Collis's office door was closed and DC Bradley Dutson was sitting at his desk and DS Rachel Killik was sitting at hers. They both turned to look when Jo walked in, but they didn't greet her as they usually did. Bradley gave a half-smile before looking back at his desk. Rachel was biting her lip.

'Is there something wrong?' Jo asked. As she finished her sentence, she heard raised voices coming from the office at the back of the room.

'DCI Collis said to send you through when you arrived. Danny's already in there,' Rachel said.

'What's happening?' Jo said.

'You'll find out. Just knock and walk in,' she said.

Jo walked over to the office. She could hear Danny's voice and she could hear DCI Collis shouting over him. She didn't really want to go in, but she'd been given her orders. She knocked on the door and opened it. She heard the tail end of Danny's sentence.

'... even Jo will agree, sir!'

Silence fell into the room as Jo gingerly entered, poking her head around the door first.

'I was told to come in, sir.'

DCI Collis was standing in front of his desk and Danny was standing in front of him, holding a piece of paper. They both looked a little red faced.

'Jo,' DCI Collis said. 'Yes. Come in and close the door.'

She stood with her back against the door as she waited to be told what was happening.

DCI Collis and DS Hughes seemed to take a moment to catch their breath before talking.

Then Danny said, 'We have to arrest Teddy.'

This sentence made Jo's stomach turn. Why would they have to arrest Teddy? Just because he lied about the scratch marks, that doesn't make him a killer. Why would Danny think this?

'What are you talking about?' she asked.

'Apparently, you and Danny stumbled across a lie he's told you and now Danny thinks that's a reason to think he's a serial killer.'

'Danny,' Jo said. 'That's ridiculous. Teddy wouldn't hurt anyone.'

'That's not what this says,' Danny said, waving the piece of paper in the air.

'What's that,' she asked.

'Evidence of him having a bad temper and being violent against women.'

'Danny,' DCI Collis shouted. 'That's not true.'

'There has to be some truth to it. There's no smoke without fire.'

'What is it?' Jo asked.

'Look,' Danny said. He stood up and held his hands out as if to calm the situation down. 'Sunday night a young couple were killed on the moors; the next night Lucy was killed. Teddy left the pub just before she did. He's going after women. The fact that the lad was killed was incidental. He lied about the scratch marks to make you think it was a panther and when I checked him out on the police computer I found out two very important facts about your friend Teddy.'

'What?' Jo asked.

'Fifteen years ago, he was arrested for beating up a woman in the pub.'

'No way,' Jo said. 'He wouldn't do that.'

'Well, the charges were dropped, but there's a statement saying that it happened.'

Jo couldn't believe it.

'Secondly, he was the one who found the campers.'

'Was he?' Jo asked.

'Yes. He called it in.'

Jo was shocked at this revelation. She didn't know what to say. She didn't know what to think. She'd known Teddy all her life and she'd never heard about him assaulting a woman before. And why didn't he tell her that he was the one who found the murder scene? Jo didn't know what to think.

DCI Collis then presented his argument. 'Teddy was arrested and charged, but that was fifteen years ago. If he had a violent temper or an urge to kill, do you not think we'd have seen a sign of this behaviour before now? You're talking about one incident and nothing else since. Why he lied about the scratches, I don't know. As for him finding the campers, that's just incidental. He's a farmer that starts early and he was probably on his way somewhere when he saw the scene.'

Danny stood a little closer to his boss. 'Sir,' he said, softly. 'If you didn't know Teddy, you'd be sending us to arrest him based on this evidence.'

'But I do know Teddy. And you going to arrest him is unnecessary stress for him and it will waste our valuable time. And don't forget the fact that we now know there's a panther on the loose. We know that for a fact.'

Jo then said, 'I think you're right, Danny. If we didn't know Teddy, we would see a connection and act upon it. But I'm with DCI Collis on this. I know Teddy and I know he wouldn't do this.'

'I'm impartial. I don't know him. So I can see the facts with more clarity than you can. I say we arrest him.'

'I also don't think that was him in the footage,' DCI Collis said.

'We couldn't see him properly,' Danny said. 'And we don't know for sure that that person is involved in Lucy's death. It looked suspicious, but we're going off five seconds of footage.'

Jo then decided to meet him in the middle. 'Why don't we go and see him and talk to him? We need to find out why he lied and take it from there.'

'And give him chance to think it all over before we arrest him? No. We need to shock him and catch him off guard.'

'But if you're right and he is the killer, then he'll already have an answer ready for you,' Jo said.

Danny paused for a moment before saying, 'OK.'

Jo saw it as a compromise. She really didn't think that Teddy was capable of murder. But she was starting to question his character now she knew he'd lied about the scratches, apparently assaulted a woman and withheld information about calling in the murder scene. Jo was struggling to understand it all.

Chapter 24

Teddy answered the door of his farmhouse in his usual jovial manner. Most people would be nervous to see two detectives standing at their front door, but to Teddy, this was just a visit from friends. He brought Jo and Danny through to the kitchen and began to make a pot of tea without even asking them if they'd like a cup. But that was just Teddy being Teddy. Whether you had the time or not he would always be a good host, and usually try to keep you there and talking to him for as long as possible.

The large old-fashioned kitchen had oak cupboards and dark wooden worktops. It was a little untidy with a few cups and plates scattered across the surfaces, but it wasn't as untidy as Jo had seen it on previous occasions. The floor was a black and white ceramic tile and there was a wooden kitchen table with four chairs in the centre of the room.

Jo and Danny sat at the table.

'Are you not wondering why we're here?' Jo asked.

'No. Ben said that you were interviewing people in the pub last night. I just presumed it was my turn.' He then stopped and turned around. 'Why, am I wrong?'

'No, not at all,' Danny said. 'We have to speak to everyone who was in the pub the night that Lucy was killed.'

Teddy turned back to pour the hot water into the teapot. 'Oh, terrible news that. Lucy was a lovely girl. She didn't deserve that. No one does, but she was such a nice, gentle person.'

'She was,' Jo said.

After preparing the teapot, he brought it to the table with three cups and a small sugar bowl and a glass bottle of milk. He poured the tea and then sat at the table opposite them.

'Right, what do you wish to know?'

'Tell me about Monday morning,' Danny said.

This seemed to surprise Teddy. He obviously thought that the questions would be in relation to Monday night.

'Monday morning?'

'Yes. You stopped Jo when she was out jogging.'

'Oh, yes. That was when I showed her the scratch marks. Yes I saw her at about seven in the morning. She wasn't happy about me taking her to see them on my quad bike. But it was quicker so she gave in, after a brief disagreement.'

Jo smiled.

'How did you find them?' Danny asked.

He seemed to think for a moment. 'Ben found them earlier that morning.'

'OK,' Danny said. This confirmed to Danny that Teddy was still lying about that so he moved on. 'What about that night?'

'In what way?'

'You left the pub just before Lucy did.'

'Did I?'

Jo thought he was starting to seem a little flustered.

'Yes. You came over to speak to Jo. That's when I first met you. You had your dog with you. You came over for a chat and then left the pub. About five minutes later, Lucy left the pub too.'

'What are you getting at?' Teddy seemed a little offended.

Jo jumped in. 'Did you see anything unusual or anybody hanging around?'

Teddy thought for a moment. 'No. I did walk home the way I normally go which takes me past Lucy's house. But I never saw anything unusual.'

'Monday morning after you showed Jo the scratches on the tree, what happened after that?' Danny asked.

Jo knew that Danny was trying to catch Teddy off guard by switching from morning to night and then back again.

'Nothing unusual,' Teddy said, while becoming a little red faced.

Jo didn't think this was a sign of guilt; she thought it was just him starting to worry about why they were actually there.

Danny sat back in his chair and looked as though he was getting slightly annoyed.

'Teddy, something did happen, didn't it?' he said.

Teddy looked even more flustered. 'I don't know what you mean.'

Danny raised his voice a little more. 'You went for a drive and stumbled across a murder scene. Do you not think that was worth mentioning?'

'I... I don't know...'

'Did you find the murder scene or not?'

'Yes...but,' Teddy began.

Danny cut him off. 'Were you hoping we wouldn't find out?'

'No... I just...'

'You lied about the scratches and amazingly you were the one that found the murder scene and you left the pub just before Lucy Webster.'

'No. I just thought...'

Danny stood up. 'Teddy Hosken, I'm arresting you on suspicion of the murder of Lucy Webster...'

As Danny read Teddy his rights, Jo was astounded at how they had gone from a calm discussion to Danny arresting him so quickly. Jo wasn't comfortable at how quickly Danny changed gear without giving Teddy the chance to explain himself. But she couldn't do anything. She couldn't argue in front of Teddy that she thought that he was being overzealous. She gestured to Teddy with raised hands and wide eyes, hoping he took the gesture as 'don't worry, it'll be OK.'

They were walking him to the car in handcuffs when Vicky came around the corner of the house.

'Grandad,' she said. 'What's going on?'

Jo walked over to her as Danny closed the car door.

'It's OK, Vicky. He's just helping us with our enquiries.'

'Have you arrested him?'

'Unfortunately, yes,' she said, talking at a level that she hoped Danny couldn't hear. 'But it's only because of circumstantial evidence. It's just procedure. We both know you're Grandad wouldn't do anything wrong.'

'What should I do?' Vicky asked.

'Just carry on with your day. He'll be home in a couple of hours. Don't worry.'

As they drove away, Jo could see by the expression on Vicky's face that she wasn't going to do anything but worry. Jo hoped they could get him home as quickly as possible.

Within the hour, Teddy was in the interview room with Danny and DS Killik. DCI Collis said that he and Jo should stay out of the room with them both being friends of Teddy's. Jo hoped that Rachel would be more impartial than she thought Danny was. She was still shocked at his demeanour during the discussion. It was as though he'd already decided to arrest him before hearing his side of things. Jo decided to knock on DCI Collis's door.

'Come in,' he shouted.

Jo walked in. 'Have you got a minute, sir?'

'Yes, Jo. Come in and take a seat.'

She closed the door and sat down opposite him.

DCI Collis gave a sympathetic smile. 'I'm guessing you're not happy at Teddy being brought in?'

'I'm not.'

'I've told DS Killik that I don't think he would do anything like this. I'm sure she'll stop DS Hughes from getting carried away.'

'I don't know what was wrong with him. One minute we're

just talking quietly, the next minute he stands up and reads him his rights. He didn't ask him enough questions to assume he'd be guilty. He didn't even challenge the lie about the scratches, and he didn't listen to his reason for not telling us that he called in the murder scene. He just shouted the facts as he saw them and then read him his rights.'

'He can be a little hot-headed sometimes, but that's what makes him a good detective. He doesn't always get it right, but he doesn't shy away from anything and he definitely doesn't leave any stone unturned. I really don't think that Teddy could do anything like this, and Danny will realise this during the interview. I'm starting to think that we're wasting our time looking for a person, to be honest.'

'Really?'

'Well try to look at it logically, Jo. Sunday, a panther escapes, Sunday night two people are killed and Monday night another person is killed. It's very coincidental if not.'

'It would be a very strange coincidence.'

'It would.'

'And what about this record of Teddy's?' Jo asked.

DCI Collis smiled softly. 'I did a little digging about that.' He reached into his desk drawer and removed a file. 'I've looked through the report. It was an incident with a tourist. She said that Teddy slapped her across the face and sent her flying across the room. He was charged with aggravated assault, but the charges were dropped a few days later.'

'Knowing Teddy, there has to be more to it than that.'

'I agree. Rachel and Danny will be asking him about it in the interview.'

'Something else I don't understand, sir.'

'What's that?'

'How long have you been at this police station?'

'Twenty-seven years.'

'And how long have you known Teddy?'

'Since we were kids.'

'Well, why didn't you know about this assault?'

DCI Collis smiled. 'There's a good reason for that.' He passed the document over the desk to Jo. 'Recognise that signature?'

She did. 'That's my dad's signature.'

'It is. Your dad, Teddy and myself were very good friends. He obviously withheld this information until he felt it necessary to tell me. The charges were dropped and that was that. He just filed it and spared Teddy the embarrassment.'

Jo smiled. 'You can't usually keep secrets in a small village.'

'Well I don't live in St Breward. I would go through periods of joining your dad and Teddy for a drink at weekends and then three or four weeks would pass without me going there. Amazingly, nobody mentioned this to me or in front of me.'

'If she dropped the charges then there's nothing to report, I suppose.'

DCI Collis smiled. 'It doesn't surprise me that your dad kept this from me to spare Teddy's humiliation. He was a good man.'

Jo smiled. She knew he was a good man, but it was still nice to hear other people say it. Especially DCI Collis who probably knew him better than anyone.

Jo thanked him and left the room.

Half an hour later Danny and Rachel came into the main office. Jo was sitting at her desk and DCI Collis came through the door of his office as he heard them enter. Danny looked a little disappointed which made Jo feel better. She hoped they were about to release Teddy and get on with their investigation. They all sat down at the large desk in the centre of the room.

'What's happening?' Jo asked.

'We're going to release him,' Rachel said.

'For now,' Danny added.

Rachel continued. 'The assault on the woman in the pub all those years ago wasn't as bad as we first thought. He said that this woman was on holiday, and she was with a few of her friends. She was drunk and staggering around the bar and she knocked Teddy's drink over. He told her off, she shouted back, it turned into an argument and she slapped him. Teddy said that he wasn't expecting it and in a reflex, he slapped her back. This sent her flying into a table and Teddy was arrested. When sober, she dropped the charges. He was very embarrassed about it, and he knows it was wrong, but it all seems plausible and I suppose, understandable. He's obviously not a violent man because we've never had any complaints about him since. It was just an impulsive reaction.'

'The scratch marks?' Jo asked.

'He's very embarrassed about this too,' Rachel said. 'He said that a few weeks ago he saw a panther on the moors and ran into the pub shouting about it.'

'That's true; I was there,' Jo said.

'Well, apparently everyone laughed at him and he's been the subject of ridicule ever since. So he carved the scratches himself to try to deflect the mocking. He's very sorry and very upset.'

'Silly old fool,' DCI Collis muttered.

'The only bit of information that we've found useful to our investigation, is that he saw Lester Hamilton on his way home from the pub the night Lucy Webster was killed.'

'Where?' Jo asked.

'He was walking past the post office where the remains were found. He said he seemed to be in hurry.'

'Why didn't he tell us that before?' DCI Collis asked.

'He said he thought nothing of it. He remembered during the interview. He didn't know his name and he didn't speak to him, but he said the bloke from London who owns Carston

Farmhouse in St Breward. That's obviously Lester; and don't forget, he doesn't know about Lester owning a panther as of yet.'

'Does that make Lester a suspect?' Jo asked.

'Well we know why he was out and about that night, so I don't think so at this stage. But it might still be worth questioning him, after all, it puts him in the vicinity of the crime,' Rachel said.

Danny was unusually quiet during this discussion.

Jo thought that he seemed to be sulking a little at the outcome; he certainly looked irritated.

'Why didn't Teddy tell me that he found the crime scene?' Jo asked.

Rachel smiled. 'He presumed you knew.'

'Really?'

'Yes. He just thought that it would've been spoken about. He didn't tell you because he thought you'd have known already.'

DCI Collis smiled and shook his head. 'Right, well arrange for him to be taken home. Meet back here in twenty minutes and we'll discuss the case again; see what we can come up with.'

'Yes, sir.'

Twenty minutes later, Jo, DS Killik, DC Dutson and DS Hughes were all sat around the centre table waiting for DCI Collis to come from his office to start the meeting. Jo could hear him talking on the phone although the door was closed so she couldn't hear what he was saying; only the muffled sound of his voice.

After a few minutes, he came through the door and sat at the desk in his usual seat. 'I've just been on the phone to HM Prison, Exeter.'

'Really?' Danny asked.

Jo wondered what this could be about. It had to be relevant for DCI Collis to discuss the phone call with them.

'Yes. It seems Vladek Boniek has slashed his wrists.'

Jo didn't quite know how she felt about this. After all, he was a murderer. Is it such a bad thing to rid the world of such a horrible person?

'Is he dead?' Rachel asked.

'No,' DCI Collis said. 'He's in hospital and it seems he's going to be OK.'

There was a confused silence in the room before Bradley finally spoke. 'Why are they ringing you then?'

DCI Collis looked at Jo. 'Because Boniek wants to see DC Green.'

'Why on earth does he want to see Jo?' Rachel said. 'And why are we even entertaining the idea?'

'It was the head warden, Robert Harvey that I spoke to. He said that Boniek hasn't eaten or spoken - except for asking to see Jo - since being sentenced. He wondered if we would oblige and send DC Green just for the sake of trying to find out what's going on with him.'

'We've got better things to do than to send one of our detectives to visit the Bodmin Butcher in hospital,' Danny said, angrily. 'Does he want her to take a bunch of grapes as well?'

'Danny,' DCI Collis said. 'Look, Boniek is a high profile prisoner and Robert's job is a difficult one. The prison service and the police department have always worked together whenever possible. I'm not going to insist upon it, Jo, but I want you to think about. OK?'

'Yes, sir.'

Chapter 25

Jo wanted to talk to Teddy rather than Vladek Boniek. She knew Teddy would be embarrassed and rightly so. How could she be anything other than annoyed with him? Lying to the police was bad enough, but wasting her valuable time on her first morning as a detective, she couldn't help but think of him as anything other than totally selfish.

Jo thought Teddy should consider himself lucky that he wasn't charged with wasting police time. He's had an obsession with the Beast of Bodmin and has for many years. It was something that Jo had heard him talk about upon many occasions, especially after a couple of pints in the King's Head. She wondered if Teddy had seen Lester's panther a few weeks earlier and maybe this wasn't the first time it had escaped. This was something Jo wanted to ask Lester.

After the meeting, she rang Lester and arranged for her and Danny to meet him. He'd been out looking on the moors again, but was heading home to eat and get changed, and also check that Raven hadn't found her way back home.

He was parked at the entrance of the road that led to his house. Danny pulled the car up behind his and they got out.

Lester came over to greet them. 'DC Green; DS Hughes.'

'I take it you haven't seen it anywhere?' Jo said.

'I haven't, unfortunately. But I'm not giving up. I want her back home.'

'You know the police marksmen are still out there?' Jo asked.

'I guessed they would be. But I'm hoping I can find her before they do.'

'How are you planning on bringing it home if you see it?' Danny asked.

'I have a choke chain in my pocket,' he said, rattling it with his hand. 'I'm pretty sure she'll let me walk her home if I find her.'

'I see.'

'Do you know who Teddy Hosken is?' Jo asked.

Lester leaned back on his car as he thought. 'No. Is he anything to do with Hosken's farm?'

'Yes. He owns it,' Jo said.

'I've seen an old chap working on the farm. He has longish grey hair.'

'That's him,' Jo said. 'Monday night, the night that Lucy Webster was killed, did you see him?'

Lester went into deep thought again. His eyes then suddenly widened as he remembered. 'As a matter of fact, yes I did. I saw him walking his dog past the shop. Why do you ask?'

'We're just piecing things together,' Danny said. 'He said he saw you walking as if you were in a hurry.'

'I was. I was out trying to find Raven.'

'He didn't seem to behave unusual in any way?' Danny asked.

'No. Why? Is he a suspect?'

'Not at all,' Danny said. 'As I said; we're just trying to piece things together.'

Jo didn't see any nervousness in Lester for being placed at the scene of Lucy's death. He could've lied about where he saw Teddy rather than mention the shop where she was as good as found. Jo didn't get the feeling he was hiding anything, but she had to still think of him as a person of interest to the case.

'I want to ask you a question,' Jo said. 'There was a sighting of a black panther on moors a few weeks back. Is this the first time Raven has escaped?'

Lester nodded. 'She's never got out before. I promise you that and I've no reason to lie about that, have I? I'm in enough trouble as it is.'

'OK.'

'I wouldn't waste too much time on that sighting. People have been going on about the Beast of Bodmin for years. It'll just be some crackpot trying to get on telly.'

Jo and Danny looked at each other, not quite smiling. Lester didn't know Jo was talking about Teddy and she felt no need to tell him.

They said their goodbyes and let him carry on with his search.

'Danny,' Jo said. 'I'm going to go to the hospital.'

Danny rolled his eyes and looked angry. 'Why? What could you possibly gain from going?'

'I don't know. But like DCI Collis said, if the governor of the prison thinks it'll help him do his job, then I should go.'

'What could he want with you? He's just going to spin you a yarn of how he didn't do it when we know he did. We have DNA evidence and a connection to all the victims.'

'He might not want that'

'What else could he want?'

Jo thought for a moment but couldn't answer the question.

Danny shook his head. 'If you want to go, then go. You waste the afternoon talking to a convicted murderer.'

'I'm sorry, Danny. I just think that if DCI Collis thinks I should go, then I should do as he asks.'

Danny then seemed to calm down a little. He obviously thought it was pointless but he couldn't go against DCI Collis.

'I'll drop you off at the station; you drive to Exeter and I'll go out to the search party on the moors.'

'OK, thanks.'

Chapter 26

Teddy, like every other farmer in Cornwall, had been hoping for rain for the last three weeks, and it was beginning to look as though he was about to get his wish. But as a man who'd lived through as much as he had, he felt his state of mind fall into a depression almost as quickly as the grey clouds formed over St Breward.

He never used to be so sensitive, but since his wife and daughter were killed in a road accident ten years earlier, he felt his moods shift as swiftly as the weather. He'd always put a brave face on things and tried his best to smile on the outside even if he wasn't smiling on the inside. But the last few days he'd felt worse than he had for a long time. He was trying his best to recover from the ridicule he'd received when he'd spotted the beast lurking on the moors. But losing Sam, his beloved dog and then getting caught out on the ridiculous lie about the scratches, he could feel himself sliding into a depression; a depression he would normally battle by opening a nice bottle of single malt. He was also upset that he had to be reminded of the spontaneous slap he'd thrust upon that drunken woman all those years ago, even though in hindsight, she only got what she deserved; not that he would ever hit a lady under normal circumstances. He remembered the instant shock at his own actions, and how ashamed he was. It was all coming back to him. He was eternally grateful to Jo's dad for keeping it a secret from Brian Collis, but now it was out in the open, he felt as though he had to make up for his behaviour.

He was so angry with himself for creating the scratch marks, partly for not covering his lie properly, but mostly for lying in the first place. Once the footage of the panther came to light, this would've made the locals believe that he had seen it anyway. The whole stupid lie needn't have been created. Had he been more patient, things would be very different now, and Jo and Brian wouldn't know of his secret.

Even though he could feel the clouds of depression creep into his mind, he wasn't going to let them win. He decided that he had two choices. One, he could go to the pub and drink until the clouds lifted, or two, he could go out onto the moors and find the panther, redeeming himself to Jo and his old friend Brian. He decided on the latter. He also hoped to come across Sam during the search. He knew that the more time went by the less likely it was that Sam would turn up. He'd never gone missing before and he didn't hold much hope for his safe return, especially with a wild cat on the loose.

He made some sandwiches and a flask of tea. He then dressed himself in his all-weather overalls. The only other thing he needed was his shotgun. Teddy knew that Jo wouldn't be happy at him taking his gun, but she would be more than happy if he caught the panther. He thought it was worth the risk.

Droplets of rain fell from the now grey sky as he walked down his gravel path towards the moors.

'Grandad!' he heard Vicky shout.

She came running from the house dressed in her jeans and denim shirt. Vicky, now eighteen was looking more and more like her mother. She had the same dark curly long hair, although unlike her mother, she never put much effort into styling it, and she very rarely wore makeup. But Teddy could see the likeness whenever they had a disagreement. They both had the same look in their eyes when they were annoyed.

'Where are you going?'

He turned away and carried on walking. 'I'm going to catch the panther.'

'Grandad, wait,' Vicky shouted. She ran after him and stood in front of him. 'Why?'

'Because I've done a stupid thing and I want to make up for it.'

'What stupid thing?'

'It doesn't matter,' he said, trying to get on his way and continuing down the path.

'Wait,' she said, jumping in front of him again.

Teddy sighed.

'If you're going looking for a panther, then I'm coming with you.'

'Don't be silly,' he said.

'I'm not being silly. If you're going, then I'm going too. I'm not letting you go out there on your own with a dangerous animal on the loose.'

Teddy was happy to go on his own; in fact, he would rather go on his own so he could carry on sulking and continue to be annoyed with himself. He didn't really feel like talking to anyone at that moment. But he knew how stubborn Vicky could be; he knew she wouldn't take no for an answer.

'OK,' he said. 'Go and get the sheep hook from the porch and get your waterproofs on.'

'Two minutes,' she said running back towards the house.

Chapter 27

It was three-thirty in the afternoon by the time Jo pulled up at Exeter hospital. The rain had started to fall by the time she'd arrived, so she ran to the front entrance from the car park. She had seen two police cars parked up outside of the hospital and wondered if they were there as extra security for the patient that would attract attention, and possibly some form of vigilante attack if news broke out of him being there. Exeter was an hour's drive from Bodmin, but there was still a chance that once the news got out, somebody known to the victims would make their way to the hospital to try and get close to him.

The large glass revolving door was full of people, some making their way in and others making their way out. After walking inside and showing her badge to one of the two women sat behind the reception desk, she was told to make her way to F ward.

She walked through the endless corridors and several sets of automatic doors. She realised that she hadn't had any lunch as she walked past the canteen. The smell of freshly ground coffee made her crave a cup, but she wanted to get the visit over with first.

As she reached the ward, there was another reception desk. After asking the woman behind the desk where Boniek was - who was reluctant until Jo showed her badge - she then pointed her in the direction of another corridor to find his room.

Jo knew she was in the right place when she turned the last corner and saw two prison officers standing outside of his room. She showed them her badge and they stood aside without speaking.

She felt a little anxious at meeting Boniek like this. She wasn't nervous, but she was wary of what he had to tell her. She was starting to think that maybe Danny was right and she shouldn't have come. But she'd already travelled this far, so she couldn't turn back now. She also remembered DCI Collis say that the prison service and police force try to work together whenever needed and so she wanted to help, even if she didn't really care about the welfare of this monster.

She opened the door. As she walked in, she saw Boniek laid asleep with his head facing towards the window. The room was very small and almost empty. There was a small cupboard in the corner for his belongings, and a door that Jo presumed led to a bathroom.

He looked even paler than she remembered and he was unshaven. He had bandages around both his wrists as he laid with his hands clasped together, fingers interlocked. There was a chair next to his bed. She went and sat down gently. She was closer to his feet than his head, and she was happy about that. He didn't look like he was in any state to cause her any problems, but this wasn't a family visit. This wasn't a visit to see how he was. This was a requested visit from a convicted serial killer and she didn't want to forget that.

She wanted to get the visit over with before the press found out about it. She imagined the newspaper headline as *Bodmin Butcher slashes wrists. Detective brings him grapes.*

Danny's comment about taking him grapes had obviously stayed in her head. This man killed four innocent people and Jo was visiting him in hospital. Maybe Danny was right, she thought. Maybe she should have said no.

His eyes briefly opened and closed. Then, seconds later, they opened wide and he quickly sat up in his bed.

'Miss Green,' he said, huskily. He then coughed and wiped his eyes. 'Thank you. I was hoping you would come.'

His broken English and mild manner wasn't endearing to

Jo. As polite as he was, he was still a murderer, a murderer who ended the lives of four innocent women.

He reached for his plastic cup of water that was resting on the table next to him. He took a sip and put it down before sitting up straight and adjusting his pillows.

Jo didn't speak first. She wanted to ask him why he wanted to see her so badly, but she didn't. She just sat there in silence and waited for him to come around from his sleep.

He cleared his throat again before saying, 'I ask to see you because you arrest me. I want to ask you why you thought I was killer?'

Danny was right, Jo thought.

She didn't know where to start. She thought back to when she first thought it might've been Boniek. It was the night she sat and observed the chess club meeting.

'I came to the chess club,' she said.

'And why you think it was me?' he asked.

'Look, Mr Boniek, I don't see what you've got to gain by going over it all again. You had your chance in court.'

This was true, but Boniek barely spoke in court. He just sat there looking guilty and answering the lawyer's questions with as fewer words as possible.

'As far as I see, I'm in prison because of my tidy house.'

'I'm sorry but I'm not going to waste any more time going over the case. The evidence was there. We proved you guilty.'

'I'm not guilty. I never kill anyone,' he said, raising his voice a little.

Jo shook her head as she sat back in her chair.

'Look, Miss Forbes and I was at the start of relationship. This is why my finger prints was there. Miss Newham I didn't really know. Miss Watts I'd spoken to in the pub and Miss Byrne from petrol station, I never seen her before. I don't even have a car.'

'A handkerchief with blood was found in your living room.'

'Yes, but think about that for moment, why you first think it was me?'

'What do you mean?' Jo asked.

'What made you first think the killer was me?'

'After I saw your OCDs at the chess club. And when I saw your house...'

'Exactly, Miss Green. My OCD is for cleaning. I don't like mess. It distracts me. So why would I put handkerchief down side of my chair?'

'I don't know. That was your lawyer's argument in court but it was your only defence. The jury obviously thought it was enough to convict you, that, plus your fingerprints at Carol Forbes's house.'

'I said before, we was beginning of relationship. I'd been to her house twice. I stand in her kitchen as she made a drink.'

Jo wasn't convinced. She looked at the time on her phone and wanted the discussion over with.

'Look, Miss Green. I am forty years old. When I get out from prison, I will be seventy. I can't stay in prison that long. I'm innocent. I tell you the truth.'

'What about the confession?' Jo asked.

'Excuse me?' he asked.

'You confessed to the murder when you were first interviewed.'

He took a deep breath before looking her in the eye. 'Have you ever lived in another country?'

'I spent a year travelling Europe.'

'On your own?'

'No. With my boyfriend.'

'Well, living on your own in a strange country is scary. Can you imagine being arrested for something you don't do? The police told me it is better to admit crime. I panicked. I say I did it. Then next day I regretted saying so. I was scared.'

Jo sat and thought for a moment. She could feel herself being drawn into seeing his side of the story. But she wasn't convinced he was telling the truth. She decided to address the problems he was causing in prison as to at least try to help the prison warden.

'Why haven't you been eating?'

'I can't face food. I also want to be heard. My not eating is a… err…protest. I want everyone to know of my innocence. I also want to stay away from other prisoners. They swear at me and threaten to be violent to me.'

Jo sat in silence for another moment. She didn't see a reason to stay any longer so she got up from the chair.

Boniek's eyes met hers. She could tell he obviously didn't want her to leave yet. The strange thing was, despite the terrible crimes of which he'd been convicted, she couldn't help to some extent liking him.

'I don't know what you want from me,' Jo said.

'I'm innocent. You arrested me. I thought if I can prove to you I didn't do the murders, you could help me.'

'I need to go.'

'No. Please, Miss Green.'

'Sorry,' Jo said.

She then left the room at a brisk pace and never turned around. She heard him shout her name again, but she didn't look back.

Chapter 28

Bodmin Moor felt very different to Teddy now the weather had changed. On a clear day he loved being able to see for miles across the majestic beauty that he felt very lucky to call home. Today, he couldn't see further than a hundred yards or so as the rain fell hard. The rattling noise of his hood was almost deafening. They had been walking for an hour and not yet seen anything so Vicky suggested they head over to the woods, presuming that the animal might be sheltering from the torrential rain.

Teddy hadn't yet spoken to Jo since he'd admitted lying to her in the interview. He wanted to do some good to make up for it before he had to face her. He knew she'd forgive him, but that didn't make him feel any better. She will probably say all the right things to make him feel a little less embarrassed once he'd apologised to her, but he didn't want that. What he wanted was to catch the panther and prove that he was right all along, and make up for his mistakes.

The Beast of Bodmin was something that he'd believed in for a long time. He shouldn't have made the scratches on the tree and he regretted that, but he was sick of being treated as a joke. The Beast of Bodmin is now very real and he wanted to catch it, not only to prove he was right, but also try to take away the stigma of him being thought of as the local idiot. He knew that he'd brought this on himself with his self-deprecating sense of humour. But although he enjoyed a laugh, he didn't enjoy being laughed at, and felt that this was something he could change if he caught the panther.

He and Vicky both walked at a brisk pace towards the woods. They both had their hoods up, Teddy was carrying the shotgun, broken over his arm, and Vicky walked with the wooden sheep hook. She carried it at her side, using it as a walking pole.

As they reached the mouth of the woods, Teddy stopped and had a good look around the moors behind them. He couldn't see very far, but he wanted to make sure that the panther wasn't behind them before they headed into the undergrowth.

The wet and misty scene behind them showed no signs of life. The grey sky had small patches of blue, but he didn't think the rain was going to stop, not for a few hours at least.

They entered the woods. The trees sheltered them from the rain enough for Teddy to remove his hood. The noise of the rain on the leaves and branches was a little quieter than the rattle of his hood. He felt as though he'd be more aware of any unusual noises in the woodland without his hood obstructing his hearing.

They made their way along the track. The flattened grass had created a dirt track like pathway that was reasonably level but scattered with shallow puddles and footprints. Teddy saw boot prints in the mud and he wondered if the marksmen had already walked this way. He wanted to get to the panther before they did. He had to make amends for his mistakes.

The trees reached over the dirt track creating a tunnel of green and brown. The water still made its way through the leaves, but it was definitely easier going for them than it was out on the moors.

'Shouldn't we walk slowly?' Vicky asked, removing her hood. 'We might walk past it if we go too fast.'

'Yes,' Teddy whispered. 'But talk quietly as well. We don't want to scare it away.'

They walked slowly, occasionally crouching down and looking under the bushes.

'Part of me is hoping that we don't find it,' Vicky said.

'Not me. I'm not going home without it.'

'Why is it so important to you?'

'I just want to help; that's all; and I'm hoping we can find Sam before the beast does.'

He'd told Vicky of what he saw the night of the sighting, but he never discussed the mocking he'd received in the pub afterwards. He hoped that nobody else had either. He definitely wasn't going to tell her about the scratches unless he had to, but he didn't think that something like that would stay a secret for long in a village like St Breward. Like Jo, he knew Vicky would forgive him and make him feel better about it, but he'd rather not have the discussion at all.

Vicky was as upset at losing Sam as Teddy was. She cried when he'd told her about his disappearance. He'd considered telling her that he'd found him dead on the farm somewhere and that he'd died naturally and not in the horrific way that they were both thinking. He thought that might be easier for her to deal with. But he'd told enough lies of late, so he decided to leave it for now.

'Do you not think we should leave it to the police?' Vicky asked.

'If you want to go home, you can, but I'm staying until I catch it.'

'Don't bite my head off.'

He realised he was being a little grumpy. 'Sorry, love. I'm just determined to get it, one way or another. And I'd have preferred it if you hadn't have come if I'm honest.'

'Well I wasn't going to let you come on your own.'

'I know. You made that very clear,' he said.

Another hour went by and they still hadn't seen anything. They continued to walk in silence, constantly checking from side to side, hoping to see the panther.

The rain had eased off a little. It was just lightly spitting by now and the sky had turned a little brighter. As they walked through the woods, Teddy suddenly grabbed Vicky by the arm and pulled her into the bushes.

'What is it?' she whispered.

'Keep quiet,' he whispered back.

Ahead of them on the track, he'd spotted two policemen. The track headed into two different directions. The policemen were both holding rifles and were dressed in black, but both had baseball caps with the black and white chequered pattern along the sides. They came from the left track and stood at the junction in the woodland, discussing which way to go, Teddy thought.

They were at least fifty yards away from them. They obviously hadn't seen Teddy and Vicky scurry from the track and into the bushes.

'Why are we hiding from the police?' Vicky asked.

'Because they'll take my gun off me. What chance have we got of catching the panther if I lose my gun?'

They waited.

After a few moments, the two marksmen headed off down the track leading to the right.

Teddy and Vicky stood up and came back onto the track.

'Well, what do we do now?' Vicky asked.

'We keep going.'

'Yes, but they've come from the way we were going and now they've headed to the right. It's pointless going where they've already checked and even more pointless walking behind them.'

'I see what you mean.'

'Well, why don't we find a dry spot to have a rest and a cup of tea? After that, we can set off again. Then we've got more chance of spotting it on the track the police have just come down once some time has passed by.'

'Good idea. What about over there?' Teddy pointed to a scattering of rocks that were sheltered by trees about ten yards along the track.

'Yes. That'll do,' Vicky said.

They walked over to the area and sat down on one of the large flat rocks and had a drink from the flask.

Ten minutes later, they returned the flask to Teddy's backpack and headed off down the track. The trees closed in a little more along this part of the woods. They had to bend down to walk under some of the overhanging branches. The rain had stopped altogether by now and the sun was intermittently revealing itself as the grey clouds moved, which Teddy thought would make it easier to find the animal.

'I'm glad the rain has...' before he could finish his sentence, there was a loud rustling of leaves ahead of them before a large black creature landed on the track about twenty feet in front of them.

The animal shook itself like a dog would do after running out of a pond. Flurries of water were flung from its thick black coat as it shook its magnificent body. The large muscular creature stood majestically in the broken sunlight that was making its way through the thick summer foliage of the forest. The panther took a step towards them but then stopped. It licked its lips before yawning and revealing to Teddy and Vicky the huge teeth that were the whitest of white in contrast to its dark black fur. Its emerald-green eyes looked straight at them as it took another couple of steps closer.

Teddy was shaking as he held his shotgun, still in the broken and therefore harmless position. He couldn't move. He wished he'd closed the gun so it was ready to fire. He felt Vicky's nails dig into his left arm.

'Grandad,' she whispered through clenched teeth.

He never spoke.

'Grandad, shoot.'

He tried to answer but no words came from his lips, even

though he felt them move. His legs felt weak and his chest hurt as he held his breath.

The panther was now about ten feet from them. Teddy looked down at his trembling hands. He tried to gently close the gun, but it wouldn't click shut. As the animal got to within six feet, he pulled the gun open wider before slamming it shut. As the gun closed, the noise scared the panther and it bolted off into the forest. He took aim and quickly fired the gun before it reached the undergrowth, but the shot went into the bushes and he presumed not into the panther. He'd missed his chance.

They both breathed a sigh of relief.

Teddy then quickly shook off the fear and started after the animal. 'Come on; we'll lose it.'

Vicky quickly followed.

They left the track and made their way into the trees. The ground was wet, muddy and uneven as they hopped from place to place, trying not to fall over the branches and roots.

Teddy tried his best to look for the panther as well as quickly checking for obstacles in his path. He could hear Vicky running behind him but he never took his eyes off the woodland in front, hoping to get another glimpse of the beast. His stomach turned with fear, but he fought past it, trying hard to think more about the mistakes of the last few days, rather than his own safety.

After covering another fifty yards or so, his lack of fitness got the better of him and he had to stop.

Vicky caught up to him and leaned on his shoulder. He looked around to see if the beast was anywhere to be seen, including behind them, but nothing.

'What...what should we do?' Vicky asked.

'I don't know,' Teddy answered. 'We shouldn't presume it's gone in a straight line.'

'It's also a lot faster than us. We're not going to catch up with it while running. Maybe we should walk slowly and hope we can surprise it.'

After resting for a brief moment and catching their breath, they decided to carry on walking in the direction the animal had headed. A few minutes later they were back on a dirt track. They continued to walk, slowly and quietly.

Teddy was ever the more determined to catch it. *Next time, it won't get away*, he thought, *next time I'll be ready.*

Chapter 29

Jo arrived back at the station just before six o'clock. She'd been stuck in traffic when she left Exeter, but she still wanted to go to the station before heading home. The rain was beating down hard again, so she ran from the car park to the entrance. After walking through the station door, she saw Danny talking to Laura at the bottom of the stairs. As she walked in, they both stopped talking and looked a little embarrassed.

'Hello,' Jo said, wondering what the problem was.

'Jo,' Danny said, smiling, albeit a fake smile, Jo thought.

'Hello,' Laura said. 'I'm off home now. See you both tomorrow.' She then walked passed her quickly, looking Jo in the eye with an expression that Jo couldn't quite understand.

She hoped that Laura hadn't told Danny about their relationship. She was still in her first week as a detective and she didn't want anything to distract her from the case she was trying hard to succeed with.

'How did you get on at the hospital?' Danny asked as he started to walk upstairs before her.

'Fine. Well, it was what you thought. He just wanted to plead his innocence.'

'So it was a total waste of an afternoon.'

'Was something wrong with Laura?' Jo asked.

'No. She was just asking how your first week was going. Why?'

'She seemed to leave in a hurry.'

'She's just finished her shift; that's all,' Danny said.

As they reached the top of the stairs Jo's mobile rang. It was Helen.

'Do you mind if I just take this?' Jo asked. 'It's Helen.'

'You answer it. I'll be in the office.'

She answered. 'Hi, Helen.'

'Can you talk?' Helen said.

'Yes. I'm OK for a minute. What's up?'

'I was just ringing to see how you are and see how the case is going?'

'I'm fine, thanks for asking,' Jo said. 'But there's nothing new to report on the case.'

'I've been watching the news; the police haven't yet confirmed that there's a panther on the loose. Is that wise?'

'We decided it was best to let video footage tell the story for now. We wanted to give the marksmen a chance to catch it first before we get people trying to interfere. Although there are probably people out there already. But once it's been confirmed, DCI Collis thinks we'll have people from all over the place searching the moors.'

'That's true,' Helen said. 'Listen, I know you're busy with the case at the moment, but I was wondering if you were free for a drink tonight.'

This made Jo's heart jump. 'Yes. I'll be free in an hour or so.'

'Excellent. We can discuss it more then.'

Helen sounded excited, Jo thought.

'I'll meet you in your local, shall we say eight?'

'Perfect.'

After ending the call, Jo couldn't help but be a little excited. It might just be a meeting to discuss the case and not a real date as such, but either way, she was happy to see her again.

She went into the office to discuss her trip to the hospital with Danny and to find out if anything else had happened in her absence. But as focused on the case as she was, she couldn't wait for eight o'clock.

Chapter 30

Another hour went by and Teddy was feeling tired. His legs felt as though they'd covered most of Bodmin Moor. He could tell that Vicky was tired too by the sluggish way she was walking through the woodland. The rain had started to fall again. It wasn't pleasant being out in the woods on the day like this, but although he was tiring, he was still as determined as ever to catch the panther.

He'd had a brief argument with Vicky about how she thought he should phone the police to tell them they'd seen the panther. But the panther could've covered a lot of ground by now and be in a completely different area. He didn't want to send them in the wrong direction by mistake and he certainly didn't want to have to meet the police anywhere to show them where they'd seen it. He would have to hide his shotgun from them and he didn't want to have to do that.

They reached the edge of the woods. There was a cobble stone wall marking the edge of the forest that had a wooden stile at the exit. The wall was still sheltered by the trees. The rain was falling hard again so Vicky suggested they stop and have another drink from the flask before leaving the shelter of the trees and heading across the open moorland. Teddy agreed, hoping that the rain might ease off once more while they have their break.

Vicky poured the drinks as Teddy stood his gun up against the wall next to his backpack before climbing up onto the wall to sit down.

Teddy held Vicky's cup as she climbed up and sat next to him. He then gave it back to her. They were beneath a large tree that kept them sheltered from the rain with only a small amount of water making its way through.

They sat with their backs facing the woods as they looked out onto the moors. The grass at the base of the wall was covered with a very large deep puddle and several smaller puddles scattered around the area.

They drank their tea and tried to regain some energy ready for the next part of their journey.

'It doesn't seem to be stop...' before Vicky could finish her sentence, a large black object hit her and sent her flying off the wall. It knocked Teddy off the wall as well, he landed face first in the deep puddle, as he landed he felt his left wrist snap under his own body weight and screamed with pain as he felt the bones crunch. He lifted his face from the puddle to see the panther on top of Vicky. The huge powerful creature sank its teeth into the base of her neck as she laid face pressed against the ground. It momentarily released her, but only to take a better bite as it buried its long white teeth into her pale wet flesh.

She screamed.

It hurt Teddy's ears, but he wanted her to scream louder, hoping that the marksmen might hear and come running.

He tried to gather himself and block out the pain from his wrist, which was now pointing in a direction that it shouldn't be. *The gun*, he thought. He looked over the panther that was mounted on top of Vicky, growling as it violently shook her. The gun was on the opposite side to them; he just knelt in the puddle, feeling helpless.

He looked around and saw a rock on the ground nearby. He stood up; the water in the puddle went above his ankles. He picked the rock up with his right hand and threw it at the panther. It caught it on the shoulder, but it just growled and spun its prey around by a few inches. Teddy saw it lift its head to stare at him, pulling Vicky's head upwards as it did.

He knew he was running out of time. He ran past the panther, heading for the gun. The animal spun around to watch him, twisting Vicky into an even more awkward position, her legs facing forwards as her torso turned the other way.

She screamed again, but this time through clenched teeth. He grasped the shotgun with his one good hand. He couldn't aim it properly and worried about hitting Vicky. So he just pointed it towards the dirt track away from the scuffle. As the shotgun lay on the ground, he threaded his index finger through the loop and pulled the trigger.

The shot went into the grass, sending water and mud flying into the air. The panther let go of its prey and bolted into the woodland.

Teddy ran over to Vicky, her face was now under water in the huge puddle next to the wall. He tried not to look at the enormous slits in her neck that were rapidly losing blood. He turned her over. She lay there wide eyed, panting for breath. Her skin was pale as the rain landed on her face. She didn't speak; she just lay there panting rapid short breaths.

'Vicky,' he cried. 'Vicky, just hold on. I'll call an ambulance; it'll be here in no time.'

The fast breaths continued, but her eyes didn't look at him anymore. Her glazed expression seemed to coincide with her breathing slowing down. The heavy rain washed away the blood from her open mouth. Her eyes no longer blinked as the downpour hit her pupils. Her head fell slightly to the side, away from Teddy. Then there was one last breath as her chest rose and fell, but it didn't rise again.

The pain in his wrist was excruciating, but it was nothing compared to the pain in his stomach as he feared his last remaining family member was drifting away. Though the rain was falling hard, he laid down next to her on the water logged grass. He hugged her hard and pressed his face against hers. He screamed as he began to cry. He couldn't go through the loss of a family member again. He wanted to die with her; he just laid there embracing her. He was soaking wet and in agonising pain. He prayed for it to be some terrible dream, but he knew that it wasn't. He cried and screamed at the top of his voice. He couldn't help her. All he could do was cry out in the hope that somebody would hear.

He rocked her almost like a baby as he knelt there in the puddle. He drifted into thoughts of his life with her. He thought back to when she was a baby, then her first day of school. He then thought of the tragedy of losing his wife and daughter in the car crash. He remembered Jo's dad coming to see him with the family liaison officer and how he couldn't tell Vicky himself. He had to let the officer deal with telling her of how her world had just been ripped apart. When the two of them were reunited they couldn't stop crying as they hugged each other. It was the most difficult thing he had ever had to deal with. He always hoped that Vicky wouldn't remember it. She was only eight years old at the time. She seemed to recover quicker than he did. But how was he going to recover from this? Not only has he lost everything, but he had caused this. If he'd have left it to the police, she'd still be OK. The mixture of guilt, shock and grief was overwhelming. He didn't even realise he was being pulled away from his granddaughter. He held onto her tight as he felt himself being dragged away. He didn't even look around to see what it was. He felt strong arms around his chest and as he was dragged away from her, he then saw a police officer drag Vicky from the puddle and slide her to slightly drier ground.

The officer who dragged him away put his face to his. 'Stay there,' he said. He then went to help Vicky who was lay motionless on the grass. One of them spoke into his radio as the other leaned over her. Teddy couldn't tell what he was doing. He couldn't move to see. He'd been told to stay there and without thinking he did exactly what he was told.

He just sat there on the wet grass staring at the scene in front of him. His body was cold and wet and his wrist wasn't wrist shaped anymore. He was just sitting there watching the two officers try to help his granddaughter. He just stared at them and stayed completely still as the rain continued to fall.

Chapter 31

The pub was very busy, most of the people were locals, but Jo also saw a few faces she didn't recognise. The news of the Beast of Bodmin being real had obviously started to bring people into the area. She could tell by the uneven numbers in the groups of people. There were three men and two women standing talking at the bar. That wasn't a usual number of people to go on holiday together, Jo thought. There was another group of people sitting at the table in front of the fire, all of them men. Again this was an unusual number of people for a trip to Cornwall. Most holiday makers are couples or two couples, usually with children. Jo could tell at a glance that these weren't your average holiday makers.

She asked Dorothy for a glass of wine and paid her before having another look around the room. As she took a sip of her wine, she then noticed Helen in the back corner of the pub sitting at a table on her own.

Helen waved and smiled at her.

Jo smiled back and made her way over to the table. She didn't recognise her at first because so far she'd only seen her dressed in her zoo uniform. Tonight she was in dark denim jeans, and a white cotton laced top. She also wore her long red curly hair down and a pair of silver earrings. This was the first time Jo saw Helen dressed for a night out. She looked much more feminine than before and even more beautiful. Her green eyes met hers and she couldn't help but stare into them. Her feelings for David had almost died, along with the passion she'd felt for Laura. The sensation she was experiencing just by looking at Helen was something she couldn't understand. She felt excited and comfortable at the same time, and Helen hadn't even spoken yet.

'I didn't see you then,' Jo said.

Helen stood to kiss her on the cheek.

'I was enjoying watching you,' Helen said. 'It was funny seeing you look around the room and not notice me.'

'Well you look so different,' Jo said.

'Were you expecting me to turn up in my zookeeper uniform?'

Jo smiled. 'Not quite. Would you like a drink?'

'No,' Helen said. 'Sit yourself down; I still have one.'

Jo sat down at the table opposite her. She still couldn't work out if this was a police meeting or friends on a night out, or an actual date. But judging by the effort Helen had made on her appearance, she thought and hoped it was the latter.

'So,' Helen said. 'How are you?'

'I'm very well.'

'This week isn't starting to get on top of you, is it?'

'It's been eventful, but in a strange kind of way I've been enjoying it.' Apart from losing Lucy, she thought.

Helen smiled. 'I suppose it's what you signed up for.'

'It is. Although I didn't expect to be dealing with panthers being loose on the moors, but like I say, it's eventful, and it sure beats working in a shop for a living. No offence to people who do work in shops, but you know what I mean.'

'I do,' Helen said. 'I think when you find a career that you really love, it's hard not to question why people do mundane jobs and don't fight to do something that they really want to do. I mean, if working in a shop or a factory is something that you love then great, but if not, then why do it?'

'I suppose we're the lucky ones. We had a good enough start in life to get a decent education and we had the choices available to us. Not everyone is so lucky.'

'I agree, but I also believe in making your own luck or at least keep trying until you get that lucky break.'

'At what point did you decide to become a zookeeper?'

'When I was eight years old.'

Jo smiled. 'As young as that?

'As young as that,' Helen repeated. 'It was during a school trip to the zoo. It was sitting next to a large glass window and having a lion on the other side come over to look at me that did it. I often think of that because I see kids doing it at the zoo now and I see how scared they are. I wasn't scared. I pressed my face up against the glass and tried to get as close to him as I could. He was a big male lion. To me at aged eight, he was huge. But I wasn't scared. I just wanted to know more about him. I could've stayed there for hours. Ever since then everything I did was big cats. I read loads of books about them; every item of clothing I ever wore had a big cat on it. My room was full of ornaments and soft toys of big cats. I must've made it very easy for my family to buy me birthday presents.'

'I find that amazing that you knew at that age what you wanted to do with your life.'

'Pick a lane and stick with it; that's what my dad used to say.'

Jo laughed. She then took a sip of her wine. She thought it was going well and hoped that the conversation continued to flow as well as it had so far.

'What made you decide to join the police?'

'My dad was a police officer. That tends to be a trend throughout the force.'

'Did he encourage you do join?'

'No; quite the opposite really. My dad and my teachers told me to stick with my education. So I did; all the way through up to and including three years at Oxford.'

'You're an Oxford graduate?' Helen asked, seeming a little surprised.

'I am. Three years at Lincoln College. I was a literary student.'

'Really?'

'You seem surprised?' Jo said.

'I am. You're obviously very intelligent. It's just a surprise career path for an Oxford graduate.'

'So I'm told. I stayed on at school and took it right to the end, then travelled Europe for a year, and when I came back I still wanted to be a police officer, so I signed up.'

'What did your dad say?' Helen asked.

Jo looked down at her glass. 'He died the week before I signed up.'

Helen's smile disappeared. 'Oh, I'm sorry to hear that.'

Jo gave a shrug.

'Is that what prompted you to go for it?'

'In a way. He wouldn't have talked me out of it. He knew how stubborn I can be. I just took my education as far as I could and then decided to join the police. I still have my degree to fall back on should I ever decide to change paths.'

'How long have you been a detective?' Helen asked.

'What time is it?' Jo said, joking.

Helen laughed. 'What does that mean?'

'This is my first week.'

Helen's eyes widened. 'Wow,' she said. 'You're having one hell of a first week.'

'I'll drink to that,' Jo said, taking another sip.

'Are you any closer to finding the killer?' Helen asked.

'Not really.'

'And have you still got people out searching the moors?'

'Yes. We're rotating teams of marksmen.'

'I don't suppose Teddy's dog has turned up?'

'I'm afraid not. It isn't like Sam to run away so it's not looking good for him.'

'Should I go out and search the moors for the panther?' Helen asked. 'I'm free tomorrow. My supervisor will let me take a tranquiliser gun and a cage. He didn't want me to break any laws, but if I tell him you asked me to, I think he'll be fine about it.'

'It might be a good idea to try. You'll be careful though, won't you?'

'Of course.'

'I can start early, six-thirty. Maybe not stay out too late tonight to make sure we get up.'

'Are you not enjoying yourself?' Jo asked, jokingly.

Helen smiled. 'Of course I am. But I don't want to be half asleep while wandering the moors at first light with a black leopard on the loose.'

'I agree.'

Helen finished her drink and then went to the bar for another. Jo was enjoying talking to her and she was hoping that this wouldn't be the last time they spent an evening together. She was so easy to talk to, ambitious, but also laid back. She was also an interesting person with an interesting background. Jo wanted to know more about her.

Helen came back to the table with their drinks.

'So,' Helen started. 'Tell me about you. Do you live on your own?'

'No,' Jo said. 'I moved back in with my mum and younger brother.'

'Moved back in from where?'

'I lived in Liskeard with my boyfriend David. We broke up about the time I arrested the Bodmin Butcher.'

'*You* arrested the Bodmin Butcher?' Helen asked, looking surprised.

'Didn't you know that? It was all over the TV.'

'I was very aware of the case, but I tend to read about things rather than watch TV. I didn't realise it was you.'

'Well anyway, David and I were having problems so I moved back home. He's a good person, we just grew apart. I started to see that we were completely different people.'

'Obviously,' Helen said.

This comment confused Jo. She didn't know anything about David at this point. Was she just saying 'obviously' because they were on a date and she knew that Jo was gay? This was a whole new experience for Jo and she didn't really know what to say. All she knew was she enjoying her company more and more.

'Look, Jo,' Helen said. 'I'm really starting to like you...' as she said this, she reached her hand across the table to gently take Jo's hand.

Jo quickly pulled her hand away and Helen stopped talking. Helen looked at her confused as Jo looked down at the table.

'Have I misread something here? I thought you liked me.'

Jo looked her in the eyes, her beautiful green eyes.

'No,' she said, softly. 'I really like you.'

'Then what's the problem. I'm happy to go slowly if that's what you want.'

'It's not that,' Jo said.

'Well, what is it?'

Jo looked around the room. The pub was full, but nobody was looking at them. The hustle and bustle of the busy pub was filled with everyone minding their own business.

'This is my local.'

Helen's face gave a little smile as the penny seemed to drop. 'Are you embarrassed about the locals knowing your business? Or are you still in the closet?'

Jo smiled at her, slightly embarrassed. Her smile answered Helen's question.

'So what is this? Are you experimenting?' Helen asked.

'No. Not at all. I am gay. It's just that nobody knows it yet.'

'Have you had a relationship since your boyfriend?'

'Yes, with a fellow officer called Laura Trevilian.'

'Really?'

'I left David for her. I just couldn't go through with it. It was all a little too much for me at the time. I'd recently lost my dad,

I was going through a lot of stress at work, and the fact of the matter was, I didn't love either of them. I loved David like a friend and Laura, well that was just...'

'Passion?' Helen asked.

Jo smiled. She was a little uncomfortable to admit it, but she nodded anyway.

'So,' Helen said, taking another sip of her drink. 'Where does that leave us?'

Jo leaned across the table a little. Not too much as to give away to the people in her village that she was on a date, but close enough to talk a little quieter.

'I'm hoping that I can get to know you more. I really like you and I struggle to get you out of my head to be honest.'

Helen smiled.

'I just don't want to be the subject of gossip just yet.'

That sentence seemed to be enough for Helen. She just continued to smile her beautiful soft smile as they gazed at each other. Jo now knew that it was in fact a date, and she was glad she got everything out in the open.

'If you caught the Bodmin Butcher you've probably already been the subject of gossip.'

'I was, and I am also aware that there are more important things going on at the minute, but I still don't want people to know just yet.'

'OK,' Helen said.

Jo enjoyed a moment of silence as she gazed into her eyes once more. But this was then interrupted as her mobile phone rang. She pulled it from her small handbag and saw it was Danny.

'Excuse me,' she said.

'No problem.'

She answered the phone. 'Danny,' she said.

'Jo. Bad news I'm afraid. Where are you?'

Jo felt her face lose its colour and she saw the concern on Helen's face at her own changing expression.

'I'm in the King's Head. What's wrong?'

'It's Teddy. He and his granddaughter have been attacked by the panther. They're on their way to Bodmin Hospital.'

'I'll be there in ten,' she said, before cutting him off.

'What is it?' Helen asked.

'It's Teddy. He's been attacked by the panther.'

Helen looked horrified. 'Oh no. Can I come with you?'

'Of course.'

They both stood and quickly left the pub.

Chapter 32

Jo and Helen arrived at the hospital. The ten minutes Jo had told Danny was more like fifteen by the time they'd arrived, mainly due to coming across oncoming traffic on the narrow country lanes heading out of St Breward. Helen and Jo raced through the Accident and Emergency doors. Jo showed the lady behind the desk her badge and asked where she could find Teddy and Vicky.

The lady pointed to the triage bay where the curtains were drawn.

As she looked over, she saw Danny standing outside of the bay. He waved them over and they made their way through the crowded waiting room to get to them.

'Jo,' Danny said. 'You need to go in. He's refusing to be seen to until he knows if Vicky's OK.'

'Is she OK?' Jo asked.

'I don't know as yet. But it's not looking too good to be honest. From what I've been told she has some very bad neck wounds. They've rushed her straight through. But Teddy is going to need surgery too. His arm is a mess.'

'I'll see if I can calm him down.'

'Jo,' Danny said, before she got to the curtain. 'You need to prepare yourself for how bad his arm looks. It's pretty terrible.'

She nodded before putting her head around the curtain. 'Is it OK to come in?' she asked.

The nurse was standing in front of Teddy while he sat on the bed with his feet on the floor. 'Who are you?' she asked.

'I'm DC Green,' she said. 'Teddy is a friend of mine.'

'Well maybe you can talk some sense into him.' She was a plump lady, only very short, in her fifties. She had a nice way about her and obviously wanted to help him, but she also looked a little stressed. She was probably feeling the pressure of a full waiting room. But Teddy obviously didn't care about himself at this point. He wanted to make sure his granddaughter was OK which Jo understood, but Jo wanted him to be OK too. At that moment his wrist was anything but OK. His left hand pointed inwards as he held his arm out in front of him. There was dried blood around his wrist and several splintered bones poking through the skin. His clothes were still wet and he was wrapped in a foil blanket.

'Teddy,' Jo said. 'What's going on?'

'This nurse wants to send me through to surgery and I've told her I'm not going anywhere until I know what's happening to Vicky,' he said, indignantly.

'Teddy, look at your wrist. That needs seeing to as quickly as possible.'

'That's what I've told him,' the nurse said.

'Can I have a minute with him?' Jo asked.

'Yes, but a quick minute. I've got a room full of people needing help.'

'I'll be quick.'

The disgruntled nurse then left the room, closing the curtain behind her.

Jo pulled a chair up towards the bed and sat down in front of Teddy. 'What happened?'

Teddy didn't speak for a moment.

Jo let the question linger until it was finally answered.

'I wanted to make up for the stupid things I'd done. I went out onto the moors, looking for the panther. Vicky insisted on coming along. We saw it at one point but I missed my chance. Then a few hours later, we were sat on a wall sheltering from the rain and suddenly...' his bottom lip trembled.

Jo put her hand on his knee as he struggled to relive what was obviously a horrific situation.

'It pounced on her from behind. I fell too and I landed badly and broke my wrist. The panther shook her like a rag doll. All I could do with my one good hand was to fire the gun into the ground. Then it ran off.'

'What've they said about Vicky?'

'Nothing, but I don't think she'll survive. I thought she was dead at the time. But the two policemen kept trying to revive her. It was horrible. They phoned for an ambulance but it seemed to take forever and we were miles away from the roads. She wasn't responding. Her skin was so white.'

He wiped a tear away. 'The Air ambulance finally arrived and they brought us here.'

'Have they not told you anything?'

'They said they'd taken her into Intensive Care.'

'She must've still been alive when you got here then.'

'They're most likely going to operate on me, but I don't want to be put out until I know what's happening with Vicky.'

'Teddy. If you don't get your wrist seen to now, you don't know what lasting damage you'll end up with.'

'I don't care. All I care about is Vicky. I've already lost my wife, my daughter and even my dog. I can't lose Vicky as well.'

'Right, listen to me, Teddy. You are in a lot of pain. The wait for hearing news of Vicky is going to be agonizing. Why not let them get on with it? The next few hours will fly past for you and when you wake up, not only will they have sorted your arm, but you'll also know one way or another about Vicky.'

Jo wasn't sure if that last part of her sentence wasn't as positive as it should've been. But she couldn't lie to Teddy and make him feel as though she was going to be OK when it was looking so bad for her. She saw him soften a little. She felt as though she was beginning to get through to him.

'Let them do their job.'

Teddy bowed his head. 'OK. Will you still be here?'

'Mine will be the first face you'll see when you open your eyes, and hopefully I'll have some good news about Vicky.'

'OK then,' he said.

Jo stood and pulled the curtains open. She nodded to the triage nurse as she came back into the cubicle.

Jo walked over to Danny and Helen who were standing in the corridor next to the waiting room.

'You two might as well go. It's going to be a long night, I think,' Jo said.

'I'll go and see if I can get any news on his Granddaughter first,' Danny said. 'DCI Collis is on his way. He'll want to know what's happening when he gets here.' He then turned away and made his way down the corridor.

'Come on, Helen,' Jo said. 'We'll get you a taxi.'

Jo rested her hand on Helens shoulder as they walked through the waiting room. Suddenly she didn't seem as embarrassed about showing affection to Helen in public. She'd come all this way, which Jo thought was nice of her, especially considering this was their first date.

'Are you sure you don't want me to stay?'

Jo smiled at her as they walked through the automatic doors.

'No. I want you to do something else for me instead.'

'What's that?'

'I want you to get a good night's sleep and then go and catch that panther in the morning.'

'I'll try my best,' she said.

'I'll find out where the attack happened and text you.'

'OK.'

'Is there someone you can go with, so that you're not on your own?'

'I'll be fine. Let me know what happens, and I hope they're both OK.'

Jo held onto both of Helen's hands as they faced each other.

'I'm sorry that our first date didn't turn out better,' Jo said.

Helen smiled. 'It's nothing to be sorry about. Hopefully we'll do it again soon.'

'I'm sure we will.'

They stared at each other. Even with the stress of the case and the sickening things that had happened to Teddy and Vicky, Jo still couldn't help but stare into Helen's eyes. Standing outside of the emergency room doors in the cold blackness of the night, with people coming and going and cars pulling up and others driving away, it didn't seem the right place for their first kiss. But Jo couldn't let her go without doing so. She leaned towards her and gently kissed her lips. The kiss continued for three or four seconds and was followed by a gaze from Helen's emerald green eyes. Neither of them spoke as Jo turned to walk back inside. Their first date had been cut short, but Jo still felt the butterflies of excitement. She couldn't wait to see her again.

As she walked through the waiting room, she tried her best to push thoughts of Helen to the back of her mind and focus on Teddy and Vicky. She hoped to God that Vicky would pull through. She couldn't imagine Teddy having to go through the loss of a family member again. He'd been strong in the past, but he had to be for Vicky. If Vicky died, he'd have no one left to be strong for.

Chapter 33

It was almost ten o'clock when PC Laura Trevilian arrived at her home in Tregoltha. She'd spent the evening at the gym and was ready to get showered and changed into her pyjamas to spend what's left of her evening in front of the television. Still dressed in her track suit and trainers, she got out of her car and made her way to the front door of her semi-detached house that backed onto Bodmin Moor. She carried her uniform in her gym bag, she never saw the point of getting dressed back into it before heading home, and she preferred to get showered at home rather than getting showered at the gym and having to get changed yet again after arriving home.

She was still missing Jo. She was finding it hard to get back to normality when all she'd done in recent months was think about her all the time and how they were going to be together. She was falling hard for Jo, and she was devastated that she'd changed her mind about moving in with her. She understood. It must've been hard leaving David and she could see why she didn't want to jump straight into another serious relationship, but she didn't see why Jo had to end it altogether. She hoped that one day they could try again, but she didn't want to pressure her. She thought it best to leave her alone and hope she comes around when she's ready.

For now, she had to get used to being alone again. She spent most evenings at the gym, unless she was on a late shift. This was her way of dealing with things. She would rather find something positive to do rather than stay at home every night on her own.

It was dark now, but the rain had stopped and the sky had started to clear. She stepped up to the front door. As she put the key into the lock, she heard a noise. It was a noise like a bang as though something had been dropped.

She removed the key from the door and walked slowly around to the side of her house. The flagstone pathway was lit up by the street light from the road. Laura could see the garage door at the end of the path was closed as usual. She waited. The rain had stopped but she could still hear water dripping from the gutter above her; something she hadn't got around to sorting as yet. It was a constant tapping that she'd heard from her bedroom on nights when the heavens had decided to open. But now, in the dark of the late evening, that's all she could hear.

She turned to go back to the front door when suddenly she heard another bang. It sounded like it came from inside her garage. It almost sounded like a paint tin being knocked over. She walked towards the garage door. She listened for any more noises, but they didn't come. She reached the door and gently grabbed the metal handle in the middle of the dark red garage door. She tried to turn it, but it was locked, just as she thought.

She wandered around to the side of the garage which meant she was now in her back garden. The garden was the length of the garage. It was a simple lawn with a low wooden fence at the bottom where in daylight she could see out onto the moors. But tonight, she could only just see as far as the fence.

Suddenly her heart jumped as she noticed the side door of the garage was slightly open. She knew she hadn't left this door open herself because she rarely used that door. She took her mobile phone from her pocket and clicked on the torch icon. She contemplated calling it in first but she was a police officer. She thought herself capable of investigating first before embarrassing herself by calling for police assistance before she even knew what she's dealing with.

She reached the door and pulled it open further. She shone her torch inside the garage. The room was filled with clutter.

There was an old couch; a dining room table stood on its side, piles of boxes with god only knows what inside. There was also a mountain bike that she bought last year and only used three or four times, and an old fridge-freezer that she hadn't got around to disposing of as yet.

She walked into the garage to try and see why her door was open. Surely if it was a burglar they'd have taken the bike first. But no, as messy as the garage was, it didn't look like anything had been disturbed. Whoever it was could still be in there. She contemplated calling it in once more, but she didn't want to waste valuable time of the police force when so much was going on. She even started to question whether she had in fact left the door open herself. She didn't think this was likely but it was possible.

She took a few more steps further into the dark garage.

As she slowly shone the light of her phone from one side of the garage to the other, her heart jumped and her breathing stopped. She saw two eyes staring at her, eyes that didn't blink, eyes that stared right into hers. She dropped her phone. It smashed onto the concrete floor and the light diminished. Her fear worsened as she now knew what was happening but couldn't see in the pitch-black room. Loud noises filled the garage as she heard things being knocked over and pushed aside. What happened next was no surprise to her. As soon as she'd seen those eyes, she knew her time was up. In a split second everything suddenly made sense to her, she knew her life was about to be brought to a sudden end. She knew she couldn't get away. She wished she had called for backup. She felt fear and then pain like no other she'd ever endured before. Then as her head hit the concrete floor hard, she felt her consciousness leave her and even at that moment, as she drifted into her next life, her last thoughts were of Jo and how she missed her, and now her life, like their relationship, was over.

Chapter 34

'Teddy,' Jo said.

Nothing.

'Teddy,' she said again.

He'd already been awake intermittently but he had yet spoken. The nurse said he'd just opened his eyes and fallen straight back to sleep.

Sleep was something that Jo needed. She'd briefly fallen asleep in the chair outside the room where they told her he was after his surgery. It was now after midnight and Jo was looking forward to the day being over and going home to bed. First she had a promise to keep. She'd told Teddy that she'd be the first to speak to him and she told him she'd let him know straight away what had happened to Vicky.

The room was small; much like Boniek's was at Exeter Hospital. There was just the bed and a chair where Jo was sitting waiting for Teddy to awaken from his operation. He didn't have any belongings there. She wondered if her mum would bring him some clothes from his house. She knew she had a key with Teddy being a family friend. This is something she would arrange the next morning.

'Teddy,' she said again, this time a little louder.

His eye lids opened a little but Jo could only see the whites of his eyes.

'Teddy,' she said one more time.

This time his eyes opened fully and he tried to sit up in his bed and looked a little confused. He looked around the room as if to try to work out where he was. After he looked down at his arm and saw the plaster with metal pins coming out of it and a strip of wood holding all the pins in place, he obviously then remembered where he was.

He muttered something but no audible words came out.

'Here, have some water,' Jo said, holding the cup to his lips.

He took a couple of gulps as Jo held onto the cup. He then leaned his head back onto his pillow and looked her in the eye. He stared at her with an expression of fear, but also acceptance. Jo thought he was expecting the worst, and looked as though he just wanted her to get it over with.

'Vicky?' he said.

Jo smiled at him.

Teddy's eyes widened.

'She's going to be OK.'

'Really?' he whispered.

'She's going to be in hospital for a while, but she's out of the woods.'

Jo smiled at him again. She was tired and weary, but it was worth it to be there to keep her promise and see Teddy's reaction to the good news.

He turned his face away and began to cry.

Chapter 35

It was Friday morning. Jo tried to conceal a yawn as she sat at the desk in the centre of the office waiting for the meeting to begin. She'd noticed DCI Collis yawn a couple of times too. He'd spent some of the previous night at the hospital as well as Jo. He also went back to see Teddy after she'd left. Jo had let him know when Teddy had come around from his operation. That was after midnight so DCI Collis must've gotten home much later, maybe even after two o'clock, Jo thought.

DCI Collis was sitting at the top of the table, DS Hughes was to Jo's left and DS Killik and DC Dutson were on the opposite side of the desk.

The bad weather had dispersed and the sun was shining through the blinds, lighting up the room once more. There was a lot to discuss at this meeting, Jo thought. A lot had happened within the last twenty-four hours. She wondered what their next move would be.

DCI Collis interlocked his fingers as he leaned on the desk. He looked around the table before starting his opening speech.

Jo had one more sip of her coffee before he began.

'Right, ladies and gentlemen,' he started. 'Sunday night, Debbie Rowland and Steve Roberts were killed while camping on Bodmin Moor near Bolventor. Teddy found the scene the next morning and as you all know, there were no bodies. Monday night, Lucy Webster was killed on the way home from her shift at the King's Head in St Breward. Again, there was a bloodied scene, but no body. That day a member of the public brought us footage of a panther he'd filmed on the moors which obviously started us down the path of there actually being a Beast of Bodmin. Lester Hamilton was reported to us, and sure enough, he has a pet panther that escaped sometime on Sunday. And yesterday, Teddy and Vicky go hunting for the panther, they see it, Teddy fails to shoot it, later on, it attacks Vicky. Teddy damaged his wrist and Vicky was very badly hurt by it, but Teddy manages to fire his gun, pointing it away as to not hit Vicky, and the animal runs off once more into the woods, and hasn't been seen since.'

A silence fell around the room.

Then Bradley said, 'One hell of a story.'

'What's everybody thinking?' DCI Collis asked.

'I'm thinking that we need to get as many people looking for this animal as we can spare,' Danny said.

'So are we back to thinking that it's the panther and not a serial killer?' Rachel said.

'I don't know,' DCI Collis said. 'Possibly.'

'You don't sound so sure, sir,' Danny asked.

'I've gone back and forth several times over this case, but the fact of the matter is, the killings only started after the panther escaped.'

'It's an unlikely coincidence if not,' Bradley said.

'Helen said it was unlikely for a whole body to be eaten. They do eat bones, but it would take them a long time to eat a full human,' Jo said.

'It wouldn't eat three people within two days though,' Rachel said.

'It's possible that the animal removed the bodies and got disturbed before eating them. But she also said that although a panther with a full belly wouldn't be able to catch any prey in the wild, but human beings don't run that fast. So it could be gorging itself on easy prey because of how easy it is for it to hunt. '

'Well let's put the panther to one side for a moment,' DCI

Collis said. 'Just think about this as if no mention of a big cat being on the loose had ever come up.'

'OK,' Danny said.

'What would connect the three victims? Five victims if we count Teddy and Vicky, but we know that the panther attacked them, so forget them for the minute, what about the first three victims?'

The detectives fell silent again as they thought about the question.

'Two first two victims,' Rachel began. 'They're from London. So as far as we're aware they don't have any connection to the barmaid.'

'Other than them all being murdered and their bodies removed from the scene, there isn't anything that connects them to each other. The couple had only just entered Cornwall so they hadn't met Lucy,' Jo said.

'The village does reside on Bodmin Moor,' Bradley said. 'We can't consider the two scenes unconnected just because one was in the village. The bodies were removed from both scenes. They are most likely to be the same killer.'

'I agree,' Jo said. 'But they must be random killings because they don't know each other.'

'I think we're wasting our time,' Danny Said.

'In what way?' DCI Collis said.

'I'm sorry, sir. I don't mean to be disrespectful, but there is a black leopard on the loose. What else could it be?'

Jo wondered why Danny was suddenly thinking it to be the panther. The day before he thought it was Teddy. Although, now a panther has actually attacked someone, it was starting to make Jo change her mind too.

'What about Lester?' Bradley said.

'What about him?' Danny asked.

'It's his panther. Is that distracting us from the fact that he's a known criminal?'

'What are you saying?' Danny asked. 'Do you think he's a murderer and he's let his panther out on purpose do cover up what he's done?'

'Twenty-four hours ago, Danny, you thought it was Teddy who killed them,' Rachel said.

'Yes because of him lying about the scratch marks on the tree and him finding the scene. We now know for a fact that the panther is attacking people.'

The discussion was beginning to get a little heated, Jo thought.

'So you're suggesting, Bradley, that Lester is the killer and he's let the panther out to deflect attention?' Rachel said.

'But again, there's no connection to the victims,' DCI Collis said.

'He was in St Breward the night Lucy was killed,' Jo said. 'But I don't see a motive or a connection to the victims. Plus he keeps saying that his panther hasn't killed anyone.'

'Hang on,' Rachel said. 'Is there a connection to the campers? They are from London and so is Lester.'

'They are from Ealing and Lester's from Rotherhithe. They're about an hour by road from each other,' Danny said.

'Get on the phone to Ealing police station and get an officer to go and ask the families if they know Lester or if they'd ever heard them talk about any trouble with a local villain,' DCI Collis said.

Jo's mobile phone began to ring.

'Sir?' Jo said, asking permission to answer.

He nodded.

She stood up and walked towards the opposite end of the room before answering. She saw that it was Helen.

'DC Green,' she said, not wanting to give away to the rest of the room that she already knew who it was. But she needed to answer because she knew Helen was searching the moors.

'Got her,' Helen said.

Jo could hear the noise in the background as if Helen was driving and talking to her on hands free.

'What d'you mean?' Jo asked.

'We've got the panther and we're taking it back to the zoo.'

Jo couldn't believe it.

'Really?' She said. 'You've caught the panther?'

'Yes. Myself and my boss have been out since six this morning. We've darted her, got her into a cage and we're now driving back to Newquay to get her into a quarantine enclosure before she wakes up.'

'Excellent,' Jo said.

'Do you need to come and see her?'

'Yes,' Jo said. 'I'll be there as quick as I can.'

'OK,' Helen said. 'Drive past the entrance and turn into the next road marked deliveries. Someone will meet you at the gate.'

'Will do. Thanks, Helen.'

'No problem.'

She then ended the call.

As Jo walked back to the table, she began to tell them who the call was from. There was a uniformed officer that had entered the room and was standing next to DCI Collis.

'That was Helen...' she stopped talking as she sensed a change in the temperature of the room. DCI Collis looked at her with pitiful eyes. Danny looked down at his desk. Bradley and Rachel seemed to be holding back tears.

'What is it?' Jo asked.

The uniformed officer was waved away by DCI Collis.

'Jo,' he said. 'Another murder scene has just been found.'

She felt the colour drain from her face. She tried hard not to speculate in her mind. 'Who is it?'

DCI Collis paused for a moment. 'A neighbour of Laura's has found what sounds like a murder scene similar to the others in her garage. Laura's gym bag was on the floor.'

Jo felt sick and almost felt as though she could pass out.

Bradley jumped up from his chair to steady her, pulling a chair out for her to sit down.

Jo waved it away.

'Jo. We can organise this without you,' DCI Collis said.

'No,' she said. 'I'm OK.'

She walked over to her place at the desk to take another gulp of her coffee. She decided to tell them about Helen's phone call, not only because they needed to know, but because she didn't want to talk or think about Laura at this point. She knew she would burst into tears if she gave it any more thought at that moment.

'My phone call was from Helen. She's been out on the moors hunting for the panther.'

'And?' Bradley said.

'She's got it.'

Even though they were all obviously struggling to come to terms with the news that they'd just lost a fellow officer, the news of the panther being caught seemed to send a wave of surprise and relief throughout the room.

'With a tranquiliser gun?' Danny asked.

'Yes,' Jo said. 'They're taking it to the zoo now.'

'Wow,' Rachel said. 'That's fantastic.'

'If it's OK, sir, I'm going to go over there now. We need to find out how to tell if it's our killer. I'll speak to Helen and her boss and...'

'Jo,' DCI Collis said. 'You don't have to do this. We can manage...'

'Yes I do, sir.'

'I'll get over to Laura's,' Danny said.

'Aren't you going to come with me?' Jo said.

'I thought I'd...' he began.

DCI Collis cut him off. 'Rachel and Bradley can go to Laura's house. Danny, you go with Jo.'

'But isn't it more important...'

'Danny, go with Jo,' he said sternly.

DCI Collis's eyes quickly shot to Jo and back to Danny.

'Yes, sir,' Danny said.

Jo realised that two detectives didn't need to go to the zoo to speak to the big cat experts. Jo presumed that DCI Collis wanted to make sure that she wasn't on her own after hearing about Laura or maybe even to make sure that Danny drove rather than Jo trying to drive, watching the road with tears in her eyes. Jo appreciated DCI Collis making this call, and although she didn't let on to him or Danny that she knew his reasons, she was glad he'd made the decision to send Danny with her. She wasn't ready for crying just yet.

Chapter 36

Jo didn't speak as Danny drove them to Newquay Zoo which was only about half an hour away from Bodmin Police Station. Danny was also upset, Jo thought, because he didn't try to start a conversation either. Jo didn't think he knew Laura as well as she did, but an officer being killed is something that every other officer feels whether they know the person or not. They just drove in silence.

Jo couldn't believe that Laura had been killed. She hoped that it was some kind of mistake, but she didn't feel as though it could be. Her bag was laid on the floor at what Jo presumed was a scene similar to the others. It wasn't likely to be anyone else.

At that moment she regretted people not knowing about how close she had become to Laura. She didn't want sympathy from anyone, but she was a little hurt by the fact that nobody knew they were once a couple. The fact that their relationship overlapped with Jo being with David made it impossible for her to reveal this information to anyone. She saw no need to hurt David any more than necessary. If things continued to go well with Helen, then sooner or later David is going to know about her being gay; but she had no plans to tell him or anyone else about Laura. Helen knew, but at that moment, no one else did.

Jo rang Lester on the way. Lester asked if he could go to see the panther too. Jo asked Danny if he could see any problem with that and he said no. Jo also thought it would be a good idea to let Lester see the animal to confirm that it was in fact his pet. Not that Jo thought it likely that there were any more black leopards on the loose on Bodmin Moor, but she thought it best to make sure.

They arrived at the zoo and drove into the turning after the main entrance as Helen had said. There was a young man, possibly still in his late teens waiting by the large wooden gate. He was dressed in the same green uniform that Jo had seen all the other keepers wearing.

He walked over to the car as Danny wound down the window.

'Can I help you?' the young man said.

Danny showed him his badge.

'We're here to see Helen Thomas.'

'Yes, sir,' he answered. 'Leave your car here and follow me.'

He turned around and opened one side of the large wooden gate. As Jo and Danny got out of the car and walked over to the gate, he looked them both up and down before saying, 'You haven't got any Wellington boots with you by any chance?'

'No,' Danny said.

'It's a bit muddy after all the rain we had. I might be able to get you some.'

'No,' Danny said. 'It's fine.'

'Your choice,' he said while closing the gate. 'This way.'

He led Jo and Danny along a concrete road that turned right after they'd passed a large wooden shed.

Jo saw several different buildings on either side of the road. She thought they looked like storage buildings of some kind, but didn't bother to ask. She was more interested in seeing the panther than a guided tour of behind the scenes of the zoo.

The young man led them through the gap between two buildings.

Jo could feel the ground squelch under her feet as they came off the concrete and onto the grass. As they reached the end of the alley, she saw a large waterlogged area of grass with a large enclosure on the other side. It was quite similar in construction to Lester's enclosure, only a lot smaller. Helen was standing in front of the cage looking inside.

'Is there no way around?' Jo asked.

Helen turned around after hearing Jo's voice. 'I'm afraid not.'

'Stuff it,' Danny said, walking over the rain-soaked ground. 'We'll go and get changed when we're done.'

Jo followed. She could feel her feet sinking with every step. She also saw Helen was wearing boots that were covered in mud.

As Jo looked into the enclosure, she could see a very beautiful creature lay on the ground. The panther was awake and lay upright, but looked a little tired as it looked around.

'You got her here before she woke up then,' Jo said.

'Yes,' Helen said. 'She's not stood up yet, but she's looking OK.'

'How did you manage to get it?' Danny asked.

'We went out first thing this morning. We saw her a hundred yards or so away from us on the moors near Blisland. We thought we'd be patient. Steve - my boss - hid with the tranquiliser gun and I called to her.'

'Really,' Danny said.

'Yes. It worked too. We had to take our time, but after five minutes or so of calling her name, she started to walk over to me. As she got closer, Steve fired the dart which hit her in the shoulder, and a few moments later she was out.'

Danny raised his eyebrows. 'Well done, Helen. Sounds like you and Steve did a great job.'

'Definitely,' Jo said.

'We need to find out if the animal is our killer or not,' Danny said. 'I'm guessing a post mortem will be necessary.'

'What?' Helen asked.

'We need to know if it's killed anyone,' Danny said.

'I've not risked my life this morning to catch this creature just you can bring its life to an end.'

'I understand that, Helen, but what else can we do?'

'Is there another way of finding out?' Jo asked.

Before Helen could answer, a voice called her name through her radio. She took it from her pocket and answered. 'Yes.'

'Helen, there's a man at the front gate,' the voice said. 'He says he's here to see the police. His name is Lester Hamilton.'

Helen looked at Jo for a confirmation that this was OK.

Jo nodded.

'Yeah, will you send him with someone to the quarantine enclosures?'

'Will do.'

'He got here fast,' Jo said.

'Did you tell him to come?' Helen asked.

'I rang him to tell him that you'd caught the panther. He asked if he could come,' Jo said. 'I thought it best just to confirm that it is his panther.'

'I hope it is,' Helen said. 'There can't be more than one panther out there, surely.'

Danny's mobile rang. 'DS Hughes,' he said.

He then walked away from them as he spoke. 'Yes, sir.'

Jo presumed it was DCI Collis.

'You're joking,' he said, turning back to look at Jo. 'Yes, sir... I will... Yes, sir... We should've known really. I don't know why I'm surprised... He's here so can you send some uniformed officers to wait at the deliveries entrance? Jo and I are full of mud and will have to go and get changed before coming back to the station... Yes, sir... We'll be done shortly... Yes, sir.' He then ended the call.

'What is it?' Jo asked.

Lester walked around the corner, following a member of staff from the zoo. After he saw the enclosure, he ran across the muddy grass to get to his pet.

Danny and Jo took a few steps away from them so they couldn't be heard.

'He's a bleeding liar,' Danny said through gritted teeth, pointing towards Lester.

'What do you mean?' Jo asked.

'DCI Collis said they've checked with the council. His licence is a forgery.'

Jo quickly shared Danny's anger. 'The lying...' She then began to walk toward him.

Danny took her by the arm. 'Wait,' he said. 'DCI Collis is sending uniform. Let's finish here first and take him to the car before we tell him we know. Helen has done us a favour here. Let's not cause a scene. After all, he's not going anywhere.'

'I suppose you're right. You were also right when you said that people like him think they're above the law.'

They walked back over to the enclosure where Helen and Lester were crouched down looking at the panther. Raven had stood by now and slowly walked over to the mesh to greet Lester. She rubbed her side along the mesh as Lester put his fingers through. 'Hello, sweetheart,' he said in a soft voice that Jo hadn't heard before. 'Where have you been?'

After a moment or two of Lester getting reacquainted with his pet, he then stood and turned to Danny and Jo before saying, 'What now?'

'How do you mean?' Jo asked.

'Well, I'm guessing it's not as simple as you letting me take her home.'

'Not yet,' Danny said. 'We need to work out how to tell if she's killed the victims or not.'

'I'm telling you, Danny, she hasn't killed those people. Even if she had attacked, she wouldn't have killed three times.'

'Four,' Jo said.

This statement seemed to bring the discussion to a halt as Lester and Helen quickly turned their heads to look at Jo.

'Four?' Lester said.

'Yes,' Danny said, taking over the conversation.

Jo presumed that Danny thought she'd find it hard to talk about. He was right.

'This morning another murder scene was found. Police Constable Laura Trevilian, who was a good friend of Jo's, was killed.'

Jo saw Helen look at her with raised eyebrows as if to ask if this was the officer she'd told her about.

Jo gave a slight nod to answer.

'Oh look, Danny. She hasn't done this. There's no way.'

'Well we know for a fact that she's attacked Teddy and Vicky,' Jo said.

'What?' Lester said, looking more and more flustered.

'Teddy Hosken and his granddaughter were attacked by a black panther yesterday. They've survived to tell us the story of what happened, but Vicky is still in a bad way.'

Lester walked back to the cage shaking his head. 'This doesn't make sense. She wouldn't do this.'

Jo didn't know what to think. She knew that Teddy and Vicky had been attacked, but had the panther killed Steve Roberts, Debbie Rowland, Lucy Webster and now Laura? She really had to agree with Lester. Although they knew it had attacked Teddy and Vicky, that didn't mean that it had to have killed the others.

Danny seemed to think about it for a moment. 'Look. We need to decide a plan of action, so let's just leave it for now. We know it's your panther, so the public are safe again.' He then turned to Helen. 'We'll head back to the station now, but we'll be in touch.'

'OK,' Helen said. 'We'll look after her until you decide what to do. We'll also speak to our vet to see if there's a way of finding out what she's been eating.'

'Thanks,' Danny said. 'Come on, Lester.'

Lester crouched down to let his pet rub up against him

through the mesh once more. 'You'll be back with me soon, Raven,' he whispered. He then stood and walked away.

Danny led Lester away from the enclosure as they made their way back to the car.

'Thanks, Helen,' Jo said.

'No problem,' Helen said. She then gestured for Jo to stay back a moment as the others walked away. She then whispered to her, 'Do you fancy a drink tonight?'

'Yes. Of course,' Jo said. Her heart spun at the excitement of a second date with Helen.

'Excellent,' Helen said. 'Give me a ring when you're free.'

'I will do,' Jo said. 'See you later.'

As they arrived at the cars, there was a police car with two uniformed officers standing next to it.

Danny then turned to Lester, who suddenly looked confused.

Danny had an expression that Jo hadn't seen before. It was a mixture of anger and elation. Jo could see his jaw twitching as he clenched his teeth while staring at Lester.

'What's going on?' Lester said.

'This is you being caught out, Lester,' Danny said, very quietly.

'I don't understand,' Lester said.

'Did you not think we'd check with the council?'

With that, Lester's shoulders dropped.

Danny took slow steps towards him.

Jo thought Danny looked like he could lose his temper and was ready to intervene if he did.

Danny stood within inches of Lester and stared into his eyes.

For the first time since Jo had met Lester, she thought he looked a little nervous. Danny was a big man and was obviously intimidating Lester a little.

'Lester Hamilton,' he said. 'I'm arresting you on suspicion of keeping a dangerous wild animal without the appropriate licence, and for obstruction of justice. Anything you say...'

As he read him his rights, Jo could see a sense of satisfaction from Danny that he finally had something to arrest him for that he couldn't worm his way out of, Danny finally had his man.'

The officers then handcuffed Lester and put him in the car before taking him back to the station.

Chapter 37

Danny and Jo decided that they'd go and get changed before heading back to the station. They called at Jo's house in St Breward first. Danny stayed in the car as she quickly removed her muddy clothes and changed into something similar to what she was already wearing, only fresh and clean.

Danny said he had a phone call to make while he waited in the car. Five minutes later they were back on the road heading to Tregoltha for Danny to change his muddy trousers and shoes.

'You really don't like him, do you?' Jo asked.

'Who?'

'Lester.'

'No, I really don't like him.'

'Was he that bad?'

Danny looked her in the eye before looking back at the road. 'People like him think they can get away with anything. I spent most of my career in London trying to get him on one thing or another. He just kept getting away with things. And now, even though he's saying he's retired from that lifestyle, he's still causing trouble.'

'True. It's stupid that he even kept an animal like that, but the fact that he went into the enclosure, and when he was drunk; it's just stupid. He's obviously a very reckless person. He must've left the door open.'

'Maybe, but why did he have a pet panther in the first place? I mean, what kind of person has an animal like that? It's all image. It's like those people you see walking around with pit bull terriers, trying to intimidate people, only a more advance version of it. He's just trying to act like he's the big man. 'Look at me, I can control a vicious beast and make it my pet. Aren't I the hard man?"

'I think you're right,' Jo said.

'And how has he paid for it? Where has he bought it from? How do you even go about doing such a thing?'

'I don't know.'

After Danny finished venting his anger, he just focused on the road as they headed to Tregoltha.

A meeting was scheduled by DCI Collis for twelve o'clock. Jo was beginning to feel hungry and suggested to Danny that they called for a sandwich somewhere.

As they reached Tregoltha, Danny pulled up on the curb behind a row of parked cars.

'The sandwich shop is just there,' he said.

Jo saw the shop, three or four doors up the road from where they were parked. As she got out, she asked him what he wanted.

'Anything,' he said. 'Ham, corned beef, something like that.'

'No problem,' Jo said.

As she walked into the shop, there was a glass counter with cakes on display, a tall fridge with cans and bottles inside and a couple of small tables and chairs. There was a young lady being served but nobody else in the shop apart from the two older ladies making the sandwiches.

The young lady in front of Jo turned around as she walked up to the counter. Jo smiled at her and she smiled back. As she turned away, Jo realised that she recognised her, but she couldn't think where from. She wore her dark hair in a short bob and had large brown eyes, and a beautiful smile.

As she was handed her order, the lady behind the counter took her money and thanked her. She then said to Jo that she wouldn't be a minute and went to the back of the room to turn some sausages that were sizzling on the grill.

As the customer walked away, Jo's curiosity got the better of her.

'Excuse me.'

The young woman stopped. 'Yes.'

'I know you from somewhere and I can't think where.'

The woman looked at Jo as if to decide if she knew her or not. She then shook her head. 'I'm sorry, I don't think so.'

As she turned to leave, Jo realised where she'd seen her before. 'Oh, I know.'

She stopped again in front of the door.

'I'm sorry. I've never met you, but I've seen a photo of you. I'm a detective; I'm working with your ex-boyfriend, Danny Hughes.'

Her face suddenly dropped and lots its colour. She turned and opened the door and quickly left the shop.

'Wait; I didn't mean to...'

She'd gone.

As the door swung back closed, Jo wondered what she'd done wrong. Obviously things didn't end well between her and Danny. Danny said she had issues but he hadn't said what they were.

As Jo ordered their dinner she decided not to tell Danny that she'd just seen his ex-girlfriend, unless he saw her leave the shop that is. She didn't see the point of causing any upset by talking about her when it clearly ended badly one way or another. She felt as though she'd been untoward by referring to him as her ex-boyfriend but she didn't know why. As she got back into the car she decided to leave well enough alone.

Ten minutes later, they parked up outside Danny's house in Tregoltha. The house was the last one on a quiet road, just at the end of the cul-de-sac. It was a reasonably large house for one person, Jo thought. It had an external porch, a bay window on the living room and an attached garage with a white door. There was a small path, big enough for one car, but Danny parked the car on the road next to the small brick wall that surrounded the small front garden.

'Your house looks nice,' Jo said.

'It keeps the rain off my head,' he said, turning off the engine. 'Come on, we'll eat inside. We've got plenty of time before the meeting.'

Danny took his muddy shoes off at the door.

As Jo walked in, she was a little surprised at how the house looked inside. The living room was open plan. There was a large television in the corner, a small black modern looking coffee table, and a large book case that covered most of the alcove. The room continued through to the dining room where there was a dark wood dining table with black leather chairs, and that was all that was in there. The carpet was cream coloured and the walls were white. There was a painting of Bodmin Moor hung on the wall in the living area, but nothing in the dining room. The place was immaculate. Not the typical bachelor pad Jo would've expected.

Danny went through to the kitchen to get some plates.

Jo walked over to the book shelves to take a closer look. 'I didn't know you were an enthusiastic reader.'

'It's all I do. The TV is rarely on.'

Jo didn't recognise many of the authors. 'All factual?' she asked.

'Yes. I'm not one for novels,' he said as he came back into the room. 'I like to read about history, and crime of course, and occasionally other things, like geography.'

'It's quite a collection,' she said, looking at the hundreds of books in front of her. She then noticed a pattern. 'Are they...' she started.

'Yes,' Danny said. 'They're all in alphabetical order. Go ahead, make fun if you want. But it makes it easier to find what I'm looking for.'

Jo shrugged. 'If it makes you happy.'

He put the plates on the table. 'You start eating if you like. I'm going to get changed first.'

He ran off upstairs and Jo sat at the table to eat her sandwich.

She was still looking at the books as she ate. She couldn't make out all the titles and authors from where she was sitting, but she could read some of them.

She saw *The History of the Decline and Fall of the Roman Empire* by Edward Gibbon, *Homage to Catalonia* by George Orwell, *This Sceptred Isle* by Christopher Lee, and even *On the Origin of Species* by Charles Darwin.

Jo was an avid reader of books, but it was novels she liked. She couldn't imagine spending countless hours reading about the things that she now knew Danny to read about. But, she was still impressed at his thirst for knowledge. She knew he was intelligent, but she never imagined him to read books like the ones she could see in front of her.

As she took another bite of her sandwich, she noticed in the bottom right hand corner, towards the end of the alphabetical collection of books, was a book that stood out to her. The name of the author caught her eye first, Martina Valentine; a very exotic name, Jo thought. But more so than the name of the author, the name of the book jumped out at her, *The Route to Chess Mastery* by Martina Valentine.

Jo walked over to the book shelf. She removed the book from the shelf and looked at the cover. The cover was a chess board faded over a picture of the author. She was beautiful. She had shoulder-length dark hair and she was looking towards the camera with a smile. She was dressed in a black blouse and black jacket and had her arms folded. She looked about forty years old.

Jo opened the cover and saw that the book had been signed. It read, *For Danny, my favourite student x.* Jo had seen a few books that had been signed before, but never with a kiss. She returned the book to the shelf as Danny came downstairs.

'I never knew you played chess?' she said.

'I don't,' he said, making his way over to the dining room table. 'I tried it a while back, but I got bored of it.'

'I see,' Jo said. She didn't pry any more about the book, the author, or why she'd signed it for him. They both sat at the table and had their lunch before heading back to the station.

Chapter 38

Jo and Danny walked into the office and were greeted by DCI Collis, DC Bradley Dutson and DS Rachel Killik. They were all sat in their usual seats waiting for the meeting to start. They weren't late; in fact they were about five minutes early so Jo was surprised to find them sat there. They all smiled as they walked into the room. They must've been discussing the events of the day, Jo thought. Danny had already told DCI Collis over the phone what happened at the zoo, so she thought that this meeting was more of a recap than a plan of action. The mood of the room was much more pleasant than when they'd left earlier that day. Although they were obviously happy about the outcome, there was still the loss of PC Laura Trevilian to deal with.

'Greetings to you both,' DCI Collis said, sounding a little happier than usual.

'Sir,' Danny said before sitting down at the desk.

Jo sat in her usual seat.

'Quite a successful outcome,' Rachel said.

'Very. What happened at PC Trevilian's house?' Danny asked.

'Same as the other scenes,' Bradley said. 'There was a puddle of blood, a few bits of flesh and nothing else.' He then turned to Jo. 'Sorry, Jo; I didn't say that in a very tactful way. I know you were friends.'

'It's OK,' Jo said. It wasn't OK. She knew that at some point it would really start to sink in what had happened to Laura, but at that point she tried not to think too hard about it. She hoped that she could see Helen that night and talk to her about it. After all, she was the only person who knew of their relationship.

'Well then,' DCI Collis started. 'What next?'

'In what way, sir?' Danny asked.

'Are we going to consider it case closed or not?'

'We'll have to order a forensic test on the animal. We may even have to destroy it and order a post mortem to see what it's been eating,' Danny said. Like Bradley, he also looked at Jo as if to apologise.

'It's OK. I don't want people sugar coating things just because Laura and I were friends. This is a serious investigation and we need to tell it as it is,' she said, almost raising her voice.

DCI Collis put his hands up to try to calm her down. 'OK,' he said.

Jo looked down at the desk.

'Look,' Danny said. 'It's most likely that the panther is our killer. We can't close the case until we've had it confirmed, but I don't think there's anything more to do until we know the results of the examination, which I presume DS Mulfra is going to be involved with, so I think we need to leave it where it is for now.'

'What if it comes back inconclusive?' Bradley asked.

'Well it's still most likely the panther is the killer,' Rachel said. 'Like Jo said, it might have dragged the body away but possibly disturbed before consuming.'

'We need to find the bodies,' DCI Collis said. 'There has to be more than a few fragments of clothing and blood tissue from the campers, and there has to be something from Lucy and Laura too.'

'We've still got officers out looking,' Rachel said.

'Well then,' Danny said. 'Let's just tell the press that we've caught the Beast of Bodmin and see what happens next.'

'We have a press conference booked for later this afternoon. Jo, I thought you could do it,' DCI Collis said.

Jo thought for a second, and then quickly decided that she'd prefer not to. 'Any chance I can sit this one out? I'm still waiting for the Bodmin Butcher fame to die down.'

DCI Collis looked at Danny with his eyebrows raised.

'Fine,' Danny said. 'I'll do it.'

'Thank you,' Jo said.

DCI Collis brought the meeting to a close. As everyone was going back to their desks, he gestured for Danny and Jo to come over to his office.

'Can you manage without Jo for the rest of the day, Danny?'

'Of course,' he said.

'Why?' Jo asked.

'I think you should go home.'

'I'm OK, sir.'

'Look, it's Friday anyway, it's been a stressful week. Your mum and Rick would probably like to see you. It's been tough on them too this week remember. Also, you've had a couple of late nights and I'm sorry to go on about it, but you've lost a good friend today.'

Jo knew DCI Collis was right to suggest this. 'OK,' she said.

'Overall, Jo, it's been a good first week and you should be happy with today's outcome.'

'I am, sir,' she said.

'Then go home and get some rest.'

Chapter 39

Jo went home to an empty house. Rick was at work and she presumed her mum had either gone out shopping, or she was maybe involved with something at the church. Jo decided to relax into a nice hot bubble bath. She would normally consider a bath a waste of time, but she was very tired, too tired to go out running, and definitely too tired to go to her weekly kick-boxing lesson.

She lay back in the bath and let her face fall below the water for a second before lifting back out and pushing her wet hair back off her face. The water was hot, almost too hot, this was relaxing her and was sending her to sleep, but images of the last week's events continued to spin around her head. It seemed like a lifetime ago since Teddy stopped her while she was out running. It also seemed a lifetime ago since she first met Danny. She'd enjoyed working with him, but she still didn't feel as though she knew him as yet. The warning from Laura about keeping an eye on him hadn't been proven necessary as yet. He'd been a perfect gentleman so far. There was the occasional disagreement where he'd raised his voice a little, but Jo just saw that as being passionate about the case.

She drifted off to sleep as she lay there surrounded by bubbles. The images continued to spin around her subconscious, but she tried to ignore them as she enjoyed the relaxation of being on her own away from the stress of the last week. This was the first time she'd felt as though she could switch off since starting her detective career. She remembered what her dad had said about detectives being a different breed and it feeling more like a lifestyle than a job. She now knew what he meant.

An hour later, Jo felt a little more energetic as she dried her hair in her bedroom. She looked in the mirror at her vast collection of books on the shelf behind her. She looked at the time and considered heading into Bodmin town centre to look for a couple of new books to add to her collection. She didn't have anything that she hadn't read before and fancied something new.

She remembered Danny's vast collection of books and wondered whether she would ever consider reading factual books on a regular basis like him. But really she fancied getting her teeth into another crime story. She eagerly awaited Rose Byron's next instalment of DI Toni Lincoln's career, but that was still a month away.

Ten minutes later she was dressed and ready to set off. As she was about to leave her bedroom, she stopped. She stared at the books. Her mind suddenly went into overdrive as she stared at them. She wasn't happy about what she was thinking but she couldn't help it. A couple of things had come to light that day and she couldn't just ignore them.

She searched for her notebook that was in her inside pocket. She opened it and wrote three separate short sentences down on one of the pages. There was a connection and she couldn't ignore it. She was starting to doubt a few things. She sat on her bed and tried to let everything fall into place in her mind, but they didn't. She needed to know more. The trip to the book store had to wait for another day. Instead, she made a flask of coffee and prepared herself for a long drive. She phoned an officer she knew was on duty and by chance they were at their desk. She gave him the name and moments later he gave her the address.

Her sat nav told her it was four and a half hours away. It would be almost six o'clock on a Friday evening when she'd arrive. She sat in the car for a moment, trying to decide if it was worth the journey or whether a phone call would suffice.

But the girl from the sandwich shop wasn't going to talk, even if she did know where to find her.

The four and a half hour journey was necessary. Jo started the engine and set off on her way.

After twenty minutes of negotiating the thin country roads, she made it to the carriageway and put her foot down. The traffic was clear for the whole journey. She presumed that most people on a Friday afternoon were driving away from London rather than towards it. Jo managed to do the journey in a little over four hours. She also had time to think throughout the journey and she was convinced that she was doing the right thing. She had to know more and she didn't want to bury her head in the sand. She knew she might not feel any the wiser after the trip, but she at least had to try.

She arrived in Ealing and found her way to Oxford road. It was a long main road with large three storey town houses either side of the road and cars parked all along each side. She couldn't park directly outside the house she was visiting and so had to walk a hundred yards or so, but she didn't mind after being sat behind the wheel for so long.

She arrived at the well kept house. She made her way up the concrete steps that led up to the large arch that sheltered the front door.

She didn't know what she would ask, she just thought she'd see what would happen once she'd told the owner of the house who she was and why she was there.

The door bell made a loud church bell sound. A moment later the door was answered by a very attractive lady. She was dressed in a long elegant gown and was wearing full makeup. She looked as though she was about to go to a ball. Her dark hair was shoulder-length, slightly longer than it was in the picture, but Jo still knew it was her.

'Miss Valentine?' Jo asked.

'Yes,' she said.

'I'm DC Green; I was wondering if I could talk to you for a moment.'

'Has something happened? Is Christopher all right?' She seemed to panic a little.

'No, no. Everything is fine. I'm just here to ask you about somebody you used to know. It'll only take a few minutes.'

She looked at her watch. 'I'm being collected very shortly.'

'Five minutes at the most.'

She thought for a moment, but then stood aside. 'OK then. You'd better come in.'

Jo walked into a very large living room. There was a black leather corner sofa, an armchair, a television, a modern looking table against the wall filled with ornaments that Jo thought looked like antiques. There were paintings hung on the wall. There was an open fire surrounded by a very large ornate fireplace. There was also a book shelf with a small collection of books upon the shelves. Jo noticed that several of them were about chess.

'I'm afraid I can't offer you a drink,' she said. 'Time is pressing.' She spoke very eloquently and came across very intelligent and confident.

'It's fine. I'll be as quick as I can and you can carry on with your evening.'

'Please sit,' she said. She then sat on the couch opposite Jo who sat in the armchair.

Jo didn't know where to start, so she decided to say the name that changed the demeanour of the young woman in the sandwich shop earlier that day. She wanted to see if it would have the same affect. 'Danny Hughes.'

It did.

Martina Valentine's face quickly went from a polite smile to a look of disgust. 'What about him?'

'I was wondering how you knew him.'

'Look, I don't want to dig up the past. That part of my life is over.'

'I just want to know how you knew him.'

Martina stood up. 'Unless this involves me directly, I don't want to continue with this conversation.'

Jo stood up and put her hands up. 'Miss Valentine. I'm here off the record. I just want to know more about him.'

Martina stopped and looked Jo up and down. 'Are you a detective?'

Jo showed Martina her badge.

She sat back down. 'What's he done?'

'Nothing.'

'Then why are you here?'

Jo thought carefully before saying, 'I've been working with him this last week, but a couple of things have made me doubt his character a little. Anything you tell me won't get back to him, I promise.'

'OK,' she said, warily.

'I was in his house and I saw your book. You'd signed it for him with a little more of a personal message than I've seen before. I'm guessing you were an item.'

She nodded. 'We were. We were together for about three months. He swept me off my feet.'

'How did you meet?'

'It was at a chess match.'

'Did he play chess?' Jo asked.

'Not at that point. I met him in the pub where the chess tournament was taking place. He was standing at the bar and he kept looking over to me. I'm guessing you've noticed that I'm a little older than he is, so as you can imagine, I was flattered at the attention.'

Jo had noticed that she was older than he was, but Jo thought that she was very attractive indeed. Although Danny was a handsome man, he wasn't in the same league as her, Jo thought.

'We began seeing each other, well to be honest; we began a very passionate relationship. I began to teach him chess one night. I don't always enjoy teaching people, I haven't usually got the patience for it, but we had lots of fun. He said he'd like to read my book, so I gave him a copy and signed it for him.'

'I see.'

'After a couple of months, I started to realise we didn't have a future. I suppose the age gap didn't help, but it was more that we weren't on the same level intellectually. I know opposites can work well together, but I just didn't feel that he was the one for me.'

'I'm guessing that he didn't take the break up well,' Jo said.

'Danny was very upset and unhappy about it, and he begged and tried to convince me to reconsider, but I refused. I thought he'd accepted it because he left me alone for a week or so.'

'What happened then,' Jo asked.

'He joined the chess club. He was getting into the sport and seemed to be taking it seriously. But I'd started seeing another member of the club, Christopher Neville.'

'Is that the Christopher you mentioned earlier?'

'Yes. We're still together now, in fact. He's picking me up shortly.'

She paused for a moment. She seemed to disappear into deep thought.

'Miss Valentine?' Jo asked.

She took a deep breath. 'It was a horrible time in my life. He phoned me constantly; he sent nasty text messages, he kept appearing outside my door. Christopher is a very good chess player, and Danny was drawn against him couple of times during our internal club games. Christopher beat him both times and Danny was really angry about it. Danny was a poor loser; he lost his temper and had to be calmed down. Then...' she trailed off.

'What happened?'

'We came home from a night out and Danny was in my house. He turned violent. He punched Christopher and knocked him unconscious. He then started on me.'

'Did he hit you?'

'No. He didn't hit me, but he threw me against the wall in a mad rage. He then started smashing my living room up.'

'Did you call the police?'

'No.'

'Why not?'

'It sounds a little silly looking back now, but with him being a police officer, I don't know... I didn't feel as though they would believe me and maybe take his side. He had this authoritarian way about him. I felt as though I couldn't phone the police because he *was* the police. It's stupid, but that's how he made me feel.'

'Did he get away with it?'

'Well, the next morning he phoned me. I answered. He was still his arrogant self, but I could tell he was worried about what I would do next. He was on the brink of a promotion and he didn't want anything to stop him advancing his career.'

'And did he leave you alone after that?'

'Once I'd said my piece.'

'What did you tell him?'

'I told him that my neighbours had heard the commotion and that they saw him leave. They hadn't, neither of them were home at the time. But I pretended that they were and I said if he didn't leave London, I'd call the police. I said that he had to move away within the week or I'd pick up the phone and end his career.'

'And he went?' Jo asked.

'Christopher drove past the flat he was renting a week later and there was a To Let sign on the front.'

'Problem solved.'

There was a beep of a horn from outside.

Martina stood and waved through the window.

Jo got to her feet too. 'Thank you for your time, Miss Valentine. Here's my number if you think of anything else I need to know.'

She took the card. 'Has he committed a crime?'

'No. There's nothing for you to worry about. I just wanted to know more about him.'

'Where is he living now?'

'Tregoltha.'

'Where's that?'

'Cornwall.'

She looked surprised. 'You've travelled all the way from Cornwall to ask me about a chess book you found on his shelf. There's more to this, isn't there?'

'Look; I don't think he's committed any crime. I just have a bit of a funny feeling about him, like he isn't quite who we think he is. Call it woman's intuition.'

'Well if I were you, DC Green, I'd stay as far away from him as possible.'

'That's a little difficult when we work in the same department.'

'Well, whatever you do, don't fall for his charms.'

'Oh, I won't be going down that road. Don't worry.'

'Well I hope I've helped you in some way. I can't say it's been a pleasure because I was hoping to live the rest of my life without hearing that name again.'

'I'm sorry. Thank you. You've been a great help.'

Chapter 40

Jo struggled with the journey home. Not because she was tired, but because of what she was thinking. She didn't know what to do next. She had to drive for four hours, which gave her time to think, but she wasn't sure if she was getting carried away. Danny was a detective with an impeccable record, but Martina Valentine had no reason to lie. During the long drive home, everything started to fall into place. Almost everything fit, and Jo knew how to find out if what she was thinking was possible. She had to go back to the office and log into the police computer.

It was approaching nine-thirty by the time she sat at her desk in the empty office. The room was dark except for the light of the computer screen. She first checked the files for the Bodmin Butcher murders and wrote down the dates and estimated times of the deaths. Then she had to search the hours lists to see who was or wasn't on duty at those times. She then checked one last thing. She looked to see who the first officers were to visit Vladek Boniek and there it was. Everything fit.

On paper it looked like her suspicions were right, but she needed to be positive before she did anything. She wished that DCI Collis was in his office, but at this time on a Friday night she didn't think he would be. She knocked on his door, she then opened it, but the room was empty.

As she walked back to her desk, she was startled as DS Killik entered the room, switching one of the lights on so the room was a little brighter, but not as bright as it usually was.

'Jo,' Rachel said. 'What are you doing here? I thought you'd finished early.'

'I had.' Jo thought for a moment. She wondered if DS Rachel Killik would be a good person to discuss the situation with.

'Is there something wrong?'

Jo took a deep breath. 'Is there anyone else here at the moment?'

'There are several officers downstairs,' Rachel said.

'No. I mean from our department.'

'No. Nobody's here apart from us.'

Jo pulled a chair out at the large desk in the centre of the room. 'Can you sit for a moment? This is pretty big. I'm not positive that I'm right, but I'm starting to think that I am, either way, I'm going to shock you.'

Rachel looked a little worried and sat down in the dark office opposite her.

Jo removed her notebook and briefly looked the three things she written down earlier. It read:

OCD

~~Hates women~~

Chess

She then put her notebook back in her pocket. She was about to say something that couldn't be taken back, something that if she was wrong she would regret forever, but if she was right, it would change everything.

'Go on,' Rachel said. 'You're starting to worry me.'

'I think Vladek Boniek might be innocent.'

Chapter 41

Rachel looked surprised. 'Is it something he said at the hospital?'

'Kind of; I didn't really believe him at the time, but some other information has come to light since then.'

'OK.'

Jo sat in silence. She still doubted herself. But she had to tell her and if Rachel could prove otherwise then great. It would still stir up trouble, but at least it would be out in the open and one way or another, she'd find out for sure if her suspicions were right.

'Jo, just spit it out. What's happened?'

Jo took another deep breath before looking Rachel in the eye.

'I think Danny is the Bodmin Butcher.'

Rachel sat back in her chair and looked shocked at Jo's declaration. She didn't speak; she just stared at her with her mouth open and her eyes wide.

'Say something,' Jo said.

'I don't know what to say. What's brought you to that ridiculous conclusion?'

Jo didn't know where to start. She decided to start with Boniek's defence.

'Vladek Boniek is a clean freak.'

'Yes,' Rachel said, looking confused.

'I connected him to the murders because of his OCDs. The murderer tidied up after himself so I thought he was worth investigating. When I went to see him, he panicked and tried to run off. We then found a handkerchief with Christine Byrne's blood on it. Case closed. His defence was why would he stuff a dirty handkerchief down the side of his armchair when he is so obsessive about cleaning?'

'Yes. He said that at the trial, didn't he?'

'Yes. But the prosecution ignored it, or at least moved past it. But it's a big thing for someone with an OCD to leave a bloodied handkerchief down the side of his sofa. If he was keeping it as a keepsake it would've been stored somewhere much neater than that.'

'So where does Danny fit in? And bear in mind you're accusing a fellow detective.'

'I know, but it all fits. Let's forget Boniek for a moment. The killer targeted women, all around the Tregoltha area, which is where Danny lives. The killer tidied up after himself and I went to Danny's house this morning and it is immaculate; I mean, look at his desk. It's just as neat as that.'

Rachel looked over to the desk in the shadows.

Jo could see that the desk was as neat as always with everything perfectly arranged.

'I don't think that's enough to...'

Jo politely interrupted. 'That's not all.'

'What else?'

'He wasn't on shift when any of the murders were thought to have been committed.'

'Coincidence?' Rachel said.

'Maybe; but he also visited Boniek at his home. He could've planted the handkerchief then.'

This seemed to spark something in Rachel's memory.

'What?' Jo asked.

'I was with him.'

'When he went to his house?'

'Yes. I remember now. He said he wanted to look around. I stayed in the kitchen while Boniek made us a cup of coffee.'

'So he could've done it then?'

'He could have,' Rachel said.

Jo thought that Rachel was now starting to see the connection.

'What started this train of thought?' Rachel asked.

'I saw an old girlfriend of his in a shop. I couldn't think who she was because I'd never seen her in person, but Danny showed me a picture of her earlier in the week. I asked her how I knew her before I realised. But as soon as I mentioned Danny, she bolted. She looked scared.'

'Really?'

'Yes. I didn't say anything at the time to Danny. I just presumed they'd had a bad break up. But then when I went to his house, not only was it ridiculously tidy and clean, but he had a book on chess. I opened it and it was signed by the author, Martina Valentine, in quite a personal way, so I drove to London today to see her. She told me how they were a couple but after she broke it off with him he turned nasty.'

'How nasty?'

'He assaulted her and her new partner. He'd been stalking her and after the assault rather than report him, she told him to leave London.'

'So he wasn't arrested?'

'No. He wanted his promotion so he moved to Cornwall.'

'It does all fit.'

'It does. I just don't know how he connects with the victims other than living in Tregoltha.'

'The chess club,' Rachel said.

'What do you mean?

'He was a member of the Tregoltha Chess Club.'

That was it, the final nail in the coffin.

'I didn't know that,' Jo said.

'Yes. He went to that chess club. He left after the murders.'

'And this is common knowledge?'

'Yes.'

'I didn't know.'

They both stared at each other, wide eyed as they tried to take in the situation. They were now both on the same page.

Jo was now certain of two things. Boniek was innocent, and Danny Hughes was the Bodmin Butcher.

'What do we do now?' Jo asked.

'We need to speak to DCI Collis.'

'Should we ring Danny and find out where he is?'

'I don't think there's any rush,' Rachel said. 'After all, if you're right, it's been a while since he's killed anyone. We'll speak to the DCI first.'

Rachel started to flick through her phone, looking for the number.

Jo suddenly went into another train of thought, caused by what Rachel had just said. She reached over the table and put her hand over her phone. 'Wait.'

Rachel looked confused. 'What now?'

Jo didn't speak. Her brain sprung into action and quickly went over the events of the last week. She thought of the campers. She then thought of Lucy and how she left the pub just before Danny. She then thought of Laura and how she interrupted an uncomfortable discussion between her and Danny. Jo thought they were talking about her, but they weren't. Danny was making a move on Laura and that night Laura was killed. It all fit, just as well as the previous murders.

'Jo, what is it?'

Jo stared into Rachel's eyes before revealing the information she'd just realised.

'Danny isn't just the Bodmin Butcher,' she said.

'What do you mean?'

'He's also the Beast of Bodmin.'

Rachel looked stunned.

'He left the pub before Lucy, I saw him having an awkward

conversation with Laura the day she died, and he was very quick to arrest Teddy with very little evidence. He wanted to frame him just like he did with Boniek.'

'Are we getting carried away here?' Rachel asked.

'I really don't think we are.'

They sat staring at each other for a moment as they let the situation sink in. Jo was scared that she was wrong, but she really didn't want this to cloud her judgement. She knew she was right.

'I'm going to ring Danny,' Jo said. 'Just to see where he is. I'll ask him if he fancies a drink or something.'

'If you're right about this, then the panther was his scapegoat. Now the animal has been caught, he doesn't have any cover so I don't think he'll do it again,' Rachel said.

'Yes, but at some point there's going to be a forensic examination of the panther, and we might find out that it hasn't killed anyone.'

'What about Teddy?'

'It obviously attacked Teddy, but I think Helen was right with her first thought; if it had have been the panther, we would've have found some remains.'

Jo searched her phone for Danny's number and pressed call.

'Relax,' Rachel said. 'You don't want him to suspect anything.'

'OK.'

It rang and rang, but he didn't answer.

'That's unusual,' Jo said. 'It's the first time he hasn't answered his phone to me.'

'What now?' Rachel said.

'We wait and see if he returns my call. Or maybe we should head over to his house. He lives in Tregoltha, so it won't take us long to get there.'

'Let's go.'

They both stood up and headed for the door.

Chapter 42

Jo felt sick at the thought of Danny being the killer. As Rachel drove quickly to Tregoltha, all Jo could think about was his reaction to being found out. He was a big man and he wasn't going to come quietly. Although they weren't one hundred percent sure it was Danny who'd killed the victims, Jo knew they had to find him. She wondered if they were doing the right thing by turning up at his house without first calling for backup in the shape of a squad car full of officers. But Rachel said they would talk to him first and try to gauge his reaction.

The street lamp spread a blanket of orange across the front garden of Danny's house as they pulled the car up onto the curb.

'His car isn't here,' Rachel said.

Jo opened the door.

'Where are you going?' Rachel said. 'He's obviously not in.'

Jo continued to get out of the car before walking over to the house. She knocked on the door and looked through the living room window. He wasn't home, but Jo wasn't prepared to just leave.

As she was looking through the window, a text message came through on her phone.

It was from Helen. It read, *'It's getting a little late. Are we going for a drink or have you been held up?'*

She didn't answer it. She thought she'd ring her when they'd finished at Danny's house.

Rachel was out of the car by now. 'What are you thinking, Jo?'

Jo turned around to her and said, 'I'm thinking that the bodies must be in his house.'

'We need to find Danny first,' Rachel said. 'We can't be breaking into his house without enough evidence for doing so.'

Jo knew Rachel was right. But she couldn't ignore the evidence they had, and she couldn't ignore her gut feeling that this would be a good place to hide the bodies.

'No one would expect to find dead bodies in a detective's house.'

'Jo,' Rachel said. 'Don't make me pull rank here. We need to go.'

'Let's just check round the back first, just in case there's a door open.'

Rachel begrudgingly agreed. 'Quickly then.'

They walked to the left of the house; they passed the attached garage and walked around the pathway that led behind his house.

As they got to the back of the house, Jo then noticed a door at the back of the garage. It wasn't a very sturdy door. It was made of wood, but it looked old and a little decayed at the edges. Jo just stared at the door.

'What?' Rachel said.

'If he's hiding four dead bodies, he's not going to keep them in the house. He's going to keep them in his garage.'

'Maybe,' Rachel said. 'But we can't just break in.'

'I suppose not.'

Rachel then walked over to the back window of the house and looked inside.

Jo stared at the door to the garage. She was almost positive about Danny. She couldn't just walk away. She had to know if she was right.

Jo quickly looked at Rachel, who was still looking through the rear window of the house. So Jo took a step forward to the wooden door. She put her fingers through the splintered gap at the top corner of the door. Both hands fit through and although she felt the broken wood digging into her hands, she quickly pulled with all her strength.

The door bent before breaking away from the lock in the

251

centre. It flew open with a loud bang as bits of wood flew and Jo fell backwards almost losing her footing.

'Jo!' Rachel hissed at her.

Jo brushed the wooden crumbs of her hands as she looked at Rachel.

'Sorry Rachel, but we can leave if I'm wrong and let him think he's been broken into.'

Jo saw Rachel look around at the other houses that overlooked them, but Jo didn't care who was watching. She wanted to see inside the garage.

As she walked into the dark garage, she took her mobile phone out and switched the torch on. She then shone it on the wall at the side of the doorway where she saw the light switch.

She turned it on and a large fluorescent light tube hanging from the ceiling flashed a couple of times before lighting up the garage.

Danny's OCDs were apparent in his garage too. There were shelves all along one side of the room where there were tools and boxes and gardening equipment all neatly arranged, neater than any garage Jo had ever seen before.

But the thing that caught Jo's eye more than anything was the blue-framed click together shelves that were standing in front of the metal garage door. There were six shelves, six feet long each at least standing three rows high.

Of the six shelves, four of them were full.

Jo's heart was pounding in her chest. She felt Rachel stand close behind her to see what she had seen.

Neither of them spoke as Jo walked over to the shelves.

The four shelves that were full had one large object on each. Jo knew what they were at first glance. The dark blue thick plastic sheeting surrounded the shape inside, a shape that Jo didn't see could be anything else.

As she reached the shelves, she focused on just one of the

bundles. She crouched down to the one on the bottom shelf on the right side. She knew what they were and she knew what was in them, but she had to look.

Her heart was beating hard and her hands were trembling as she reached for the plastic.

She pulled hard on the flap of plastic but it was wrapped around too tight.

Jo turned to look at Rachel who was standing behind her, leaning over her shoulder.

Rachel then said, 'Hang on.' She walked away to the shelves where the gardening tools were and rummaged in one of the boxes before returning with some secateurs.

Jo took them from her.

Rachel gave a nod, telling her to go ahead.

Jo then cut the thick plastic from the top, working her way to the middle.

Even though she knew what was inside, the shock of seeing Lucy's face come into view sent Jo falling backwards.

She was overwhelmed with a sickening feeling as she coughed and spluttered to try and remove the smell and taste of decay from her mouth and lungs.

She then covered her face with her arm and walked back to see Lucy, staring up at her from the body bag. Her skin was grey and her hair matted with black blood. Her lips were dark blue and her eyes were wide.

Jo thought of what kind of girl Lucy was. She certainly didn't deserve to have ended up on a shelf in the garage of a cold-blooded murderer.

Rachel took Jo by the arm and led her outside.

Once outside, she asked, 'Are you OK?'

Jo took a deep breath and nodded. 'I'm fine.'

'I'm going to call it in,' Rachel said. 'You go and sit down somewhere.'

Jo nodded and walked around to the front of the house. She sat on the front wall.

She took her phone out to check the time when she remembered Helen's message.

She decided to ring her.

'Oh, hello, Jo,' Helen answered.

'Sorry, Helen; I don't think I'll be able to see you tonight.'

'It's OK, Jo. I understand if you're busy. There will be a lot going on at the station I can imagine.'

'Quite a lot to be honest.' Jo paused a moment before asking, 'Where are you at the moment?'

'I'm in my kitchen at home, making a coffee; why?'

'Just wondering. I hate the thought of you waiting for me and feeling stood up.'

'Well Danny's here anyway.'

Jo's heart almost stopped at the shock of what Helen just said. 'Danny?'

'Yes, he's here now.'

Jo's stomach churned with fear, not fear for herself, fear for Helen's safety.

'He's just called for me to sign the forms for us helping with the panther.'

Jo had to think fast. She didn't want to risk making things worse or maybe even prompt an attack from Danny.

'I forgot about that. Listen, Helen, don't tell him I've called. I don't want him to think I wasn't listening to him,' she said, putting on a fake laugh. 'He can't hear you now can he?'

'No. He's in the living room.'

'OK. Well, I'll let you make your coffee and I'll ring you later on tonight, if that's OK?'

'Of course. I'll look forward to it.'

'One more thing, Helen, I need your address for *my* paperwork,' she said, grabbing a pen and notebook from her pocket.

'Number seven, Woodlands Drive, Tregoltha.'

'OK, thanks for that. I'll speak to you later,' Jo said. She then hung up the phone.

She quickly ran around the back of the house to get Rachel.

Rachel had just hung up her phone. 'They're on their way.'

'We need to go,' Jo said.

'Why? What's wrong?'

'I just phoned Helen. Danny's there.'

Rachel seemed to think for a second before saying, 'Let's go. Uniform will be here shortly anyway.'

Jo knew they shouldn't leave a crime scene unattended, but they had to go and help Helen, so they jumped in the car and drove off at speed.

Chapter 43

Helen couldn't help but smile at the fact that Jo had phoned her and she couldn't wait to give her a call back once Danny had left. It was only that morning when she saw her last, but she was still excited to see her again. She found it a little strange that Jo asked her not to tell Danny that she'd phoned. But she understood that Danny was her superior and didn't want to come across as incompetent to him.

Jo seemed anything but incompetent to Helen. Helen was impressed by her intelligence when they'd first met at the zoo. Normally Helen had little patience for people who didn't understand animals. It was the one thing she disliked about her job when visitors stopped her and asked her questions because more often than not, they were the same questions she'd heard many times before. But Jo was different. Jo seemed to have an understanding of animals and she asked intelligent questions. Helen could also tell that she'd done a little research before going to the zoo. This made it so much easier to help her.

Helen was also impressed by the fact that Jo was an Oxford graduate. She found the story of how she went from wanting to become a writer to becoming a detective fascinating. She found everything about her fascinating. She couldn't wait to see her again. She couldn't wait to kiss her again. She hoped that their relationship didn't just exist because of the events that brought them together and just left to die once the case was finished. She hoped they had a future.

After she'd made the coffees, she took them through to the living room where Danny was looking through a book on big cats that Helen had left on her coffee table.

As she walked into the room, Danny stood up and took the

cup of coffee from her, still holding the book open with his other hand.

'It says here that panthers can be black leopards or black jaguars.'

'That's right,' Helen said. 'Ours is a black leopard.'

'What's the difference?'

'Jaguars are a bigger, stockier. They come from South America whereas leopards are from Africa. There's a difference in the rosettes too.'

'Panthers don't have markings,' Danny said.

'Yes they do. You can only see them when the light hits them a certain way, but they're there.'

'Hmm. I didn't notice that today.'

He closed the book before taking a sip of his coffee.

Helen sat on the opposite couch. There was a moment of uncomfortable silence as Danny looked at her. She felt uneasy in his company. She didn't know why, but she didn't really like him that much. She thought he came across as a little arrogant, and possibly thought a lot of himself. Or it might have been the lack of sympathy he showed when they'd discussed whether or not the panther should be destroyed.

'I suppose you found today an exciting change of pace?' he asked.

'It was certainly different,' Helen said. 'I didn't expect to...'

'Are you not married?' Danny said.

Helen was taken back at how rude he was to interrupt her. She answered anyway. 'No. No I'm single.'

'Do you fancy going out with me one night?'

Helen was even more shocked by his manner of asking such a question. She felt a slight quiver in her stomach. Surely this was against the rules for a detective to ask a member of the public out like this, especially on a police related visit. Helen had never wasted too much time on manners before and didn't want to start now. 'No,' she said. 'No, I don't.'

'OK,' he said.

Helen was beginning to feel more uneasy and couldn't help but fidget in her seat.

He just stared at her. He didn't look nervous when he asked her out and he didn't look disappointed when she said no.

'Look,' Helen started. 'Can we get on with signing these forms? I have an early start tomorrow.'

'Yes,' he said, still staring. 'No problem.'

He still didn't move.

Then Helen realised that she couldn't see any forms. 'Where are...'

'They're in the car. I'll go and get them.' He took a gulp of his coffee and then stood up.

He left the room and Helen heard the front door open.

She stood up and took the cups into the kitchen. He hadn't finished his drink but she wanted him to go so she poured away what was left and started to wash the cups. After rinsing them, she put the cups onto the draining board; she then turned around and almost screamed as she saw Danny standing in the doorway of the kitchen.

'You scared me to death,' she said.

He just stood there looking at her.

She became more nervous as his arrogant demeanour seemed to exacerbate.

He stood in the doorway of the kitchen, still dressed in his suit, but there was something different about him. He was wearing black leather gloves. He wasn't wearing them before, and why would anyone wear leather gloves in the height of summer? She also realised that he wasn't holding any pieces of paper.

He slowly walked over to her.

Helen stood back against the sink as she watched him gradually come closer.

Without taking his eyes off her, he slowly reached out and opened the top drawer next to her; he then looked inside and took out a knife, the biggest knife from the drawer. The knife wasn't as big as the ones in the knife rack on the worktop next to the sink. This one had a metal handle and an eight-inch blade.

Helen felt her temperature change, almost like she was freezing cold on the outside, but boiling hot on the inside. 'What are you doing?' She asked, nervously. Her heart began to beat harder and her legs felt weak.

'What do you think I'm doing?' he said. He spoke very politely and calmly.

Helen wondered if it was some sort of joke, but if it was she didn't see the funny side. She had a six foot four inch muscular man standing in front of her with a knife in his hands. She couldn't imagine this being a joke of any kind.

'The thing is, Helen,' he said, very slowly. 'At some point, we're going to discover that the panther hasn't eaten anybody.'

Helen started to understand what was happening. Her hands began to sweat and her leg muscles tightened. She could hear her breaths becoming more rapid.

'You're going to see that these people who have lost their lives, haven't got any connection to the animal you caught today.'

'Why are you telling me this?'

'I think you know why.'

'I don't.'

She didn't care why he was telling her; she just wanted him out of her house. She tried to think of a way to make this happen.

'You and Jo,' he said. 'You two are becoming close aren't you?'

Helen wondered why he was changing the subject. 'I suppose,' she said. 'Why?'

'I was just wondering how close.'

'I like her a lot, yes.'

He looked her straight in the eye. 'You're a dyke, aren't you?' he said. This was a statement more than a question. 'I've seen the way you look at her.'

'What if I am?'

'I think she likes you too.'

'I don't understand what this has to do with anything,' she said, raising her voice a little.

'Just a funny coincidence, that's all. I killed Laura last night. She was a dyke as well.'

Although Helen already knew by now that Danny was the killer, hearing him say it was confirmation that he was in fact going to kill her. He wouldn't have shared this with her if he wasn't planning on doing something dreadful to her. Once a statement like that has been spoken, it can't be taken back.

'You know I can help you, don't you?' she said.

'How?'

'I have keys to the zoo.' This wasn't true, but she thought it might buy her some time at least.

He frowned. 'Why is that going to help me?'

'Because if we go to the zoo, we can take the cat and release it again and nobody will know what happened.'

Danny started to laugh. 'You expect me to believe that? We go and remove the panther, then I let you go and you want me to believe that you won't say anything? And you expect me to believe that the zoo hasn't got cameras everywhere?'

'I can help you avoid them.'

'I'd give it up if I was you. It's over.'

He took another step towards her. His eyes briefly shot to the knife rack behind her. He seemed to give a gentle laugh to himself, almost as if he was annoyed for choosing a smaller knife from the drawer when there are six, larger ones there waiting for him.

His wide, blue eyes fixed on her once more. 'I am going to kill you and then I'm going to go home. There's no need for me to remove the bodies anymore. I'm going to kill you, leave you here, and being a detective, I'll be the last person they will suspect. It's better to kill you now before they realise that there is still a killer on the loose. Then tomorrow, I'll be sent here to investigate the scene.'

'Maybe I was too hasty before,' Helen said, shuddering.

'What?'

'Maybe we could go out.'

Danny laughed. 'Now you're reaching.'

He was right. She didn't think he would fall for that now, but she was running out of ideas.

'I don't understand,' she said. Her stomach began to hurt.

'Understand what?' he asked calmly.

'Why do you have to kill me?' Helen said. The shaking in her voice was getting worse. 'Why?' she shouted.

He took another step closer to her and put his face to hers.

His wide eyes were only a few inches from her as she leaned back as far as she could. She felt his breath on her face and could smell coffee and aftershave blending together.

He then whispered, 'Why not?'

Chapter 44

Jo called DCI Collis to let him know what was happening as DS Rachel Killik drove them to Helen's house. He took some convincing in the fact that one of his detectives was the murderer they'd been looking for, and that there was an innocent man in prison. But eventually, Jo convinced him that this situation was very real.

Jo hoped there would be a squad car following them, or maybe even one already there by the time they arrived. But this wasn't the case: Rachel pulled into the quiet cul-de-sac in Tregoltha and threw the car up onto the pavement across the street from Helen's house. Jo said it would be better to run the last ten yards rather than inadvertently cause an attack with the sound of screeching tyres and slamming car doors. Rachel agreed.

The street was a very quiet one that only had a dozen small semi-detached houses, six either side. Helen's row backed onto a forest that Jo could see between the gaps in the houses. There were two street lamps, making it bright enough to see the forest behind Helen's house that was situated in the middle of the street.

They both got out of the car and ran over the road to the cottage. Jo ran just in front of Rachel and opened the unlocked door and ran straight inside. They should've looked through the windows first, Jo thought, but she didn't want to delay and risk Helen getting hurt.

Jo quickly walked along the hallway. She was just going to turn right into the living room when she saw Danny and Helen in the kitchen ahead of her. Danny was standing in front of the sink, very close to Helen. He was holding a kitchen knife as if he were about to thrust it into Helen's stomach. He was staring at her with a look of utter hatred, still wearing his suit, but he was also wearing black leather gloves.

Jo dashed through the doorway and into the kitchen. As soon as Danny saw Jo, he turned away from Helen and glared at her.

Jo felt sick. She was terrified that at any moment Danny might stab Helen to death and furious that Danny was obviously the murderer. Jo knew now that Danny had killed Lucy and Laura, along with the other victims.

Jo made a lunge for the knife.

'Jo, no!' Rachel shouted, trying to stop her.

But Jo wasn't going to be stopped. Danny was holding a knife to Helen. Quite apart from the prime directive Jo felt as a police officer to protect life, she knew she was falling for Helen, and there was no way she was going to let Danny hurt her.

Danny was quick, but Jo was quicker. She grabbed both his wrists with both hands as he began to swing the knife towards Helen. Helen, who looked scared beyond belief, swung herself away from Danny, who had already begun to thrust the knife at her. With Jo holding Danny's wrists and Helen moving, the knife, when it thrust at Helen, didn't go deep into her body but nicked her on her left side as she leaned back against the cupboards to try to avoid it.

Helen screamed as the knife cut her.

'You bastard!' Jo shouted at Danny. She was still grasping both his wrists and used all her strength to pull him away from Helen. But Danny managed to get his left hand free and punched Jo on the right side of her face

Her face suddenly felt full of fire where Danny had punched her. She felt dizzy and in pain, but what made her feel even worse was that a man she had trusted and even liked could've behaved this way towards her and Helen. Now, through the fog of her dizziness, she saw over her right shoulder Rachel rushing towards them and bringing down her now extended baton onto Danny's hand with a loud smack. Danny groaned with pain as he dropped the knife. He elbowed Jo in the mouth before stepping forwards and punching Rachel full in the face before she could swing her baton again. Rachel fell backwards landing hard on the white tiled floor but not -'thank god', Jo thought - hitting her head on the tiles. Yet it was obvious that Rachel was out cold.

Jo could only hope Rachel wasn't too badly hurt but there was no time to get to her to check. Jo grabbed her baton, gave a vigorous flick to extend it and pointed it at Danny as if it were a sword. Danny raised his left hand in front of him to protect himself. The expression on his face was one Jo hadn't seen before on Danny or anyone. His eyes were wide as he snarled at her, baring his teeth in anger.

She swung the extended the baton at him. He nimbly dodged backwards avoiding the blow.

Jo jumped in front of Helen to protect her.

Danny looked around frantically as he tried to decide his next move. His eyes quickly shot around the room.

He'd just been revealed as the Beast of Bodmin, he'd injured Helen and seriously hurt Rachel, a fellow detective. Jo knew Danny's options were running out.

He dashed towards Jo as she swung the baton at him again. Once more he avoided it by dodging out of the way.

Jo momentarily considered running at Danny and trying to knock him down, using the baton to try to knock him out. But the trouble was, Danny was a big man, and Helen and Rachel were both hurt. Jo wanted to make sure they were OK and she knew if Danny got the better of her he'd more than likely kill her, Helen and Rachel too.

Danny feigned to the right but moved to the left. He grabbed a chair from next to the wooden dining table. He shouted 'Bitch!' as he lifted the chair above his head before throwing it at Jo.

Jo turned her back towards the chair as it came at her. It crashed against her back and shoulders, knocking the wind from her before it smashed to the floor.

The next thing Jo saw was Danny bolting through the back door of the house.

Jo felt flooded with relief that he'd gone. She quickly turned to Helen and took Helen's arm with her left hand. Touching her, despite the horrible circumstances and hurt face and the pain in her back from where the chair had hit her, Jo felt flooded with electric excitement. 'Are you OK?' she asked Helen.

Helen raised her shirt with her shaking hands to reveal a four-inch scratch above her left hip that was just starting to bleed. She grabbed a towel from the kitchen worktop and pressed it against the cut. 'Jo, I'll be fine,' she said. 'Check your friend.'

Jo crouched down next to Rachel who lay unconscious on the white tiled floor. Her right eye socket was red and swollen.

Jo leaned closely to Rachel's face. She could feel her breath. 'Please stay with her,' she said to Helen. 'Help should be here soon. I'll radio for an ambulance.'

'Don't worry,' Helen said. 'I'll look after her. What are you going to do?'

'Danny's the murderer. He'd have killed you if I hadn't have stopped him. I have to catch him.'

'I know,' Helen said. 'But Jo, please be careful.'

Jo felt sure she'd seen love in Helens eyes, but she didn't dare to hope she was right about that.

Helen smiled.

Jo smiled back at Helen and kissed her on the lips. Right then, at that moment, despite everything that was going on, despite Rachel being unconscious, and Danny having got away for the time being, despite now knowing who the Beast of Bodmin really was, and Vladek Boniek being unjustly locked up and living on prison food, doubtless with no 500 ml bottle of Evian water in sight, at that moment, Helen was the only important element in Jo's world.

Jo would've liked the kiss to have gone on forever, but then she thought of Danny roaming free like a wild dog, searching for his next victim to get another murder or two under his belt before he was locked up forever. Very reluctantly Jo broke the kiss.

'I've got to go,' she whispered at Helen.

Helen gave her a nod.

The next moment, Jo turned and ran through the open doorway, still holding the baton stretched out like a sword, in pursuit of Danny. She knew she was never going to let him escape.

Jo pulled her radio up to her mouth and asked for any available officers to come to the scene, and for them to send an ambulance. She knew there would be help on its way, but she couldn't wait. She had to stop him.

There wasn't time to assess the situation; Jo had to try her best to catch him. She ran across the garden to the wooden gate that was open in the middle of the six foot wooden fence. As she came through the fence, still holding her baton, the lights from the kitchen window lit up the garden but not the land at the back of the houses. Her eyes started to focus. The fields to the left led to another estate about three hundred yards away. She couldn't see Danny. To the right was a wooded area, starting about twenty feet down the hill. She wondered if he'd made his way back around to the front of the houses, but he would've had to have been fast as the fences at the rear of the houses continued for another fifty yards. He must've gone into the woods.

From where Jo stood, it looked more like a spinney than a wood. She couldn't tell, but she thought it was about the size of a football field, judging by the length of the row of trees along the left hand side. The houses at the other end of the field seemed to surround the area.

She switched on the torch icon on her phone and held it out in front of her with her left hand as she held the baton in her right.

As she made her way to the dark entrance of the woods, she heard a rustle in the distance. It was quite a way from where she was, but she was pretty sure the rustling was Danny. It wasn't the kind of sound that an animal would make. This was more like a person stumbling in the dark woodland.

She went into the woods.

She'd driven to and from London all in one day and should've been ready for sleep by now, but she was running on adrenaline. She'd been hailed as a hero for catching Boniek, but now she knows he's innocent, and she can't allow Danny to escape.

The woods would've been almost pitch-black if it wasn't for the torch on her phone. She was aware that using this would give away her whereabouts to Danny, but she still felt it was the best option rather than making her way through the woods in the dark.

As she shone the torch light from side to side, she realised just how scared she was. Although there had been a panther on the loose, there was something more terrifying about trying to find Danny Hughes. He couldn't see in the dark and he couldn't move as silently as a panther, but he was deadly, and he'd shown his relentless non-negotiable malice when he swung an elbow at Jo's face; and the way he punched Rachel. Jo knew if she managed to catch him she couldn't give him an inch. She had to put him down and she had to make sure whatever happened, she didn't believe anything he said. If he could hurt Rachel so quickly and mercilessly, he wouldn't think twice about hurting Jo, especially considering she'd only known him for a week, and especially now that he had nothing to lose. At that moment, Danny was far more deadly than any big cat that had ever roamed the moors.

Jo pointed the torch side to side as she walked along the track that led into the woods. The shadows and sporadic movement of the bushes and trees in the light breeze played tricks on her. She saw eyes looking at her with every movement, but when she returned the light to the area where she thought she saw them, the eyes were gone.

She was twenty yards along the track and the woods closed in around her; giving her less room to retreat should Danny appear. She continued to walk, she wanted to run, but that would almost certainly give Danny another advantage. He already had the bonus of being able to see the light from her phone, because of this she had to walk slowly.

The phone light cut out. Possibly because she'd touched the screen by mistake, or maybe it had a timeout, she didn't know. She quickly reset the icon, still holding the baton in her hand and still aware that Danny was most likely watching her. She lit the phone up again and continued through the woods.

The dirt track went downhill and slightly to the right. Butterflies were flying in swarms around her stomach as she played the deadly game of cat and mouse with her former mentor. She wanted to find him, she wanted to catch him, but above all she wanted it to be over. It quickly crossed her mind as she wandered through the ever increasing darkness of the woods, that she could turn back and wait for help. She could wait for the dogs to arrive, or even the helicopter. But Danny had to be caught. Turning back isn't what DI Lincoln would do, and it certainly wasn't what DC Jo Green was going to do. Danny Hughes had killed eight people so far including a police officer, and he couldn't be allowed to escape.

She heard a rustling noise ahead of her. She stopped and shone the torchlight into the trees. The thick green summer leaves of the bushes could've been hiding her assailant, she didn't know. She waited for another noise. It didn't come. She waited.

As she contemplated continuing along the track, the phone light went out again. It must have a timeout, she thought. She quickly pressed the icon, as the light came back on, there was a sudden loud rustling noise accompanied by the appearance of a huge six foot four inch man coming towards her. Before she could react, a leather covered fist pounded her left cheek hard, harder than anything she was used to at her kickboxing lessons. She felt dazed. She didn't even feel herself hit the ground as her mind momentarily left the scene. She had a millisecond of a dream; she was with Helen, they were sat in the pub, Helen gazing longingly into her eyes. But she quickly snapped out of it and back into consciousness as she felt Danny land on top of her and hit her again. This strike didn't hurt as much as the first, but it awakened her into the reality of what was happening.

She fought back. She tried to grab his arms.

He swung at her again, but her self defence experience triggered her into folding her arms across her face. After the third strike, she stuck out a jab and felt his mouth against her knuckles. She knew this wouldn't be enough to stop him, but anything to slow him down would help.

He grabbed her wrists and slammed her arms to the ground at her sides.

Her left hand could feel the baton, but he was now kneeling on her arms and she couldn't swing. The phone was lying on the ground with the light facing upwards. She could see his silhouette; she could also make out his expression of pure rage.

He sat there staring at her with a wild look in his eye.

She stopped struggling; she hoped he would take this as a sign of defeat. Once she stopped struggling, his pressure seemed to lighten a little. They just stared at each other. Jo's eyes adjusted to the dark and she could make out his face a little better. She could see how much he hated her for exposing him as the Beast and Butcher of Bodmin.

She stared at him a moment longer before putting her plan into action. She quickly shot her gaze to her right and looked over his shoulder. She then attempted half a smile, trying to show relief. There was nobody there, but her acting must've been good, it was good enough to cause Danny to look behind him. As soon as he'd turned his head, she used all her strength to throw her hips into the air, pushing hard against the ground with her legs and back. He turned back to her, but not before he'd began to fall to his right.

Jo groaned as she forced him off of her, she then punched him hard in the face before scrambling to her feet.

Danny looked a little dazed but quickly stood up.

They stood there looking at each other, just five feet apart.

Jo then reached down for the baton.

The light on her phone had gone out but there was just enough light from the slight-moon for her to see him as they stood in the clearing of the woods.

Danny didn't have a weapon but she was still aware of how difficult it was going to be to get the better of him.

After a moment of them staring, Danny finally spoke. 'Bitch,' he said, through gritted teeth.

Jo could hear the anger in him, she could see how aggressive he'd become and she was in no doubt that Martina Valentine had told her the truth.

'You had to work it out, didn't you,' he said. 'And now, because of you interfering, you're going to have to die.'

'Why?' Jo said. 'Why did you have to kill all those people?'

Danny laughed. 'So you've figured it out then?'

'What, that you're the Bodmin Butcher as well as the Beast of Bodmin? Yes, I figured it out.'

He took a step towards her. 'How?' he asked.

'The evidence is all there,' Jo said. 'You were never on shift at the times of the Bodmin Butcher murders, you planted the bloodied handkerchief at Boniek's house, and you were connected to all the victims.'

He didn't reply.

'I saw your old girlfriend, the one you showed me a picture of, and when I spoke to her and told her who I was, she ran. She actually looked scared.'

He didn't show any guilt, he just stood there.

'I saw the chess book by Martina Valentine at your house and read the signature, so I then went to see her. She told me of how you'd treated her and that you'd assaulted her and her new partner.'

'You went to see her?'

'Yes. Then after I found out you was a member of the Tregoltha Chess Club, it all tied in. You killed the four women, you planted the handkerchief at Boniek's house and then you sat back and watched me become famous for catching him.'

He laughed. 'That was brilliant. I was planning on arresting him the next day, but the fact that you stuck your nose in made it all the more convincing.'

'Then, you sat back for six months and let the dust settle while an innocent man began a life sentence for something you did. You then killed the campers, then Lucy, then Laura and tried your best to frame Teddy for it.'

'Well, that didn't work,' he said. 'But the panther was a great distraction. People were going to think that the panther had done it all along. It was beautiful.'

'You had to change your tactics though. Whereas the Bodmin Butcher murders, you tidied the scenes, now as the Beast of Bodmin you removed the bodies.'

'I had to so people thought the panther was to blame. That's why I removed the bodies and planted the bloodied clothing in the woods. The bodies are all wrapped up in my garage.'

'I know.'

Danny looked confused. 'What do you mean?'

'Rachel and I went to your house. We broke into your garage.'

'How did you know they were there?'

'I knew that you were arrogant enough to think that nobody would check a detective's garage.'

Danny smirked. 'I was going to wait until the searches were called off and then bury them on the moors.

Jo pictured this but quickly pushed it to the back of her mind. She had to concentrate. 'Lester's panther escaping was a lucky coincidence to help you cover it up.'

'Oh no,' he said. 'It wasn't a coincidence.'

'What d'you mean?'

'I let the panther loose.'

'What?' Jo said.

'Yes. I already knew Lester was living in St Breward, I'd been watching him. He *was* drunk and he *did* fall asleep in the enclosure. After he woke up and went back inside, I pulled the door open while the panther was in its sleeping quarters and left. I knew when I first saw that he was keeping a big cat that it was the perfect cover for me to start a new chapter. I just had to bide my time and find the right opportunity to release it.'

Jo couldn't believe what she'd just heard.

'Now, removing the bodies was hard work, and obviously I wanted to tidy the scenes like before. But I had to make sure that no one connected the two together. I didn't want the Bodmin Butcher file reopening, you see?'

'So you released a dangerous animal, and then went looking for another victim.'

'Yes. I drove around for a while, and then came across the campers.'

'If you thought that the panther was going to take the blame, why try to kill Helen?' her voice trembled as she shouted.

'Because they're most likely going to know sooner or later that it hasn't killed anyone.'

'That's no reason to kill Helen.'

'I was hoping the panther would never be caught.'

'Why did you try to kill Helen?' Jo asked again.

He didn't reply.

'You can't help yourself, can you?' she snarled.

He still didn't answer.

'You've got a taste for it and you can't stop.'

He shrugged his shoulders.

'Who was next? Was it me?'

Again he didn't answer.

'Why? Why do you have to kill these people?'

'I don't have to explain to you.'

'And apart from one, they're all women.'

'So?'

'I'll tell you what I think,' she said.

'I don't care what you think.'

'Well, I'm going to tell you anyway. You killed those women because they rejected you. I saw you talking to Laura and I thought you were talking about me, but you weren't. You were making a move on her, and because she said no, you killed her. And I'm guessing that's what happened with the first four women from Tregoltha?'

He stepped towards her and began to shout. 'You don't know what you're talking about.'

'No?' Jo asked.

'You don't think those women deserved what they got?' He shouted.

This scared Jo a little more. He already looked and sounded angry, but now he looked like he could explode.

'Carol Forbes flirted with me over and over again at the chess club, but when I showed an interest in her, she tells me she "doesn't like me in that way." Women are always saying that sort of stuff to me. Stephanie Newham used to talk to me in the pub all the time, and again, she was just stringing me along. Claire Watts even kissed me outside the pub one night. When I declared an interest in her, she said no. And Christine Byrne from the petrol station, she laughed when I suggested us going for a drink, she actually laughed at me. I can't tell you I didn't enjoy stabbing her in the throat that night. The look of fear and regret on her face when she saw the knife, it was priceless.'

'So it is rejection?'

'Rejection I can handle. What pisses me off is when you string us along. You act like you're interested but you're not. You're all just playing some stupid game.'

'You say "us" like we're all the same.'

'You are,' he said, still looking angry.

'What about the campers?' Jo asked. She knew that the longer she kept him talking, the more chance of help arriving.

'I saw the campsite. I went over to see who it was. I enjoyed killing Steve Roberts, but not as much as I enjoyed killing the little bitch girlfriend of his.'

'Why?' Jo asked.

He shook his head. 'I just did, just like I enjoyed killing Lucy too. She deserved it for stringing along your brother.'

Jo felt infuriated at this, but tried not to let it affect her control of the situation.

'And Laura, well she probably didn't deserve it as much as the others, but yes, I asked her out, she laughed too, but that was because she was gay. I didn't know that. But I still put an end to her.'

'From what Martina Valentine said it was only a matter of time before you did something terrible. You're no different to

274

all the other serial killers out there. Only you had the cover of being a detective to give you the inside track and to lead people away from the truth.'

'It worked, didn't it?' he said with an angry smirk.

Jo thought he was about to strike. 'Until now.'

He took another step closer. 'You haven't caught me yet.'

That was true. Jo figured out that he was the killer but she still had to catch him, and he wasn't going to come easily.

He took another step towards her. 'I'm not going to enjoy this as much as I enjoyed killing the other women,' he said. 'I don't know why.'

'I do,' Jo said.

'Do enlighten me,' he said, through gritted teeth.

'You prefer your victims to be just that, victims. You don't like it when we fight back.'

This seemed to enrage him even more. 'I don't just pick on weak women.'

'Of course you do,' Jo said, raising her voice. 'That's why I wasn't on your list. You knew that if it came to it, you'd struggle to get the better of me.'

'Really?' he asked.

'Yes, and you know it.'

He seemed to think about this for a moment. He obviously didn't like his masculinity being questioned. But then he seemed to get even angrier than he already was. His chest rose and fell with deeper and deeper breaths.

He suddenly lunged at Jo.

She reacted quickly and swung the baton and caught him across the face.

He dropped to one knee before jumping straight back up again.

Jo swung again, this time he blocked it with his arm, but he groaned with pain as it landed.

He lunged at her once more, this time ducking underneath the swinging baton and grabbing Jo and tackling her to the ground.

Jo dropped the baton but managed to roll herself over with the momentum of the tackle and sent Danny over the top of her so she could quickly get back to her feet.

She swung her right leg and caught him on his jaw, this threw him backwards but he managed to stay on his feet.

As he stepped back towards her, she stuck out a left jab before swinging hard with her right fist. This punch landed hard and knocked him to the ground.

Jo was used to throwing punches, but not without her protective mitts on. She tried her best to ignore the pain in her knuckles as she prepared for another round.

He got up again and Jo swung another fist, this time she felt his jaw buckle as he fell to the floor. He landed on his back and was breathing hard as he lay flat on the ground. He wasn't unconscious, but he looked dazed as he writhed and squirmed on the ground.

Jo stood over him. She contemplated trying to put the handcuffs on him that she had in her pocket, but she didn't feel as though he was quite finished.

He lifted his head and winced as he focused on her. 'You're a tough bitch, aren't you?'

She was out of breath, but still felt strong enough to carry on if he should get up and continue to fight.

'I am.'

'Well,' he said. 'I'm not done yet.'

With that he swung his leg out, kicking Jo in her left knee. This caused her leg to buckle and before she could correct her balance, a leather gloved fist hit her hard on the cheek and sent her flying backwards onto the ground.

She stood up quickly but she then felt a hard hit on her jaw from the baton. She hadn't seen him pick it up, she hadn't even seen him swing it, but she sure as hell felt it.

She collapsed to the floor and he hit her again, this time catching her in the temple. She fell back against the ground and immediately felt blood run down her face. She lifted her head up to try and focus on her attacker, but the baton struck her again, this time on her left cheek.

She lay on her back and looked up at the dark sky. Her left eye wouldn't focus and she felt warm sensation make its way down her face. One more hit across her cheek was enough to stop her from moving.

She lay still. Everything hurt. She could hardly breathe with the pain and her vision wouldn't come into focus. Her head was spinning. She tried her best to stay awake; she tried her best to see.

She could hear his footsteps as he stood over her. He'd stopped swinging the baton for now, but she waited, wondering when the next hit would come.

She could taste a metallic taste in her mouth she was sure was blood. She hurt all over and felt as though that was it. She was beaten. She'd figured out that he was the murderer, but she hadn't stopped him. He was about to finish her off and escape once more. She took small comfort in the fact that she'd called DCI Collis so at least his guilt wasn't a secret anymore. But he was about to get away.

Her eyes began to focus on the huge shape of a man that was Danny Hughes.

He towered over her, still with the baton in his hand.

'I still caught you,' Jo said. The words came out slurred, but she knew he'd heard her.

'Not really,' he said. 'I'm going to get away with this.'

'No you're not,' Jo said. 'We called DCI Collis before we got here.'

'That doesn't surprise me. But I won't be caught. I have a plan.'

Jo lifted her head a little more and sat back on her elbows.

'I knew that sooner or later someone would get close to figuring it all out. Do you not think I have a plan B?'

'No,' she said. 'I don't think you have. And by morning, you'll be in a cell.'

'I don't think so.'

'You will be. You're not that clever.'

'I'm tired of this conversation. I'm tired of you and your big mouth. I hadn't finished yet, not by a long shot. But you know what, Jo? You are.'

He raised the baton above his head. The anger in his face made Jo realise that her time was up. There was nothing more she could do. She lay there on the ground with blood pouring from her head. She was feeling very weak and she knew she didn't have much left. She quickly thought about what to do and thought that she'd wait until he was down thrusting with the baton before trying to roll over. She had nothing to lose. She thought she'd spin away and then try to grab him once more.

She waited.

He didn't move.

He stood with his arm in the air, still clutching the baton. The look of anger disappeared from his face as his eyes softened and he started to smile.

What was he doing? Jo thought. Had he changed his mind? Did he want to let her go?

His evil smile almost turned to a laugh as he just stood there.

She didn't know what he was doing.

His arm fell to his side and he dropped the baton. His smile then grew bigger as his eyes rolled backwards before he fell, face first, onto the ground at the side of her. Jo then spotted the knife in the nape of his neck before she saw the figure standing behind him.

It was Helen.

Jo couldn't believe what had happened.

Helen ran to Jo and crouched down next to her.

The pain in Jo's head was still there, but the overwhelming feeling of not only being saved from certain death, but being saved by Helen, over took the pain she was feeling.

'Are you OK?' Helen asked.

'Thanks to you,' Jo said, tiredly.

Helen smiled. 'Help will be here any minute.'

'It's been great getting to know you,' Jo whispered. 'Really great.'

'We're not done yet, Jo. We still have to finish our date.'

'What about Rachel...?' Jo trailed off and fell silent.

Her vision was fading, she felt her hands shaking. The loss of blood was now affecting her and she could feel herself drifting.

She saw two blurry figures she presumed were police officers come running through the woods. She heard one calling for an ambulance over his radio; the other one pulled Helen away from her and knelt down next to her.

'Rachel's fine. Her head hurts but she's fine,' she heard Helen say.

Jo's blood loss then got the better of her and she drifted off into unconsciousness.

Chapter 45

Jo's eyes opened briefly as she felt herself lying on a bed and being lifted into what she presumed was an ambulance. As she lifted her heavy eyelids she was forced to close them again because of the multiple flashes of blue that hit the backs of her eyes from several angles. She heard voices, but she couldn't concentrate on what they were saying. She heard a mumbled sentence from a man who said her name, but the rest of the sentence was inaudible to her. The movement of the bed stopped but then she was reminded of the pain in her head, worse than any headache she'd ever experienced. Her mind drifted once more as the engine started. She could feel a plastic mask over her face. Then the noise and the voice and the movement disappeared once more as she fell into a deep sleep. She heard a voice try to wake her, but she didn't want to be awake. She wanted the pain in her head to stop.

She slipped into unconsciousness again, and mercifully the pain stopped.

Chapter 46

Jo heard voices. This time they weren't the paramedics, but they were voices she knew. They were all talking quietly as if they didn't want to disturb her. She began to wake up, but she didn't yet open her eyes. She heard her mum's voice, then Rick's. Then a deeper voice spoke, she thought it was DCI Collis but she wasn't sure. She tried to open her eyes, but she struggled. She then thought of the events at the woods.

She forced her eyes open and she saw that she was in a hospital bed. She could see her mum was smiling at her through tears. Standing next to her was Rick. The other side of the bed was DCI Collis. She didn't recognise him at first because he wasn't wearing his suit. He was dressed in a woollen patterned jumper with a shirt collar. There was also a man standing next to him in a white overcoat and light blue shirt underneath. He leaned over her and seemed to be looking straight into her eyes.

'Jo,' he said. 'Can you hear me?'

Jo tried to speak but her voice just croaked. She tried to lift her head, but couldn't.

'Stay still,' the doctor said.

Jo tried to speak again, but still nothing came out but a croaky whisper.

She wasn't in pain now, but she felt restricted as if she couldn't move, and she felt very tired, she wanted to close her eyes again.

The doctor shone a light into her eyes, which gave her an instant headache, but it went as quickly as it came once he turned the torch away.

'Jo, you're in Bodmin Community Hospital. I'm Doctor Reeves. You've had a few nasty blows to the head, but you're going to be OK?'

Jo muttered once more, she then coughed and cleared her throat, which helped her finally say the one word she really wanted to say.

'Danny.'

'Danny's dead,' DCI Collis said.

That was enough for Jo. Things started to come back to her. Danny was the killer, which was devastating to her. The fact that a fellow detective was the murderer all along was something she struggled to take in. She was also devastated at losing Laura as well as Lucy.

She had mixed feelings about Danny's death, even though she knew he didn't deserve to live, she felt that death was an easy way out for him. Above all, even with all these things going around her head, she wanted to see Helen. She closed her eyes once more and drifted off back to sleep.

Chapter 47

Jo went home the next evening, having slept through most of the day in her hospital bed. Her doctor told her to stay at home and rest and drink lots of fluids. Jo followed these instructions, for the first hour at least. Her mum and Rick fussed around her. Rick brought her quilt downstairs and put it on the sofa for her. Her mum offered to make her any meal she fancied as she gave her the remote control to the television.

They stopped fussing as the evening went on. Rick went to the pub, and her mum, who'd lost a lot of sleep the previous night, went to bed at around nine-thirty. She made sure she had her mobile phone with her and told Jo to ring her from downstairs even if she just needed a drink.

Jo told her that she was fine and didn't need to be fussed over, but these statements had so far been falling on deaf ears.

Just after ten o'clock, Jo went upstairs and quietly got dressed. Physically she was still in pain, but mentally she was still all over the place. She knew she wouldn't have slept that night had she not addressed something that was eating away at her.

She drove for just over an hour. The car park was as good as empty so she parked close to the hospital building. She didn't have to ask at the desk for directions this time; she knew where she was going.

She made her way along the corridors until she finally came to the private secure ward where the prison guards were sat outside. They had a small table close to them and were playing cards. They both stood up as Jo approached.

'Can I help you?' the bigger man said.

Before she could reply, the smaller of the two said, 'It's OK, John. She's a detective.'

Jo was momentarily confused by how he knew this, but it was most likely on the news the night before. She was obviously about to go through another bout of unwanted notoriety. She didn't think that the news of Danny Hughes being the Bodmin Butcher would've come out yet, but she didn't know for sure. She couldn't remember what she'd put on the television when her mum had given her the remote control, but she knew it wasn't the news.

She walked into the room. Vladek Boniek was lying in his bed. He was still bandaged, but he wasn't asleep, even though it was late. He was watching a television that was attached to a bracket which hung from the wall in front of him. He was listening through earphones. When he saw Jo walk in, he quickly unplugged the earphones and pushed the TV out of the way. He looked at Jo wide-eyed. Neither of them spoke for a second as she closed the door behind her and just stood there looking at him. She didn't know where to start.

Boniek sat up in his bed and straightened the covers but still didn't take his eyes off her.

Finally he spoke. 'The TV says Detective Hughes was the Beast of Bodmin. He killed those people.'

'Yes,' Jo said, quietly.

'Did he kill the women in Tregoltha?'

Jo nodded.

Boniek's head fell back against his pillow. Jo was aware Boniek would have realised Danny was the Bodmin Butcher as soon as he'd seen the news of him being the Beast of Bodmin.

Jo was overwhelmed at seeing the relief on Boniek's face as he pushed his head back into the pillow and stared up at the ceiling. His eyes filled with tears and his shoulders began to shake.

He then wiped his eyes and sat up on his bed and looked hard at Jo. 'What… what happens now?' he asked.

Jo sat down next to Boniek, on his right, and took his right hand in her left. 'Vladek,' she said quietly, 'I don't exactly know. This isn't a procedure I'm familiar with. But you'll be released soon.'

'How soon?'

'Within a week or so, I think. And you'll qualify for compensation.'

'Thank you,' he said.

Jo gently let go of his hand, then turned to him. 'I'm sorry, Vladek, I really am. I really thought it was you. I never imagined it was one of ours. I'm so sorry.'

Boniek gave a nod. 'I never thought I would be free again.'

'I'm glad you are. What will you do when you're out?'

Boniek had a think. Jo wondered what he was going to say. Then he gave a faint smile and said, 'I'll play a chess match.'

Jo smiled back.

Jo knew her dad would've been proud of her, just like she knew her mum was now.

Jo was thankful that she'd trusted her instincts when it came to Danny. If she hadn't realised he was the killer, she could've watched countless other people fall victim to one of the most prolific serial killers of modern times. A detective would've been the last person that anyone would've thought to be the killer. People were still suspecting Lester's panther. It could've gone on for a lot longer had she not acted. For this she felt relieved.

Jo also knew that the panther would be kept alive, now it was known that Danny was the killer. She hadn't yet discussed with Helen's superiors at the zoo if it was possible to find out if there was any forensic connection to the people who were killed without destroying the animal. Now they knew for sure Danny was the Beast of Bodmin, Raven could now be kept alive. Jo was very happy about that. Where Raven would spend the rest of her days was as yet to be decided. Jo remembered Helen telling her that it wasn't easy to introduce a big cat to an existing collection. But one way or another, Raven would be looked after.

Jo looked forward to her blossoming relationship with Helen. She had loved David and she felt something for Laura that she hadn't felt before. But Jo knew she had much stronger feelings for Helen. She hoped she could look forward to a life with Helen, and she couldn't wait to see her again.

On her long drive home Jo contemplated her next steps. She looked in the rear-view mirror at her battered face and wondered how long it would be before DCI Collis would let her go back to work. That was what she was struggling to understand. Her dad was right; being a detective was more of a way of life than a job. She couldn't believe that after the week she'd just had, the pain she was in, and losing people close to her, she still couldn't wait to go back to work.

Jo wondered if maybe she was in the same league as DI Lincoln. Jo had help in bringing Danny Hughes to a halt from Helen, but it was Jo that realised that he was the killer.

Jo began to wonder if what she was feeling was normal, or was there something wrong with her. She wondered if most people would want to stay at home for a while and recover from such an ordeal, but not Jo. Jo wanted to get straight back on the horse as soon as possible. Jo felt a certain amount of guilt for wrongly arresting Vladek Boniek. But Danny was the one who orchestrated the whole thing, and who knows what would've happened if Jo hadn't discovered the truth. How long would he have stayed in prison and how many more people would've lost their lives?

Jo looked back at her first week and couldn't help but be happy at the outcome. It was one hell of a start to her detective portfolio and a very successful first case, and in spite of the pain she was feeling, inside and out, she couldn't wait for the next.

Chapter 48

Jo's cuts and bruises still hurt, but the pain was dispersing only to be taken over by the sensation of her insides spinning as she eagerly waited for Helen to answer the door. She'd felt like this ever since turning and heading for Tregoltha instead of heading back to St Breward. It was late by now, but this visit - like the journey to the hospital - couldn't wait until morning.

There were no lights on but Jo saw the curtains gently swinging in the upstairs window as if they'd just been disturbed. Moments later the door opened and Helen stood there wearing a white oversized T-shirt.

Her dark red hair hung down and her beautiful green eyes stared into hers. Helen's lips parted, but she didn't speak. She tilted her head slightly to one side as she smiled.

Jo's pulse raced as she felt her chest rise and fall with her deep breaths. Her hands were trembling as she waited for Helen to say something, but she didn't say a word.

Suddenly Helen stepped forward and kissed her more passionately than Jo had ever been kissed in her life. Jo felt dizzy with happiness. She threw her arms around Helen, clutching this beautiful woman, this woman she knew she was falling for, in an embrace Jo never wanted to end.

They just went on kissing. It was almost midnight, and they were finally alone. There would be no interruptions, no phone calls, nothing that could stop them having the night to themselves.

As the kiss ended, with great reluctance on both their parts, Helen smiled deeply at Jo and took Jo by the hand and led her inside the house. As the door closed, leaving them both in delicious privacy, Jo felt overwhelmed with a surging, wonderful sense of happiness that a fabulous new chapter was about to begin in her life.

She didn't care anymore about what people thought. She wouldn't be refusing to hold Helen's hand in public again, like she had the night in the pub.

Helen glanced at Jo again, smiled and shook her head slowly, as if amazed at how lucky she was to have met Jo. Then, with more of a sense of purpose now, she led Jo towards the stairs.

Neither of them said a word as they climbed the stairs. Still holding Jo's hand, Helen led Jo into her bedroom.

They glanced at each other and smiled, then embraced and kissed. After holding each other for a long time, they slowly began removing each other's clothes, kissing passionately as they did so.

Chapter 49

Vladek Boniek had struggled to hold back the tears as everyone from the chess club welcomed him back. He had a big lump in his throat as they all greeted him with a handshake or a hug. He couldn't hold any grudges against any of them. He didn't know how many of them believed in his innocence and how many would've thrown away the key; but none of that mattered now. He was free, and he was back doing what he loved the most.

Vladek sat down opposite his opponent. He straightened all the pieces as he always did before a game. He turned his 500 ml bottle of Evian mineral water so that the label faced him. That made him feel good and relaxed. It was a warm summer's evening, but he still wore his lucky faded green chess jumper.

Vladek thought of Jo. He wondered what she was doing now. He hoped she was happy.

Even though it was Jo who'd arrested him, he was eternally grateful for her catching Danny Hughes and discovering his, Vladek's, innocence. He hoped to see Jo again and even considered inviting her to the club. He thought she'd make a good chess player. Maybe she'd let him teach her. He hoped that she would. He'd never taught anyone to play chess before but he wouldn't mind sharing some of his techniques and secrets with Jo.

Vladek was now ready to begin the game. He was White. He knew he would open with pawn to king four, which was always his favourite first move. He liked familiarity; it made him feel comfortable. The world was a difficult and often frightening place; familiarity made it easier to cope with.

The table was clear, the stage was set.

For the first time since his release he had to force himself to stop smiling. He liked to play chess with a poker face, but today he thought he might be smiling throughout the game, even if he lost. But somehow he was confident of winning. He quickly gazed up at his opponent before looking back down at the table.

After taking a deep breath, Vladek made his first move.

THE END

Acknowledgements

It's true what they say, nobody writes a book alone.

First of all I'd like to say a huge thank you to my lovely and very tolerant wife, Maggi, for putting up with me being locked away in my office for so long, and for reading every draft of this story.

I'd like to thank PC Nick Slater for all your police procedural advice, my friend Amy Vaughan for creating Vladek's pseudonym, 'The Bodmin Butcher,' and all my family and friends for your continuing support.

I'd also like to thank Charlotte Mouncey for her amazing cover design and brilliant typesetting skills.

Thanks to all at The Conrad Press, and last but not least, I'd like to thank my agent, James Essinger for giving me the tools with which to build this story.